WISDOM OF THE WORLD

The happy, sad and wise parts of life

ROBERTA CAVA

Wisdom of the World
The happy, sad and wise parts of life
Roberta Cava

Published by Cava Consulting
info@dealingwithdifficultpeople.info

Discover other titles by Roberta Cava at
www.dealingwithdifficultpeople.info

National Library of Australia
Cataloguing-in-publication data:

ISBN 978-0-9923579-6-2

BOOKS BY ROBERTA CAVA

Non-Fiction

Dealing with Difficult People
(21 publishers – in 16 languages)
Dealing with Difficult Situations – at Work and at Home
Dealing with Difficult Spouses and Children
Dealing with Difficult Relatives and In-Laws
Dealing with Domestic Violence and Child Abuse
Dealing with School Bullying
Dealing with Workplace Bullying
Retirement Village Bullies
Keeping Our Children Safe
What am I going to do with the rest of my life?
Before tying the knot – Questions couples Must ask each other
Before they marry!
How Women can advance in business
Survival Skills for Supervisors and Managers
Human Resources at its Best!
Human Resources Policies and Procedures - Australia
Employee Handbook
Easy Come – Hard to go – The Art of Hiring, Disciplining and
Firing Employees
Time and Stress – Today's silent killers
Take Command of your Future – Make things Happen
Belly Laughs for All! – Volumes 1 to 4
Wisdom of the World! The happy, sad and wise things in life!

Fiction

That Something Special
Something Missing
Trilogy: Life Gets Complicated
Life Goes On
Life Gets Better

Wisdom of the World

WISDOM OF THE WORLD!

The happy, sad and wise parts of life

Table of Contents:

Wisdom of the World

INTRODUCTION

I had just completed writing four joke books and enjoyed writing them. However, I did have quite a bit of left-over information that was about the more serious side of life. So I got busy and this book is the result.

You will find some side-splitting humour; parts that will educate you about things you might not have known and tell you stories that will likely bring a tear to your eye.

Wisdom of the World

CHAPTER 1 - IS THAT RIGHT?

Oddities of life

- A door that's open is ajar; what is it called when a jar is open?
- Would you buy a solar-powered flashlight?
- They call it a hot-water-heater, but why would you need to heat hot water?
- They call it a building, but after it's completed shouldn't they call it a built?
- Why do women wear evening gowns to nightclubs ... shouldn't they wear nightgowns?
- If vegetarians eat only vegetables, then what do humanitarians eat?
- If a person kills his/her clone, is it murder or suicide?
- What does the Q in Q-tip stand for?
- Why do they call warm water, luke warm ... did someone named Luke discover it?
- What do you call two Mexicans playing basketball? Juan on Juan.
- What do you see when the Pillsbury Dough Boy bends over? Doughnuts.
- Why did OJ Simpson want to move to West Virginia? Everyone has the same DNA.
- What does it mean when the flag at the Post Office is flying at half-mast? They're hiring.
- Why is there no Disneyland in China? No one's tall enough to go on the good rides.
- Why do bagpipers walk when they play? To get away from the noise.
- If you throw a cat out a car window does it become kitty litter?
- If there is no God, who pops up the next Kleenex in the box?
- If nothing sticks to Teflon, how do they stick Teflon to the pan?
- What do they use to ship Styrofoam?
- Why is abbreviation such a long word?
- Why do kamikaze pilots wear helmets?
- Why do they call it taking a dump instead of leaving a dump?
- Why is there only one Monopolies Commission?

- Why do they say new and improved ... because how can it be new if it was improved?
- If you worked at a fire hydrant plant, where would you park?
- What happens to that other sock you lost in the laundry?
- Why is it that when you're at the beach swimming and it starts to rain, everyone gets up and leaves?
- Why when a kid is running, will his mother say, *'Don't come running to me if you break your leg?'*
- Why do people look up when they think?
- Why does a serving of frosted flakes have the same number of calories as regular flakes?
- Why do women wear shoes that hurt their feet?
- Why do men wear something that resembles a hangman's noose?
- Why does 1 kilogram of groceries generate 50 kilograms of garbage?
- What do you plant to grow a seedless watermelon?
- Why do you need a driver's license to buy liquor when you can't drink and drive?
- Why isn't phonetic spelled the way it sounds?
- Why are there interstate highways in Hawaii and Singapore?
- How do you know when it's time to tune your bagpipes?
- Is it true that cannibals don't eat clowns because they taste funny?
- If this is the land of the free, why is someone always trying to sell me something?
- Why do people who know the least, know it the loudest?
- How do you know when you've run out of invisible ink?
- If a vampire can't see himself in a mirror, why is his hair always so neat?
- Why do women have a pair of underwear, but just one bra?
- If a 7-11 is open 24 hours a day, 365 days of the year, why are there locks on the doors?
- How does the guy who drives the snow plough get to work in the morning?
- Why is it that when you transport something by truck, it's called a shipment, but when you transport something by ship, it's called cargo?
- It is said that if you line up all the cars in the world end to end, someone would be stupid enough to try and pass them.

- It is hard to understand how a cemetery raised its burial cost and blamed it on the cost of living.
- Why is it that when you're driving and looking for an address, you turn down the radio volume?
- I know what you're thinking and you should be ashamed of yourself.
- Despite the cost of living, have you noticed how it remains so popular?
- You have the right to remain silent. Anything you say will be misquoted then used against you.
- What's the difference between snowmen and snowwomen? Snowballs.
- I have six locks on my door all in a row. When I go out, I lock every other one. I figure no matter how long somebody stands there picking the locks, they are always locking three.
- Ever wonder if illiterate people get the full effect of alphabet soup?
- What do you call cheese that isn't yours? Nacho Cheese.
- What do Eskimos get from sitting on the ice too long? Polaroids.
- What do you call four bullfighters in quicksand? Quatro sinko.
- What do you get from a pampered cow? Spoiled milk.
- What do you get when you cross a snowman with a vampire? Frostbite.
- What do you get when you cross an elephant and a skin doctor? A pachydermatologist.
- What has four legs is big, green and fuzzy and if it fell out of a tree would kill you? A pool table.
- Did you hear about the Buddhist who refused his dentist's Novocain during root canal work? He wanted to transcend dental medication!
- What kind of coffee was served on the Titanic? Sanka. And what kind of lettuce? Iceberg.
- What lies at the bottom of the ocean and twitches? A nervous wreck.
- What's the difference between an oral thermometer and a rectal one? The taste.
- Where do you find a no-legged dog? Right where you left him.
- Where do you get virgin wool from? Ugly sheep.

- What's the difference between roast beef and pea soup? Anyone can roast beef.
- Why are there so many Smiths in the phone book? They all have phones.
- Why do gorillas have big nostrils? Because they have big fingers ...
- What is a zebra? 26 sizes larger than an 'A' bra.
- If you yelled for 8 years, 7 months and 6 days you would have produced enough sound energy to heat one cup of coffee. (Hardly seems worth it.)
- If you farted consistently for 6 years and 9 months, enough gas is produced to create the energy of an atomic bomb. (Now that's more like it!)
- If Barbie is so popular, why do you have to buy her friends?
- Corduroy pillows: They're making headlines!
- I intend to live forever - so far, so good.
- Many people quit looking for work when they find a job.
- Everyone has a photographic memory. Some just don't have film.
- If you choke a smurf, what colour does it turn?
- Energiser Bunny arrested - charged with battery.
- I poured Spot remover on my dog. Now he's gone.
- I used to have an open mind, but my brains kept falling out.
- Shin: a device for finding furniture in the dark.
- Join the Army, meet interesting people and kill them.
- Wear short sleeves! Support your right to bare arms!
- All those who believe in psycho kinesis raise my hand.
- The Human heart creates enough pressure when it pumps out to the body to squirt blood 30 feet. [O.M.G.!]
- A cockroach will live nine days without its head before it starves to death! [Creepy!]
- Banging your head against a wall uses 150 calories an hour. [Don't try this at home - maybe at work.]
- The male praying mantis cannot copulate while its head is attached to its body. The female initiates sex by ripping the males head off. [*'Honey, I'm home. What the ...?!'*]
- The flea can jump 350 times its body length. It's like a human jumping the length of a football field.
- Some lions mate over 50 times a day. (Wow)

- The catfish has over 27,000 taste buds. [What could be so tasty on the bottom of a pond?]
- Butterflies taste with their feet. [Something I always wanted to know.]
- The strongest muscle in the body is the tongue. [Hmmmmmm.]
- Right-handed people live, on average, nine years longer than left-handed people. So if you're ambidextrous - do you split the difference?
- Polar bears are left-handed. [If they switch, they'll live a lot longer.]
- Elephants are the only animals that cannot jump. Okay - so that would be a good thing.
- A cat's urine glows under a black light. [I wonder who was paid to figure that out?]
- An ostrich's eye is bigger than its brain. [I know some people like that.]
- Starfish have no brains. [I know some people like that too.]
- Humans and dolphins are the only species that have sex for pleasure.
- 'Stewardesses' is the longest word typed with only the left hand and 'lollipop' with your right.
- 'Typewriter' is the longest word that can be made using the letters only on one row of the keyboard.
- The sentence: 'The quick brown fox jumps over the lazy dog' uses every letter of the alphabet.
- Maine is the only state with a name that's just one syllable.
- No word in the English language rhymes with month orange, silver or purple.
- Our eyes are always the same size from birth, but our nose and ears never stop growing. [Ugh!]
- The words 'race car,' 'kayak' and 'level' are the same whether they are read left to right or right to left [palindromes].
- There are only four words in the English language that end in 'dous:' tremendous, horrendous, stupendous and hazardous
- There are two words in the English language that have all five vowels in order: 'abstemious' and 'facetious.'
- All 50 states are listed across the top of the Lincoln Memorial on the back of the US $5 bill.
- A dime [10¢] has 118 ridges around the edge.
- A cat has 32 muscles in each ear.

- A crocodile cannot stick out its tongue. [But who really cares?]
- A dragonfly has a life span of 24 hours.
- A *'jiffy'* is an actual unit of time for 1/100th of a second
- A shark is the only fish that can blink with both eyes.
- A snail can sleep for three years!
- Al Capone's business card said he was a used furniture dealer.
- Almonds are members of the peach family.
- February 1865 is the only month in recorded history not to have a full moon.
- In the last 4,000 years, no new animals have been domesticated.
- If the population of China walked past you, eight abreast - the line would never end because of the rate of reproduction. [How do they do that standing up and walking?]
- If you are an average person living in a developed country, in your whole life, you will spend an average of six months waiting at red lights.
- Leonardo Da Vinci invented the scissors. [I didn't know that either!]
- On the old Canadian two-dollar bill, the flag flying over the Parliament building was an American flag. [Canada now has $2 coins - nicknamed toonies - could that be why?]
- Peanuts are one of the ingredients of dynamite!
- Rubber bands last longer when refrigerated.
- The average person's left hand does 56% of the typing.
- The cruise liner QE2, moves only six inches for each gallon of diesel that it burns.
- The microwave was invented after a researcher walked by a radar tube and a chocolate bar melted in his pocket. [Good thing he did that.]
- The winter of 1932 was so cold that Niagara Falls froze solid.
- There are more chickens than people in the world [so far].
- Winston Churchill was born in a ladies' room during a dance.
- Your stomach has to produce a new layer of mucus every two weeks, otherwise it will digest itself. [Yuck!]
- If you take an Oriental person and spin him around several times, does he become disoriented?
- If people from Poland are called Poles, why aren't people from Holland called Holes?
- If FedEx and UPS were to merge, would they call it FedUp?
- Do Lipton Tea employees take coffee breaks?

- Why do we say something is out of whack? What's a whack?
- If a pig loses its voice, is it disgruntled?
- When someone asks you, *'A penny for your thoughts'* and you put your two cents in, what happens to the other penny?
- When cheese gets its picture taken, what does it say?
- Why is a person who plays piano called a pianist, but a person who drives a race car not called a racist?
- Why are a wise man and a wise guy opposites?
- Why do overlook and oversee mean opposite things?
- Why isn't 11 pronounced onety-one?
- If lawyers are disbarred and clergymen are defrocked, doesn't it follow that electricians can be delighted, musicians denoted, cowboys deranged, models deposed, tree surgeons debarked and dry cleaners depressed?
- Do older people read the Bible a whole lot more as they get older because they're cramming for their final exam?
- Why do they put pictures of criminals up in the Post Office? What are we supposed to do - write to them? Why don't they just put their pictures on the postage stamps so the mailmen can look for them while they deliver mail?
- Ever wonder what the speed of lightning would be if it didn't zigzag?
- Latest survey shows that 3 out of 4 people make up 75% of the world's population.
- It was recently discovered that research causes cancer in rats.
- Everybody lies, but it doesn't matter, since nobody listens.
- I wish the buck stopped here, as I could use a few.
- I started out with nothing and I still have most of it.
- How do you get holy water? Boil the Hell out of it.
- What did the fish say when he hit a concrete wall? *'Damn.'*
- What do prisoners use to call each other? Cell phones.
- The statistics on sanity are that one out of every four is suffering from some form of mental illness. Think of your three best friends. If they're okay - then it's you.
- I always wanted to be somebody, but I should have been more specific.
- How do crazy people go through the forest? They take the psycho path.
- Two wrongs don't make a right, but three rights make a left.

- Why don't blind people sky dive? Because it scares the hell out of their dog.
- How do you confuse a retard? Put him in a round room and tell him to pee in a corner. How do you confuse him even more? Ask him what corner he peed in.
- What do you call a boomerang that doesn't come back? A stick.
- When is Mother's Day? Nine months after Father's Night!
- What's the difference between an evening gown and a nightgown? About fifteen minutes if you're lucky.
- What do all constipated people have in common? None of them give a crap!
- How did Dairy Queen get pregnant? Burger King forgot to wrap his Whopper.
- Notice: to person or persons, who took the large pumpkin on Highway 87 near Southridge Storage, please return the pumpkin and be checked. Pumpkin may be radioactive. All other plants in vicinity are dead.
- Last night I played a blank tape at full blast. The mime next door went nuts.
- If a cow laughed, would milk come out of her nose?
- Whatever happened to Preparations A through G?
- I went for a walk last night and my kids asked me how long I'd be gone. I replied, *'The whole time.'*
- Isn't Disney World a people-trap operated by a mouse?
- Whose cruel idea was it for the word *'lisp'* to have an *'s'* in it?
- Person #1: *'Do you know what the capital of Alaska is?'* Person #2: *'Juneau?'* Person #1: *'If I knew, I wouldn't be asking you!'*
- So what's the speed of dark?
- How come you don't ever hear about gruntled employees? And who has been diss-ing them anyhow?
- After eating, do amphibians need to wait an hour before getting out of the water?
- I just got skylights put into my place. The people who live above me are furious.
- Do they have reserved parking for non-handicapped people at the Special Olympics?
- Some people are like slinkies - not really good for anything but they bring a smile to your face when pushed down the stairs.
- Why is a carrot more orange than an orange?

16

- If it's zero degrees outside today and it's supposed to be twice as cold tomorrow, how cold is it going to be?
- Why do you press harder on the remote control when you know the battery is dead?
- Why do banks charge you a non-sufficient funds fee on money they already know you don't have?
- If the universe is everything and scientists say that the universe is expanding, what is it expanding into?
- If you got into a taxi and the driver started driving backward, would the taxi driver end up owing you money?
- What would a chair look like if your knees bent the other way?
- If a tree falls in the forest and no one is around to see it, do the other trees make fun of it?
- When two airplanes almost collide why do they call it a near miss? [It sounds like a near hit to me!]
- Do fish get cramps after eating?
- Why are there five syllables in the word *'monosyllabic?'*
- Why do they call it the Department of Interior when they are in charge of everything outdoors?
- Why do scientists call it research when looking for something new?
- When I erase a word with a pencil, where does it go?
- Tell a man there are 400 billion stars and he'll believe you. Tell him a bench has wet paint and he has to touch it.
- What would you call it when an Italian has one arm shorter than the other? A speech impediment.
- Always keep several get well cards on the dining room table so if unexpected guests arrive, they will think you've been sick and weren't able to clean the house.
- Did you hear about the Chinese couple that had a retarded baby? They name him *'Sun Ting Wong.'*
- How come Superman could stop bullets with his chest, but always ducked when someone threw a gun at him?
- Why is it lemon juice contains mostly artificial ingredients, but dishwashing liquid contains real lemons?
- Why buy a product that it takes 2,000 flushes to get rid of?
- Why do we wait until a pig is dead to *'cure'* it?
- Do Roman paramedics refer to IV's as *'4's?'*
- What do little birdies say when they get knocked unconscious?
- Is boneless chicken considered to be an invertebrate?

- Do married people live longer than single people or does it just seem longer?
- Two Eskimos sitting in a kayak were chilly, but when they lit a fire in the craft - it sank proving once and for all that you can't have your kayak and heat it too.
- If man evolved from monkeys and apes, why do we still have monkeys and apes?
- If all those psychics know the winning lottery numbers, why are they all still working?
- Isn't the best way to save face to keep the lower part shut?
- War doesn't determine who's right - just who's left.
- A little known fact: The first testicular guard was used in cricket in 1874 and the first helmet was used in 1974. It took a hundred years for men to realise that the brain is also important.
- Why do they call it an asteroid when it's outside the hemisphere, but call it a haemorrhoid when it's in your butt?
- Why do they use sterilised needles for death by lethal injection?
- Why doesn't Tarzan have a beard?
- Did you ever notice that when you blow in a dog's face, he gets mad at you, but when you take him for a car ride, he sticks his head out the window?
- Why is it that no matter what colour bubble bath you use the bubbles are always white?
- Is there ever a day that mattresses are not on sale?
- Why do people constantly return to the refrigerator with hopes that something new to eat will have materialised?
- Why do people keep running over a string a dozen times with their vacuum cleaner, then reach down, pick it up, examine it, then put it down to give the vacuum one more chance?
- Why is it that no plastic bag will open from the end on your first try?
- How do those dead bugs get into those enclosed light fixtures?
- When we are in the supermarket and someone rams our ankle with a shopping cart then apologises for doing so, why do we say, *'It's all right?'* Well, it isn't all right, so why don't we say, *'That really hurt, why don't you watch where you're going?'*
- Why is it that whenever you attempt to catch something that's falling off the table you always manage to knock something else over?
- How come you never hear father-in-law jokes?

- In winter why do we try to keep the house as warm as it was in summer when we complained about the heat?
- If you have sex with a prostitute against her will, is it considered rape or shoplifting?
- Can you cry under water?
- How important does a person have to be before they are considered assassinated instead of just murdered?
- Once you're in heaven, do you get stuck wearing the clothes you were buried in for eternity?
- Why does a round pizza come in a square box?
- What disease did cured ham actually have?
- How is it that we put man on the moon before we figured out it would be a good idea to put wheels on luggage?
- Why is it that people say they *slept like a baby* when babies wake up like every two hours?
- If a deaf person has to go to court, is it still called a hearing?
- Why are you in a movie, but you're on TV?
- Why do people pay to go up tall buildings and then put money in binoculars to look at things on the ground?
- Why do doctors leave the room while you change? They're going to see you naked anyway.
- Why do toasters always have a setting that burns the toast to a horrible crisp, which no decent human being would eat?
- If Jimmy cracks corn and no one cares, why is there a stupid song about him?
- If the professor on Gilligan's Island can make a radio out of a coconut, why can't he fix a hole in a boat?
- Why does Goofy stand erect while Pluto remains on all fours? They're both dogs!
- If Wile E. Coyote had enough money to buy all that ACME crap, why didn't he just buy dinner?
- If corn oil is made from corn and vegetable oil is made from vegetables, what is baby oil made from?
- If electricity comes from electrons, does morality come from morons?
- Do the Alphabet song and Twinkle, Twinkle Little Star have the same tune? [Why did you just try singing these two songs?]
- I love cooking with wine. Sometimes I even put it in the food.
- Money isn't everything, but it sure keeps the kids in touch.
- Reality is only an illusion that occurs due to a lack of alcohol.

- Don't sweat the petty things. Don't pet the sweaty things.
- I want to die while asleep like my grandfather, not screaming in terror like the passengers in his car.
- I have kleptomania, but when it gets bad, I take something for it.
- Sometimes too much to drink isn't enough.
- My short-term memory is not as sharp as it used to be.
- Also, my short-term memory's not as sharp as it used to be.
- In just two days from now, Tomorrow will be yesterday.
- A bartender is just a pharmacist with a limited inventory.
- I may be schizophrenic, but at least I have each other.
- I am a nobody. Nobody is perfect. Therefore I am perfect.

Heaven is where:

- The Police are British,
- The Chefs are Italian,
- The Mechanics are German,
- The Lovers are French and
- It's all organised by the Swiss.

Hell is where:

- The Police are German,
- The Chefs are British,
- The Mechanics are French,
- The Lovers are Swiss and
- It's all organised by the Italians.

The wisdom of Larry the cable guy

1. 42.7 percent of all statistics are made up on the spot.
2. 99 percent of lawyers give the rest a bad name.
3. Remember, half the people you know are below average.
4. He who laughs last, thinks slowest.
5. Depression is merely anger without enthusiasm.
6. The early bird may get the worm, but the second mouse gets the cheese in the trap.
7. Support bacteria. They're the only culture some people have.
8. A clear conscience is usually the sign of a bad memory.
9. Change is inevitable, except from vending machines.
10. If you think nobody cares, try missing a couple of payments.
11. Okay; so what's the speed of dark?

12. When everything is coming your way, you're in the wrong lane.
13. Hard work pays off in the future. Laziness pays off now.
14. How much deeper would the ocean be without sponges?
15. Eagles may soar, but weasels don't get sucked into jet engines.
16. What happens if you get scared half to death, twice?
17. Why do psychics have to ask you your name?
18. Inside every older person is a younger person wondering, *'What the heck happened?'*
19. Light travels faster than sound. That's why some people appear bright until you hear them speak.
20. Life isn't like a box of chocolates. It's more like a jar of jalapenos. What you do today, might burn your butt tomorrow.

Flight Safety

After every flight, UPS pilots fill out a form, called a *'gripe sheet,'* which tells mechanics about problems with the aircraft. The mechanics correct the problems, document their repairs on the form and then pilots review the gripe sheets before the next flight.

Never let it be said that ground crews lack a sense of humour. Here are some actual maintenance complaints submitted by UPS pilots (marked with a P) and the solutions recorded (marked with an S) by maintenance engineers.

P: Left inside main tire almost needs replacement.
    S: Almost replaced left inside main tire.
P: Test flight OK, except auto-land very rough.
    S: Auto-land not installed on this aircraft.
P: Something loose in cockpit.
    S: Something tightened in cockpit.
P: Dead bugs on windshield.
    S: Live bugs on back-order.
P: Autopilot in altitude-hold mode produces a 200-feet-per-minute descent.
    S: Cannot reproduce problem on ground.
P: Evidence of leak on right main landing gear.
    S: Evidence removed.
P: DME volume unbelievably loud.
    S: DME volume set to more believable level.
P: Friction locks cause throttle levers to stick.
    S: That's what friction locks are for.
P: IFF inoperative in OFF mode.
    S: IFF is always inoperative in OFF mode.

P: Suspected crack in windshield.
S: Suspect you're right.
P: Number 3 engine missing.
S: Engine found on right wing after brief search.
P: Aircraft handles funny. [I love this one!]
S: Aircraft warned to straighten up, fly right and be serious.
P: Target radar hums.
S: Reprogrammed target radar with lyrics.
P: Mouse in cockpit.
S: Cat installed.
And the best one for last:

P: Noise coming from under instrument panel. Sounds like a midget pounding on something with a hammer.
S: Took hammer away from the midget.

By the way, UPS is the only major airline that has never, ever, had an accident.

Actual exchanges between pilots and control towers

From an unknown aircraft waiting in a very long takeoff queue: *'I'm bored!'*
Ground Traffic Control: *'Last aircraft transmitting, identify yourself immediately!'*
Unknown aircraft: *'I said I was bored, not stupid!'*

O'Hare Approach Control to a 747: *'United 329 heavy, your traffic is a Fokker, one o'clock, three miles, Eastbound.'*
United 329: *'Approach, I've always wanted to say this ... I've got the little Fokker in sight.'*

A student became lost during a solo cross-country flight. While attempting to locate the aircraft on radar, ATC asked, *'What was your last known position?'*
Student: *'When I was number one for takeoff.'*

Tower: *'TWA 2341, for noise abatement turn right 45 Degrees.'*
TWA 2341: *'Centre, we are at 35,000 feet. How much noise can we make up here?'*
Tower: *'Sir, have you ever heard the noise a 747 makes when it hits a 727?'*

A DC-10 had come in a little hot and thus had an exceedingly long roll out after touching down in San Jose

Tower Noted: *'American 751, make a hard right turn at the end of the runway, if you are able. If you are not able, take the Guadeloupe exit off Highway 101, make a right at the lights and return to the airport.'*

Tower: *'Delta 351, you have traffic at 10 o'clock, 6 miles!'*

Delta 351: *'Give us another hint! We have digital watches!'*

The German air controllers at Frankfurt Airport are renowned as a short-tempered lot. They not only expect one to know one's gate parking location, but how to get there without any assistance from them. So it was with some amusement that we (a Pan Am 747) listened to the following exchange between Frankfurt ground control and a British Airways 747, call sign Speedbird 206.

Speedbird 206: *'Frankfurt, Speedbird 206! clear of active runway.'*

Ground: *'Speedbird 206. Taxi to gate Alpha One-Seven.'*

The BA 747 pulled onto the main taxiway and slowed to a stop.

Ground: *'Speedbird, do you not know where you are going?'*

Speedbird 206: *'Stand by, Ground, I'm looking up our gate location now.'*

Ground (with quite arrogant impatience): *'Speedbird 206, have you not been to Frankfurt before?'*

Speedbird 206 (coolly): *'Yes, twice in 1944, but it was dark, - And I didn't land.'*

Tower: *'Eastern 702, cleared for takeoff, contact Departure on frequency 124.7.'*

Eastern 702: *'Tower, Eastern 702 switching to Departure. By the way, after we lifted off we saw some kind of dead animal on the far end of the runway.'*

Tower: *'Continental 635, cleared for takeoff behind Eastern 702, contact Departure on frequency 124.7. Did you copy that report from Eastern 702?'*

BR Continental 635: *'Continental 635, cleared for takeoff, roger; and yes, we copied Eastern ... we've already notified our caterers.'*

One day the pilot of a Cherokee 180 was told by the tower to hold short of the active runway while a DC-8 landed. The DC-8 landed, rolled out, turned around and taxied back past the Cherokee. Some quick-witted comedian in the DC-8 crew got on the radio and said, *'What a cute little plane. Did you make it all by yourself?'*

The Cherokee pilot, not about to let the insult go by, came back with a real zinger: *'I made it out of DC-8 parts. Another landing like yours and I'll have enough parts for another one.'*

A Pan Am 727 flight, waiting for start clearance in Munich overheard the following:

Lufthansa (in German): *'Ground, what is our start clearance time?'*

Ground (in English): *'If you want an answer you must speak in English.'*

Lufthansa (in English): *'I am a German, flying a German airplane, in Germany - Why must I speak English?'*

Unknown voice from another plane (in a beautiful British accent): *'Because you lost the bloody war!'*

While taxiing at London's Gatwick Airport, the crew of a US Air flight departing for Ft. Lauderdale made a wrong turn and came nose to nose with a United 727.

An irate female ground controller lashed out at the US Air crew, screaming: *'US Air 2771, where the hell are you going? I told you to turn right onto Charlie taxiway! You turned right on Delta! Stop right there. I know it's difficult for you to tell the difference between C and D, but get it right!'*

Continuing her rage to the embarrassed crew, she was now shouting hysterically: *'God! Now you've screwed everything up! It'll take forever to sort this out! You stay right there and don't move till I tell you to! You can expect progressive taxi instructions in about half an hour and I want you to go exactly where I tell you, when I tell you and how I tell you! You got that, US Air 2771?'*

'Yes, ma'am,' the humbled crew responded.

Naturally, the ground control communications frequency fell terribly silent after the verbal bashing of US Air 2771. Nobody wanted to chance engaging the irate ground controller in her current state of mind. Tension in every cockpit out around Gatwick was definitely running high. Just then an unknown pilot broke the silence and keyed his microphone, asking: *'Wasn't I married to you once?'*

Restroom Signs

- Beauty is only a light switch away. [Perkins Library, Duke University, Durham, NC]

- If life is a waste of time and time is a waste of life, then let's all get wasted together and have the time of our lives. [Armand's Pizza, Washington, DC]
- Fighting for peace is like having sex for virginity. [The Bayou, Baton Rouge, LO]
- No matter how good she looks, some other guy is sick and tired of putting up with her shit. [Men's room, Linda's Bar and Grill, Chapel Hill, NC]
- At the feast of ego, everyone leaves hungry. [Bentley's House of Coffee and Tea, Tucson, AZ]
- It's hard to make a comeback, when you haven't been anywhere. [Written in the dust on the back of a bus, Wickenburg. AZ]
- Make love, not war. Hell, do both – get married! [Women's restroom, The Filling Station, Bozeman, MT]
- If voting could really change things – it would be illegal. [Revolution Books, New York, NY]
- If pro is the opposite of con, then what is the opposite of progress? Congress! [Men's restroom House of Representatives, Washington, DC]
- Express Lane: Five beers or less. [Sign over one of the urinals Ed Deb Evic's, Phoenix, AZ]
- You're too good for him! [Sign over mirror in women's restroom Ed Deb Evic's, Beverly Hills, CA]
- No wonder you always go home alone. [Sign over mirror in Men's restroom, Ed Deb Evic's, Beverly Hills, CA]
- A woman's rule of thumb: If it has tires or testicles, you're going to have trouble with it! [Women's restroom, Dick's Last Resort, Dallas, TX]

Newspaper ads 'For Sale:'

- 1 Man, 7 women hot tub - $850/best offer.
- Amana washer $100. Owned by clean bachelor who seldom washed.
- Free puppies: ½ Cocker Spaniel - ½ sneaky neighbour dog.
- Free puppies. Mother, a Kennel Club registered German Shepherd. Father, Super Dog. Able to leap tall fences in a single bound.
- Wedding dress for sale. Worn once by mistake. Call Stephanie.
- Snow blower for sale - only used on snowy days.

- Eye of round roast - $1.99 lb. - bonerless.
- Complete set of Encyclopaedia Britannica, 45 volumes. Excellent condition - £200 or best offer. No longer needed, Got married last month. Wife knows everything.
- 2 wire mesh butchering gloves, 1 5-finger, 1-3 finger, pair $15
- Our sofa seats the whole mob - and it's made of 100% Italian leather.
- Joining nudist colony, must sell washer and dryer - $300.
- Tickle Me Elmo, still in box, comes with its own 1988 mustang, excellent condition $6,800.
- Tickle Me Elmo - new in box, hardly tickled, $700.
- 2 Tinkle Me Elmo Dolls - best offer.
- Black face cows, calves. Also 1 gay bull for sale.
- '83 Toyota Hunchback - $2,000.
- Do something special for your valentine - have your septic tank pumped.
- Free Yorkshire Terrier. 8 years old - unpleasant little dog.
- Soft and genital bath or facial tissues - 89 cents.
- German Shepherd 85 lbs. Neutered. Speaks German. Free.
- Full-sized mattress. 20 year warranty - like new - slight urine smell.
- Free 1 can of pork and beans with purchase of 3-bedroom 2-bath home.
- For sale: Lee Majors (6 million dollar man) - $50.
- Nordic Track $300 - hardly used - call Chubbie at xxx-1275.
- Bill's septic cleaning - *'We haul American-made products.'*
- Shakespeare's pizza - free chopsticks.
- Found: dirty white dog - looks like a rat - been out a while - better be a reward.
- Hummels - largest selection ever - *'If it's in stock, we have it!'*
- Get a little John - the travelling urinal - holds 2 ½ bottles of beer.
- Harrisburg postal employees gun club.
- Georgia peaches - California grown - 89 cents lb.
- Cute kitten for sale, 2 cents or best offer.
- Nice parachute - never opened - used once - slightly stained
- Whirlpool built in oven - frost free!
- Barbie Country Ride – [Note most dolls cannot pedal the bike].
- '93 Pontiac Lemon - low miles.
- Free, farm kittens. Ready to eat.

- Kittens 8 weeks old - seeking good Christian home.
- Ground beast: 99 cents lb.
- Free puppies - Part German Shepherd, part dog.
- Open house - body shapers toning salon - free coffee and donuts.
- Kellogg's pot tarts - $1.99 box.
- Alzheimer's Centre prepares for *'An Affair to Remember.'*
- Gas cloud clears out Taco Bell.
- Battery charger for sale - batteries not included.
- Lost: small apricot poodle. Reward. Neutered. Like one of the family.
- A superb and inexpensive restaurant. Fine food expertly served by waitresses in appetising forms.
- Dinner Special - Turkey $2.35; Chicken $2.25: Children $2.00.
- For sale: Antique desk suitable for lady with thick legs and large drawers.
- Wanted: 50 girls for stripping machine operators in factory.
- We do not tear our clothing with machinery. We do it carefully by hand.
- For sale: Three canaries of undetermined sex.
- Get rid of your aunts: Zap does the job in 24 hours.
- Great Dames for sale.
- Stock up and save. Limit: one.
- Dog for sale: Eats anything and is fond of children.
- Mt. Kilimanjaro, the breathtaking backdrop for the Serena Lodge. Swim in the lovely pool while you drink it all in.
- The hotel has bowling alleys, tennis courts, comfortable beds and other athletic facilities.
- Sheer stockings. Designed for fancy dress, but so serviceable that lots of women wear nothing else.
- Men wanted to work in dynamite factory. Must be willing to travel.
- Three-year-old teacher needed for pre-school. Experience preferred.
- And now, the Superstore - unequalled in size, unmatched in variety, unrivalled inconvenience.
- Our bikinis are exciting. They are simply the tops.
- Wanted. Man to take care of cow that does not smoke or drink.

- Our experienced Mom will take care of your child. Fenced yard, meals and smacks included.
- Auto repair service. Free pick-up and delivery. Try us once; you'll never go anywhere again.
- Illiterate? Write today for free help.
- Mixing bowl set designed to please a cook with a round bottom for efficient beating.
- Semi-annual after-Christmas sale.

Words of wisdom:

✓ Feel safe tonight ... sleep with a cop.
✓ Remember folks: Stop lights timed for 60 kph are also timed for 120 kph.
✓ Sign seen in restaurant: **GUYS**: No shirt, no shoes - no service. **GALS**: No shirt - no charge.
✓ If walking is so good for you, then why does my mailman look so bad?
✓ Impotence: Nature's way of saying, *'No hard feelings.'*
✓ Necrophilia: That uncontrollable urge to crack open a cold one.
✓ We have enough youth, how about a fountain of smart?
✓ What is the difference between Bird Flu and Swine Flu? For bird flu you need tweetment and for swine flu you need oinkment.
✓ Cat: the other white meat.
✓ Caution - Driver legally blonde!
✓ Don't be a sexist - broads hate that.
✓ Eat well, stay fit and die anyway.
✓ Heart attacks - God's revenge for eating his animal friends.
✓ Honk if you've never seen an Uzi fired from a car window.
✓ If you lived in your car, you'd be home by now.
✓ I'm an imbecile and I vote.
✓ Money isn't everything, but it sure keeps the kids in touch.
✓ Saw it - wanted it - had a fit - got it!
✓ What has four legs and an arm? A happy pit bull terrier.
✓ Do not walk behind me, for I may not lead. Do not walk ahead of me, for I may not follow. Do not walk beside me either, just leave me alone.
✓ The journey of a thousand miles begins with a broken fan belt and a flat tyre.
✓ If at first you don't succeed, avoid skydiving.
✓ A closed mouth gathers no feet.

- ✓ The darkest hours come just before the dawn. So if you're going to steal your neighbour's milk and newspaper, that's the time to do it.
- ✓ Sex is like air. It only becomes really important when you aren't getting any.
- ✓ Don't aspire to become irreplaceable. If you can't be replaced, you can't be promoted.
- ✓ If you think nobody cares whether you're dead or alive, try missing a couple of mortgage payments
- ✓ Before you judge someone, you should walk a mile in his or her shoes. That way, when you judge them, you're a mile away and you have their shoes.
- ✓ Have you ever lent someone $20 and never seen that person again? It was probably worth it.
- ✓ If you tell the truth, you don't have to remember anything.
- ✓ Some days we are the flies; some days we are the windscreens.
- ✓ Don't worry; it only seems kinky the first time.
- ✓ Good judgment comes from experience; experience comes from bad judgment.
- ✓ The quickest way to double your money is to fold it in half and put it back in your pocket.
- ✓ There are two theories about how to win an argument with a woman. Neither one works.
- ✓ Generally speaking, you aren't learning much if your lips are moving. Never miss a good chance to shut up.
- ✓ Experience is something you don't get until just after you need it.
- ✓ When we are born we are naked, wet, hungry and we get smacked on our arse. From there on in, life gets worse.
- ✓ The most wasted day of all is one in which we have not laughed.
- ✓ Remember not to forget that which you do not need to know.
- ✓ Childhood – the time in life when you make funny faces in the mirror. Old Age – is the time when the mirror gets even.
- ✓ It takes your food seven seconds to get from your mouth to your stomach.
- ✓ One human hair can support 3 kg (6.6 lb).
- ✓ The average man's penis is three times the length of his thumb.
- ✓ Human thighbones are stronger than concrete.
- ✓ A woman's heart beats faster than a man's.
- ✓ There are about one trillion bacteria on each of your feet.
- ✓ Women blink twice as often as men.

- ✓ The average person's skin weighs twice as much as the brain.
- ✓ Your body uses 300 muscles to balance itself when you are standing still.
- ✓ If saliva cannot dissolve something, you cannot taste it.
- ✓ Women reading this will be finished now but men are still busy checking their thumbs.

Paying your debts

It's August. In a small town on the South Coast of France, the holiday season is in full swing, but it is raining so there's not too much business happening.

Everyone is heavily in debt.

One day a rich Aussie arrives in the foyer of the small local hotel. He asks for a room and puts a €100 note on the reception counter, takes a key and goes to inspect the room located up the stairs on the third floor.

The hotel owner takes the banknote and rushes to his meat supplier to whom he owes €100.

The butcher takes the money and races to his supplier to clear his debt.

The wholesaler rushes to the farmer to pay €100 for pigs he purchased some time ago. The farmer triumphantly gives the €100 note to a local prostitute who gave him her services on credit.

The prostitute goes quickly to the hotel, as she owes €100 for her hourly room use to entertain clients. Just as she hands the owner the cash, the rich Aussie comes back down to reception. He informs the hotel owner that the proposed room is unsatisfactory. He takes back his €100 and departs.

Sure, there was no retained profit in these transactions, but everyone no longer has any debt and the people of the small town can look more optimistically towards their future.

How to keep a healthy level of insanity and drive other people insane:

- At lunchtime, sit in your parked car and point a hair dryer at passing cars to see if they slow down.
- Page yourself over the intercom. [Don't disguise your voice].
- Insist that your e-mail address be Zena-goddess-of-fire@companyname.com or Elvis-the-king@companyname.com

- Every time someone asks you to do something, ask if they want fries with that.
- Encourage your colleagues to join you in a little synchronised chair dancing.
- Put your garbage can on your desk and label it *'IN.'*
- Develop an unnatural fear of staplers.
- Put decaf in the coffee maker for three weeks. Once everyone has gotten over his or her caffeine addiction, switch to espresso.
- In the memo field of all your cheques, write, *'For sexual favours'*
- Reply to everything someone says with, *'That's what you think.'*
- Finish all your sentences with, *'In accordance with the prophecy.'*
- Adjust the tint on your monitor so that the brightness level lights up the entire working area. Insist to others that you like it that way.
- Don't use any punctuation or capital letters.
- As often as possible, skip rather than walk.
- Ask people what sex they are.
- Specify that your drive-through order is a *'to go.'*
- Sing along at the opera.
- Go to a poetry recital and ask why the poems don't rhyme.
- Find out where your boss shops and buy exactly the same outfits. Wear them one day after your boss does. [This is especially effective if your boss is the opposite gender.]
- Send e-mail to the rest of the company and tell them what you're doing. For example: *'If anyone needs me, I'll be in the bathroom.'*
- Put mosquito netting around your cubicle.
- Five days in advance, tell your friends you can't attend their party because you're not in the mood.

Good information to know

Shampoo Warning - I don't know why I didn't figure this out sooner! I use shampoo in the shower! When I wash my hair, the shampoo runs down my whole body and printed *very clearly* on the shampoo label is this warning, *'For extra volume and body.'* No wonder I have been gaining weight!

Well! I have gotten rid of that shampoo and I am going to start showering with Dawn Dish Soap instead. Its label reads, *'Dissolves fat that is otherwise difficult to remove.'* Problem solved!

If I don't answer the phone, I'll be in the shower!

Now if I can just figure out how to use those wrinkle free bounce sheets!

Nutritrional Health

For those of you who watch what you eat, here's the final word on nutrition and health. It's a relief to know the truth after all those conflicting nutritional studies.

1. The Japanese eat very little fat and suffer fewer heart attacks than Americans.
2. The Mexicans eat a lot of fat and suffer fewer heart attacks than Americans.
3. The Chinese drink very little red wine and suffer fewer heart attacks than Americans.
4. The Italians drink a lot of red wine and suffer fewer heart attacks than Americans.
5. The Germans drink a lot of beer and eat lots of sausages and fats and suffer fewer heart attacks than Americans.

Conclusion:

Eat and drink what you like. Speaking English is apparently what kills you.

Wise words on a Sunday evening.

1. My husband and I divorced over religious differences. He thought he was God and I didn't.
2. I don't suffer from insanity; I enjoy every minute of it.
3. Don't take life too seriously; No one gets out alive.
4. You're just jealous because the voices only talk to me.
5. Beauty is in the eye of the beer holder.
6. Earth is the insane asylum for the universe.
7. I'm not a complete idiot -- Some parts are just missing.
8. Being *'over the hill'* is much better than being under it!
9. Wrinkled was not one of the things I wanted to be when I grew up.
10. A hangover is the wrath of grapes.
11. A journey of a thousand miles begins with a cash advance.

12. Stupidity is not a handicap. Park elsewhere!
13. They call it PMS because Mad Cow Disease was already taken.
14. He who dies with the most toys is nonetheless DEAD.
15. Ham and eggs ... A day's work for a chicken, a lifetime commitment for a pig.
16. I smile because I don't know what the hell is going on.

You don't say?

✓ A mate of mine recently admitted to being addicted to brake fluid. When I quizzed him on it he reckoned he could stop any time ...

✓ The secret of enjoying good red wine: Open the bottle to allow it to breathe. If it doesn't look like it's breathing, give it mouth-to-mouth.

✓ My daughter asked me for a pet spider for her birthday, so I went to our local pet shop and they were $70!!! Blow this, I thought, I can get one cheaper off the web.

✓ I was at an ATM yesterday when a little old lady asked if I could check her balance, so I pushed her over.

✓ I was driving this morning when I saw an AA van. The driver was sobbing uncontrollably and looked very miserable. I thought to myself that guy's heading for a breakdown.

✓ Statistically, 6 out of 7 dwarves are not happy.

✓ My neighbour knocked on my door at 2:30 am this morning, can you believe that, 2:30 am?! Luckily for him I was still up playing my Bagpipes.

✓ Paddy says *'Mick, I'm thinking of buying a Labrador.'*
'I wouldn't do that' says Mick. *'Have you seen how many of their owners go blind?'*

✓ I saw a poor old lady fall over today on the ice!! At least I presume she was poor - she only had £1.20 in her purse.

✓ I was explaining to my wife last night that when you die you get reincarnated but must come back as a different creature. She said, *'I would like to come back as a cow.'* I said, *'You're obviously not listening.'*

✓ A teddy bear is working on a building site. He goes for a tea break and when he returns he notices his pick has been stolen. The bear is angry and reports the theft to the foreman. The foreman grins at the bear and says *'Oh, I forgot to tell you, today's the day the teddy bears have their pick nicked.'*

✓ Murphy says to Paddy *'What ya talkin to an envelope for?'*

'I'm sending a voicemail ya thick sod!'

✓ A wife says to her husband, *'You're always pushing me around and talking behind my back.'* He says, *'What do you expect? You're in a wheelchair.'*

✓ When I was in the pub I heard a couple of losers saying that they wouldn't feel safe on an aircraft if they knew the pilot was a woman. What a pair of sexists. I mean, it's not as if she'd have to reverse the plane!

✓ I bought some 'rocket salad' yesterday but it went off before I could eat it!

✓ Just got back from my mate's funeral. He died after being hit on the head with a tennis ball. It was a lovely service.

✓ 19 Irishmen go to the cinema, the ticket lady asks *'Why so many of you?'* Mick replies, *'The film said 18 or over.'*

Ever wonder

- Why the sun lightens our hair, but darkens our skin?
- Why women can't put on mascara with their mouth closed?
- Why is it that doctors call what they do *'practice?'*
- Why is the man who invests all your money called a broker?
- Why is the time of day with the slowest traffic called rush hour?
- Why isn't there mouse-flavoured cat food?
- Why didn't Noah swat those two mosquitoes?
- Why do they sterilise the needle for lethal injections?
- You know that indestructible black box that is used on airplanes? Why don't they make the whole plane out of that stuff?!
- Why don't sheep shrink when it rains?
- Why are they called apartments when they are all stuck together?
- If flying is so safe, why do they call the airport the terminal?

Paraprosdokians: (Winston Churchill loved them!)

I had to look up *'paraprosdokian.'* Here is the definition: *'Figure of speech in which the latter part of a sentence or phrase is surprising or unexpected; frequently used in a humorous situation.'*

- Where there's a will, I want to be in it.
- The last thing I want to do is hurt you. But it's still on the list.

- We live in a society where pizza gets to your house before the police.
- If I agreed with you, we'd both be wrong.
- Men have two emotions: Hungry and Horny. If you see him without a sandwich, look out.
- I used to be indecisive. Now I'm not so sure.
- War does not determine who is right – only who is left ... left. Oh ya they are the ones holding the protest signs.
- Knowledge is knowing a tomato is a fruit; Wisdom is not putting it in a fruit salad.
- I want to die peacefully in my sleep, like my grandfather... Not screaming and yelling like the passengers in his car.
- To be sure of hitting the target, shoot first and call whatever you hit the target.
- Money can't buy happiness, but it sure makes misery easier to live with.
- I didn't say it was your fault, I said I was blaming you.
- A bus station is where a bus stops. A train station is where a train stops. On my desk, I have a work station.
- Never, under any circumstances, take a sleeping pill and a laxative on the same night.
- I didn't fight my way to the top of the food chain to be a vegetarian.
- Whenever I fill out an application, in the part that says, If an emergency, notify: I put 'doctor.' What's my mother going to do?
- Why does someone believe you when you say there are four billion stars, but check when you say the paint is wet?
- Women will never be equal to men until they can walk down the street with a bald head and a beer gut and still think they are sexy.
- Crowded elevators smell different to midgets.
- Good girls are bad girls that never get caught.
- Why do Americans choose from just two people to run for president and 50 for Miss America?
- Behind every successful man is his woman. Behind the fall of a successful man is usually another woman.
- He who smiles in a crisis has found someone to blame.
- Always borrow money from a pessimist. He won't expect it back.

- Never get into fights with ugly people, they have nothing to lose.
- Hospitality: making your guests feel like they're at home, even if you wish they were.
- I intend to live forever. So far, so good.
- I discovered I scream the same way whether I'm about to be devoured by a great white shark or if a piece of seaweed touches my foot.
- Some cause happiness wherever they go. Others whenever they go.
- I got in a fight one time with a really big guy and he said, *'I'm going to mop the floor with your face.'* I said, *'You'll be sorry.'* He said, *'Oh, yeah? Why?'* I said, *'Well, you won't be able to get into the corners very well.'*
- Never hit a man with glasses. Hit him with a baseball bat.
- I always take life with a grain of salt ... plus a slice of lemon ... and a shot of tequila.
- Jesus loves you, but everyone else thinks you're an asshole.
- I like work. It fascinates me. I sit and look at it for hours.
- I thought I wanted a career. Turns out I just wanted paycheques.
- When tempted to fight fire with fire, remember that the Fire Department usually uses water.
- Knowledge is power and power corrupts. So study hard and be evil.
- With sufficient thrust, pigs fly just fine.
- A bargain is something you don't need at a price you can't resist.
- If winning isn't everything why do they keep score?
- Nostalgia isn't what it used to be.
- A bus is a vehicle that runs twice as fast when you are after it as when you are in it.
- There's a fine line between cuddling and holding someone down so they can't get away.
- Some people hear voices. Some see invisible people. Others have no imagination whatsoever.
- Change is inevitable, except from a vending machine.
- A clear conscience is usually the sign of a bad memory.

- Never argue with an idiot. He'll drag you down to his level and beat you with experience. . [That is why I don't argue with a politician.]
- You don't need a parachute to skydive, but you do need one to skydive again.
- You're never too old to learn something stupid.
- The voices in my head may be fake, but they have good ideas!
- Sometimes my mind wanders and other times it goes away completely.
- Never complain about growing old, far too many people have been denied that privilege.

The geography of a woman

➢ Between 18 and 22, a woman is like Africa, half discovered, half wild, fertile and naturally beautiful!

➢ Between 23 and 30, a woman is like Europe, well developed and open to trade, especially for someone with cash.

➢ Between 31 and 35, a woman is like Spain, very hot, relaxed and convinced of her own beauty.

➢ Between 36 and 40, a woman is like Greece, gently aging but still a warm and desirable place to visit.

➢ Between 41 and 50, a woman is like Great Britain, with a glorious and all conquering past.

➢ Between 51 and 60, a woman is like Russia, has been through war and doesn't make the same mistakes twice, takes care of business.

➢ Between 61 and 70, a woman is like Canada, self-preserving, but open to meeting new people.

➢ After 70, she becomes Tibet, wildly beautiful, with a mysterious past and the wisdom of the ages ... only those with an adventurous spirit and a thirst for spiritual knowledge visit there.

The geography of a man

Between 1 and 70, a man is like Iran, ruled by nuts.

My Years of Job Hunting

1. My first job was working in an Orange Juice factory, but I got canned. I couldn't concentrate.

2. Then I worked in the woods as a Lumberjack, but just couldn't hack it, so they gave me the axe.
3. After that, I tried being a Tailor, but wasn't suited for it - mainly because it was a sew sew job.
4. Next, I tried working in a Muffler Factory, but that was too exhausting.
5. Then, tried being a Chef - figured it would add a little spice to my life, but just didn't have the thyme.
6. Next, I attempted being a Deli Worker, but any way I sliced it ... I couldn't cut the mustard.
7. My best job was a Musician, but eventually found I wasn't noteworthy.
8. I studied a long time to become a Doctor, but didn't have any patients.
9. Next, was a job in a Shoe Factory. I tried hard but just didn't fit in.
10. Then I became a Professional Fisherman, but discovered that I couldn't live on my net income.
11. I managed to get a good job working for a Pool Maintenance Company, but the work was just too draining.
12. So then I got a job in a Gymnasium/Workout Centre, but they said I wasn't fit for the job.
13. After many years of trying to find steady work, I finally got a job as a Historian - until I realised there was no future in it.
14. My last job was working in Starbucks, but had to quit because it was the same old grind.
15. So this year, I tried Retirement and ... guess what ... I found that I'm perfect for the job.

Amazingly simple home remedies:

1. Avoid cutting yourself when slicing vegetables by getting someone else to hold the vegetables while you chop.
2. Avoid arguments with the females about lifting the toilet seat by using the sink.
3. If you have a bad cough, take a large dose of laxatives. Then you'll be afraid to cough.
4. If you can't fix it with a hammer, you've got an electrical problem.
5. For high blood pressure sufferers ~ simply cut yourself and bleed for a few minutes, thus reducing the pressure on your veins. Remember to use a timer.

6. A mouse trap placed on top of your alarm clock will prevent you from rolling over and going back to sleep after you hit the snooze button.

7. You only need two tools in life - WD-40 and duct tape. If it doesn't move and should, use the WD-40. If it shouldn't move and does, use the duct tape.

Thought for the day:

Never hold farts in. They travel up your spine into your brain and that is where shitty ideas come from.

More Words of wisdom

- Nothing is foolproof to a sufficiently talented fool.
- The 50-50-90 rule: Anytime you have a 50-50 chance of getting something right, there's a 90% probability you'll get it wrong.
- The things that come to those who wait will be the things left by those who got there first.
- The shin bone is a device for finding furniture in a dark room.
- A fine is a tax for doing wrong. A tax is a fine for doing well.
- When you go into court, you are putting yourself in the hands of 12 people who weren't smart enough to get out of jury duty.
- Is it true that you never really learn to swear until you learn to drive?
- As income tax time approaches, did you ever notice: When you put the two words *'The'* and *'IRS'* together, it spells *'theirs?'*
- What hair colour do they put on the driver's licenses of bald men?
- I thought about how mothers feed their babies with tiny little spoons and forks, so I wondered what do Chinese mothers use - toothpicks?
- If 4 out of 5 people suffer from diarrhea ... does that mean that one out of five enjoys it?
- Why do croutons come in airtight packages? Aren't they just stale bread to begin with?
- If it's true that we are here to help others, then what exactly are the others here for?

Sex education in the 1960's

This is an actual extract from a sex education school textbook for girls printed in the early 1960's in the UK and explains why the world was much happier and peaceful for men – [But how about the women?]

When retiring to the bedroom, prepare yourself for bed as promptly as possible. Whilst feminine hygiene is of the utmost importance, your tired husband does not want to queue for the bathroom, as he would have to do for his train. But remember to look your best when going to bed. Try to achieve the look that is welcoming without being obvious. If you need to apply face cream or hair rollers, wait until he is asleep as this can be shocking to a man last thing at night.

When it comes to the possibility of intimate relations with your husband, it is important to remember your marriage vows and in particular your commitment to obey him.

If he feels that he needs to sleep immediately, then so be it. In all things be led by your husband's wishes; do not pressure him in any way to stimulate intimacy. Should your husband suggest congress then agree humbly, all the while being mindful that a man's satisfaction is more important than a woman's. When he reaches his moment of fulfilment, a small moan from yourself is encouraging to him and quite sufficient to indicate any enjoyment that you may have had.

Should your husband suggest any of the more unusual practices, be obedient and uncomplaining, but register your reluctance by remaining silent. It is likely that your husband will then fall promptly asleep, so adjust your clothing, freshen up and apply your night-time face and hair care products.

[This was obviously written by a man!]

Observations

1. The nicest thing about the future is that it always starts tomorrow.
2. Money will buy a fine dog, but only kindness will make him wag his tail.
3. If you don't have a sense of humour, you probably don't have any sense at all.
4. Seat belts are not as confining as wheelchairs.
5. A good time to keep your mouth shut is when you're in deep water.

6. How come it takes so little time for a child who is afraid of the dark to become a teenager who wants to stay out all night?

7. Business conventions are important because they demonstrate how many people a company can operate without.

8. Why is it that at class reunions you feel younger than everyone else looks?

9. Scratch a dog and you'll find a permanent job.

10. No one has more driving ambition than the boy who wants to buy a car.

11. There are no new sins; the old ones just get more publicity.

12. There are worse things than getting a call for a wrong number at 4 am. It could be a right number.

13. Think about this ... No one ever says *'It's only a game'* when his team is winning.

14. I've reached the age where the happy hour is a nap.

15. Be careful reading the fine print. There's no way you're going to like it.

16. The trouble with bucket seats is that not everybody has the same size bucket.

17. Do you realise that in about 40 years, we'll have thousands of old ladies running around with tattoos? (And RAP music will be the Golden Oldies!)

18. Money can't buy happiness - but somehow it's more comfortable to cry in a Corvette than in a Datsun.

19. After a certain age, if you don't wake up aching in every joint, you are probably dead.

True or False?

Can you guess which of the following are true and which are false?

1. Apples, not caffeine, are more efficient at waking you up in the morning.

2. Alfred Hitchcock didn't have a belly button. It was eliminated when he was sewn up after surgery.

3. A pack-a-day smoker will lose approximately 2 teeth every 10 years.

4. People do not get sick from cold weather; it's from being indoors a lot more.

5. When you sneeze, all bodily functions stop, even your heart!

6. Only 7 percent of the population are lefties.

7. Forty people are sent to the hospital for dog bites every minute.

8. Babies are born without kneecaps. They don't appear until they are 2-6 years old. [I didn't know that!]
9. The average person over 50 will have spent 5 years waiting in lines.
10. The toothbrush was invented in 1498.
11. The average housefly lives for one month.
12. 40,000 Americans are injured by toilets each year.
13. A coat hanger is 44 inches long when straightened.
14. The average computer user blinks 7 times a minute.
15. Your feet are bigger in the afternoon than any other time of day.
16. Most of us have eaten a spider in our sleep.
17. The REAL reason ostriches stick their head in the sand is to search for water.
18. The only two animals that can see behind themselves without turning their heads are the rabbit and the parrot.
19. John Travolta turned down the starring roles *in 'An Officer and a Gentleman'* and *'Tootsie.'*
20. Michael Jackson owned the rights to the South Carolina State anthem.
21. In most television commercials advertising milk, a mixture of white paint and a little thinner is used in place of the milk.
22. Prince Charles and Prince William NEVER travel on the same airplane, just in case there is a crash.
23. The first Harley Davidson motorcycle, built in 1903, used a tomato can for a carburettor.
24. Most hospitals make money by selling the umbilical cords cut from women who give birth. They are used in vein transplant surgery.
25. Humphrey Bogart was related to Princess Diana. They were 7th cousins.
26. If colouring weren't added to Coca-Cola, it would be green.

Answers below ...

They are all TRUE. Now go back and think about #16!!!

Bits and Pieces

Put your ear to the ground, your shoulder to the wheel and your nose to the grindstone. We all know this saying - now try to work in that position!

Bank president, advising Henry Ford's lawyer not to invest in the Ford Motor Company, 1903: *'The horse is here to stay, but the automobile is a novelty, a fad.'* [With the high petrol prices, it may well become a novelty again!]

David Sarnoff's associates in response to his urgings for investment in the radio in the 1920's: *'The wireless music box has no imaginable commercial value. Who would pay for a message sent to nobody in particular?'*

'Rock and Roll - It will be gone by June.' - Variety Magazine, 1955.

'This little computer,' said the sales clerk *'will do half your job for you.'* The senior manager studying the machine made his decision; *'Fine, I'll take two.'*

A girl involved with the women's lib group boarded a crowded bus and one man rose to his feet. *'No, no, you must not give up your seat. I insist,'* she said.

The man replied; *'You may insist as much as you like, Lady, this is the street where I get off.'*

A little boy was attending his first wedding. After the service, his cousin asked him, *'How many women can a man marry?'*

'Sixteen,' the boy responded.

His cousin was amazed that he had an answer so quickly.

'How do you know that?'

'Easy,' the little boy said. *'All you have to do is add it up, like the Bishop said: 4 better, 4 worse, 4 richer, 4 poorer'*

A family was on its way to the hospital where their 16-year-old daughter was scheduled to undergo a tonsillectomy. During the ride, the teenager and her parents talked about how the procedure would be performed.

'Dad,' the teenager asked, *'How are they going to keep my mouth open during the surgery'?*

Without hesitation, he said, *'They're going to give you a phone.'*

John O'Reilly hoisted his beer and said, *'Here's to spending the rest of me life, between the legs of me wife!'*

That won him the top prize at the pub for the best toast of the night! He went home and told his wife, Mary, *'I won the prize for the Best toast of the night'*

She said, *'Aye, did ye now. And what was your toast?'*

John said, *'Here's to spending the rest of me life, sitting in church beside me wife.'*

'Oh, that is very nice indeed, John!' Mary said.

The next day, Mary ran into one of John's drinking buddies on the street corner. The man chuckled leeringly and said, *'John won the prize the other night at the pub with a toast about you, Mary.'*

She said, *'Aye, he told me and I was a bit surprised myself. You know, he's only been there twice in the last four years. Once he fell asleep and the other time I had to pull him by the ears to make him come.'*

While fishing off the Queensland coast, a tourist capsised his boat. He could swim, but his fear of crocodiles kept him clinging to the overturned craft. Spotting an old beachcomber standing on the shore, the tourist shouted, *'Are there any crocs around here?'*

'No,' the man shouted back, *'They haven't been around for years!'*

Feeling safe, the tourist started swimming leisurely toward the shore. About halfway there he asked the guy, *'How'd you get rid of the crocs?'*

The beachcomber said, *'The sharks got 'em.'*

Definitions:

- Marriage: It's an agreement wherein a man loses his bachelor degree and a woman gains her master.
- Lecture: An art of transmitting information from the notes of the lecturer to the notes of students without passing through the minds of either.
- Cigarette: A pinch of tobacco rolled in paper with a fire at one end and a fool at the other.
- Conference: A confusion of one man multiplied by the number present.
- Conference room: A place where everybody talks, nobody listens and everybody disagrees later on.
- Compromise: The art of dividing a cake in such a way that everybody believes he got the biggest piece.
- Tears: The hydraulic force by which masculine will power is defeated by feminine water power!
- Ecstasy: A feeling when you feel you are going to feel a feeling you have never felt before.
- Classic: A book which people praise, but never read.

- Smile: A curve that can set a lot of things straight!
- Office: A place where you can relax after your strenuous home life.
- Yawn: The only time when some married men ever get to open their mouth.
- Experience: The name men give to their mistakes.
- Diplomat: A person who tells you to go to Hell in such a way that you actually look forward to the trip.
- Optimist: A person who while falling from the Eiffel Tower says when midway, *'See I'm not injured yet!'*
- Miser: A person who lives poor so that he can die rich.
- Father: a banker provided by nature.
- Boss: Someone who is early when you are late; and late when you are early.
- Politician: One who shakes your hand before elections and your confidence later.
- Doctor: A person who kills your ills by pills and kills you by his bills.

I never knew

Q: Why do men's clothes have buttons on the right while women's clothes have buttons on the left?

A: When buttons were invented, they were very expensive and worn primarily by the rich. Since most people are right-handed, it is easier to push buttons on the right through holes on the left. Because wealthy women were dressed by maids, dressmakers put the buttons on the maid's right! And that's where women's buttons have remained since.

Q: Why do ships and aircraft use *'mayday'* as their call for help?

A: This comes from the French word *m'aidez* -meaning *'help me'* - and is pronounced, approximately, *'mayday.'*

Q: Why are zero scores in tennis called *'love?'*

A: In France, where tennis became popular, round zero on the scoreboard looked like an egg and was called *'l'oeuf,'* which is French for *'egg.'* When tennis was introduced in the US, Americans (mis) pronounced it *'love.'*

Q. Why do X's at the end of a letter signify kisses?

A: In the Middle Ages, when many people were unable to read or write, documents were often signed using an X. Kissing the X represented an oath to fulfil obligations specified in the document. The X and the kiss eventually became synonymous.

Q: Why is shifting responsibility to someone else called *'passing the buck?'*

A: In card games, it was once customary to pass an item, called a buck, from player to player to indicate whose turn it was to deal. If a player did not wish to assume the responsibility of dealing, he would *'pass the buck'* to the next player.

Q: Why do people clink their glasses before drinking a toast?

A: It used to be common for someone to try to kill an enemy by offering him a poisoned drink. To prove to a guest that a drink was safe, it became customary for a guest to pour a small amount of his drink into the glass of the host. Both men would drink it simultaneously. When a guest trusted his host, he would only touch or clink the host's glass with his own.

Q: Why are people in the public eye said to be *'in the limelight?'*

A: Invented in 1825, limelight was used in lighthouses and theatres by burning a cylinder of lime which produced a brilliant light. In the theatre, a performer *'in the limelight'* was the centre of attention.

Q: Why is someone who is feeling great *'on cloud nine?'*

A: Types of clouds are numbered according to the altitudes they attain, with nine being the highest cloud. If someone is said to be on cloud nine, that person is floating well above worldly cares.

Q: In golf, where did the term *'Caddie'* come from?

A. When Mary Queen of Scots went to France as a young girl, Louis, King of France, learned that she loved the Scots game *'golf.'* So he had the first course outside of Scotland built for her enjoyment. To make sure she was properly chaperoned (and guarded) while she played, Louis hired cadets from a military school to accompany her. Mary liked this a lot and when returned to Scotland (not a very good idea in the long run) she took the practice with her. In French, the word cadet is pronounced *'ca-day'* and the Scots changed it into *'caddie.'*

Q: Why are many coin banks shaped like pigs?

A: Long ago, dishes and cookware in Europe were made of a dense orange clay called *'pygg.'* When people saved coins in jars made of this clay, the jars became known as *'pygg banks.'* When an English potter misunderstood the word, he made a container that resembled a pig. And it caught on.

Q: Did you ever wonder why dimes, quarters and half dollars have notches (milling), while pennies and nickels do not?

A: The US Mint began putting notches on the edges of coins containing gold and silver to discourage holders from shaving off

46

small quantities of the precious metals. Dimes, quarters and half dollars are notched because they used to contain silver. Pennies and nickels aren't notched because the metals they contain are not valuable enough to shave.

Daft Tourists

These *were* '*allegedly*' posted on an Australian Tourism Website and the answers are the actual responses by the so-called website officials, who obviously have a great sense of humour:

Q: Does it ever get windy in Australia? I have never seen it rain on TV, how do the plants grow? (UK).

A: We import all plants fully grown and then just sit around watching them die.

Q: Will I be able to see kangaroos in the street? (USA)

A: Depends how much you've been drinking.

Q: I want to walk from Perth to Sydney - can I follow the railroad tracks? (Sweden)

A: Sure, it's only three thousand miles, take lots of water.

Q: Are there any ATMs (cash machines) in Australia? Can you send me a list of them in Brisbane, Cairns, Townsville and Hervey Bay? (UK)

A: What did your last slave die of?

Q: Can you give me some information about hippo racing in Australia? (USA)

A: Africa is the big triangle shaped continent south of Europe ... Australia is that big island in the middle of the Pacific which does not ... Oh forget it. Sure, the hippo racing is every Tuesday night in Kings Cross ... Come naked.

Q: Which direction is North in Australia? (USA)

A: Face south and then turn 180 degrees. Contact us when you get here and we'll send the rest of the directions.

Q: Can I bring cutlery into Australia? (UK)

A: Why? Just use your fingers like we do.

Q: Can you send me the Vienna Boys' Choir schedule? (USA)

A: Austria is that quaint little country bordering Germany, which is ... Oh forget it. Sure, the Vienna Boys Choir plays every Tuesday night in Kings Cross, straight after the hippo races. Come naked.

Q: Can I wear high heels in Australia? (UK)

A: You are a British politician, right?

Q: Are there supermarkets in Sydney and is milk available all year round? (Germany)

A: No, we are a peaceful civilisation of vegan hunter/gatherers ... Milk is illegal.

Q: Please send a list of all doctors in Australia who can dispense rattlesnake serum. (USA)

A: Rattlesnakes live in America, which is where YOU come from. All Australian snakes are perfectly harmless, can be safely handled and make good pets.

Q: I have a question about a famous animal in Australia, but I forget its name. It's a kind of bear and lives in trees. (USA)

A: It's called a Drop Bear. They are so called because they drop out of Gum trees and eat the brains of anyone walking underneath them. You can scare them off by spraying yourself with human urine before you go out walking.

Q: I have developed a new product that is the fountain of youth. Can you tell me where I can sell it in Australia? (USA)

A: Anywhere significant numbers of Americans gather.

Q: Can you tell me the regions in Tasmania where the female population is smaller than the male population? (Italy)

A: Yes, gay night clubs.

Q: Do you celebrate Christmas in Australia? (France)

A: Only at Christmas.

Q: I was in Australia in 1969 on R+R and I want to contact the girl I dated while I was staying in Kings Cross. Can you help? (USA)

A: Yes and you will still have to pay her by the hour.

Q: Will I be able to speak English most places I go? (USA)

A: Yes, but you'll have to learn it first.

Interesting Facts:

- Every drop of seawater contains approximately 1 billion gold atoms.
- During WW II, IBM built counting machines the Nazis used to manage their death/concentration camps.
- The first computer was ENIAC, short for Electronic Numerical Integrator And Computer, unveiled on Feb 14, 1946.
- The total combined weight of the world's ant population is heavier than the weight of the human population.

- The deadliest war in history excluding WW II was a civil war in China in the 1850's in which the rebels were led by a man who thought he was the brother of Jesus Christ.
- Just about 3 people are born every second and about 1.333 people die every second. The result is about a 2 and 2/3 net increase of people every second. Almost 10 people more live on Earth now, than before you finished reading this.
- Ever notice how the people who tell you to calm down are often the ones who made you angry in the first place?
- Lack of planning on your part does not constitute an emergency on my part.
- Proceed and Procedure is the last hiding place of people without the wit and wisdom to do their job properly.
- Remember that age and treachery will always triumph over youth ad ability.
- Never do today that which will become someone else's responsibility tomorrow.
- Every time you open your mouth you have this wonderful ability to continually confirm what I think.
- Show me a good loser and I'll show you a loser!
- Put the key of despair into the lock of apathy. Turn the knob of mediocrity slowly and open the gates of despondency – welcome to a day in the average office.
- It's the team that matters. Where would The Beatles be without Ringo? If John got Yoko to play drums, the history of music would be completely different.
- What does a squirrel do in the summer? It buries nuts. Why? Because then in winter time he's got something to eat and he won't die. So, collecting nuts in the summer is worthwhile work. Every task you do at work think, would a squirrel do that? Think squirrels. Think nuts.
- When confronted by a difficult problem, you can solve it easier by reducing it to the question, *'How would the Lone Ranger handle this?'*
- Accept that some days you are the pigeon and some days you are the statue.
- If your boss is getting you down, look at him through the prongs of a fork and imagine him in jail.

- If you can't keep your head when all around you have lost theirs, then you probably haven't understood the seriousness of the situation.
- Some mistakes are too much fun to only make them once.
- You don't have to be mad to work here! In fact we ask you to complete a medical questionnaire to ensure that you are not.
- If you treat the people around you with love and respect, they will never guess that you're trying to get them sacked.
- If at first you don't succeed, remove all evidence you ever tried.
- You have to be 100% behind someone before you can stab them in the back.
- If work was so good, the rich would have kept more of it for themselves.
- Those of you who think you know everything are annoying to those of us who do.
- There's no 'I' in 'Team,' but there's no 'I' in 'useless smug colleague,' either. And there are four in 'platitude-quoting idiot.' Go figure.
- Know your limitations and be content with them. Too much ambition results in promotion to a job you can't do.
- Make good use of your cylindrical filing unit, the one you mainly keep under the desk.
- Quitters never win, winners never quit. But those who never win and never quit are idiots.
- If you're going to be late, then be late and not just 2 minutes – make it an hour and enjoy your breakfast.
- Statistics are like a lamp post to a drunken man – more for leaning on than illumination.
- A problem shared is a problem halved, so is your problem really yours or just half of someone else's?
- You don't have to be mad to work here, but you do have to be on time, well presented, a team player, customer service focused and sober.
- I thought I could see the light at the end of the tunnel, but it was just some b'stard with a torch, bringing me more work.
- Living on earth is expensive, but it does include a free trip around the sun every year.
- How long a minute is, depends on what side of the bathroom door you're on.

- Birthdays are good for you, the more you have, the longer you live.
- Happiness comes through doors you didn't even know you left open.
- Ever notice that the people who are late are often much jollier than the people who have to wait for them?
- Most of us go to our grave with our music still inside of us.
- If Wal-Mart is lowering prices every day, how come nothing is free yet?
- You may be only one person in the world, but you may also be the world to one person.
- Don't cry because it's over, smile, because it happened.
- A truly happy person is one who can enjoy the scenery on a detour.

Wise words and sage advice

✓ Men have two emotions: Hungry and Horny. If you see him without a sandwich, look out.

✓ Politicians and diapers have one thing in common. They should both be changed regularly and for the same reason.

✓ Going to church doesn't make you a Christian any more than standing in a garage makes you a car.

✓ Evening news is where they begin with *'Good evening,'* and then proceed to tell you why it isn't.

✓ I asked God for a bike, but I know God doesn't work that way. So I stole a bike and asked for forgiveness.

✓ Sex is not the answer. Sex is the question. *'Yes'* is the answer.

✓ We never really grow up; we only learn how to act in public.

✓ Children: You spend the first 2 years of their life teaching them to walk and talk. Then you spend the next 16 years telling them to sit down and shut-up.

✓ To steal ideas from one person is plagiarism. To steal from many is research.

✓ Better to remain silent and be thought a fool, than to speak and remove all doubt.

✓ How is it one careless match can start a forest fire, but it takes a whole box to start a campfire?

✓ Did you know that dolphins are so smart that within a few weeks of captivity, they can train people to stand on the very edge of the pool and throw them fish?

✓ No one is listening until you fart.
✓ Never test the depth of the water with both feet.
✓ Give a man a fish and he will eat for a day. Teach him how to fish and he will sit in a boat and drink beer all day.
✓ Some days you are the dog, some days you are the tree.

They walk amongst us!

- A man bought a new fridge for his house. To get rid of his old fridge, he put it in his front yard and hung a Sign on it saying: *'Free to good home. You want it, you take it.'*

  For three days the fridge sat there without anyone looking twice. He eventually decided that people were too mistrustful of this deal. So he changed the sign to read: *'Fridge for sale $50.'* The next day someone stole it!

- One day I was walking down the beach with some friends when someone shouted ... *'Look at that dead bird!'* Someone looked up at the sky and said ...*'where?'*

- While looking at a house, my brother asked the Estate Agent which direction was north because he didn't want the sun waking him up every morning. She asked, *'Does the sun rise in the north?'* My brother explained that the sun rises in the east and has for some time.

  She shook her head and said, *'Oh, I don't keep up with all that stuff ...'*

- My colleague and I were eating our lunch in our cafeteria when we overheard an admin girl talking about the sunburn she got on her weekend drive to the beach. She drove down in a convertible, but said she didn't think she'd get sunburned because the car was moving.

- My sister has a lifesaving tool in her car which is designed to cut through a seatbelt if she gets trapped. She keeps it in the trunk.

- I couldn't find my luggage at the airport baggage area and went to the lost luggage office to report the loss. The woman there smiled and told me not to worry because she was a trained professional and said I was in good hands. *'Now,'* she asked me, *'Has your plane arrived yet?'* [I work with professionals like this.]

- While working at a pizza parlour I observed a man ordering a small pizza to go. He appeared to be alone and the cook asked him if he would like it cut into four pieces or six. He thought about it for some time then said 'Just cut it into four pieces; I don't think I'm hungry enough to eat six pieces.

- A man was driving when he saw the flash of a traffic camera. He figured that his picture had been taken for exceeding the limit, even though he knew that he was not speeding ... Just to be sure, he went around the block and passed the same spot, driving even more slowly, but again the camera flashed. Now he began to think that this was quite funny, so he drove even slower as he passed the area again, but the traffic camera again flashed. He tried a fourth time with the same result ... He did this a fifth time and was now laughing when the camera flashed as he rolled past, this time at a snail's pace ... Two weeks later, he got five tickets in the mail for driving without a seat belt.

And last, but not least:

- A noted psychiatrist was a guest speaker at an academic function where Nancy Pelosi happened to appear. Ms. Pelosi took the opportunity to schmooze the good doctor a bit and asked him a question with which he was most at ease.

     'Would you mind telling me, Doctor,' she asked, *'how you detect a mental deficiency in somebody who appears completely normal?'*

     'Nothing is easier,' he replied. *'You ask a simple question which anyone should answer with no trouble. If the person hesitates, that puts you on the track ...'*

     'What sort of question?' asked Pelosi.

     Well, you might ask, *'Captain Cook made three trips around the world and died during one of them. Which one?'*

     Pelosi thought a moment and then said with a nervous laugh, *'You wouldn't happen to have another example would you? I must confess I don't know much about history.'*

Sadly, they walk amongst us!

An Old Farmer's Advice:

- ✓ Your fences need to be horse-high, pig-tight and bull-strong.
- ✓ Keep skunks and bankers at a distance.
- ✓ Life is simpler when you plough around the stump.
- ✓ A bumble bee is considerably faster than a John Deere tractor.
- ✓ Words that soak into your ears are whispered ... not yelled.
- ✓ Meanness don't jes' happen overnight.

- ✓ Do not corner something that you know is meaner than you.
- ✓ It don't take a very big person to carry a grudge.
- ✓ You cannot unsay a cruel word.
- ✓ Every path has a few puddles.
- ✓ When you wallow with pigs, expect to get dirty.
- ✓ The best sermons are lived, not preached.
- ✓ Don't interfere with somethin' that ain't bothering you none. [If it ain't broke – don't fix.]
- ✓ Most of the stuff people worry about ain't never gonna happen anyway.
- ✓ Remember that silence is sometimes the best answer.
- ✓ Live a good, honourable life. Then when you get older and think back, you'll enjoy it a second time.
- ✓ Timing has a lot to do with the outcome of a Rain dance.
- ✓ If you find yourself in a hole, the first thing to do is stop diggin'.
- ✓ Sometimes you get and sometimes you get got.
- ✓ The biggest troublemaker you'll probably ever have to deal with watches you from the mirror every mornin'.
- ✓ Always drink upstream from the herd.
- ✓ Good judgment comes from experience and a lotta that comes from bad judgment.
- ✓ Lettin' the cat outta the bag is a whole lot easier than puttin' it back in.
- ✓ If you get to thinkin' you're a person of some influence, try orderin' somebody else's dog around.
- ✓ Live simply. Love generously. Care deeply.
- ✓ Don't pick a fight with an old man. If he is too old to fight, he'll just kill you.

As I mature

I've learned that:

1. you cannot make someone love you. All you can do is stalk them and hope they panic and give in.
2. it takes years to build up trust and it only takes suspicion, not proof to destroy it.
3. you can get by on charm for about fifteen minutes. After that, you'd better have a big willy or big boobs.
4. you shouldn't compare yourself to others – they are more screwed up than you think.
5. you can keep vomiting long after you think you're finished.

6. I've learned that we are responsible for what we do, unless we are celebrities or politicians.
7. regardless of how hot and steamy a relationship is at first, the passion fades and there had better be a lot of money to take its place!
8. 99% of the time when something isn't working in your house, one of your kids did it.
9. the people you care most about in life are taken from you too soon and all the less important ones just never go away.

I Didn't Know that!

Alaska: More than half of the coastline of the entire United States is in Alaska.

Amazon: The Amazon rainforest produces more than 20% of the world's oxygen supply.

The Amazon River pushes so much water into the Atlantic Ocean that, more than one hundred miles at sea off the mouth of the river; one can dip fresh water out of the ocean. The volume of water in the Amazon River is greater than the next eight largest rivers in the world combined and three times the flow of all rivers in the United States.

Antarctica: Antarctica is the only land on our planet that is not owned by any country. Ninety percent of the world's ice covers Antarctica. This ice also represents seventy percent of all the fresh water in the world. As strange as it sounds, however, Antarctica is essentially a desert; the average yearly total precipitation is about two inches. Although covered with ice (all but 0.4% of it, ice.), Antarctica is the driest place on the planet, with an absolute humidity lower than the Gobi desert.

Russia: The deepest hole ever drilled by man is the Kola Superdeep Borehole, in Russia. It reached a depth of 12,261 meters (about 40,226 feet or 7.62 miles). It was drilled for scientific research and gave up some unexpected discoveries, one of which was a huge deposit of hydrogen - so massive that the mud coming from the hole was boiling with it.

Brazil: Brazil got its name from the nut, not the other way around.

Canada: Canada has more lakes than the rest of the world combined. Canada is an Indian word meaning *'Big Village.'*

United States: The Eisenhower interstate system requires that one mile in every five must be straight. These straight sections are usable as airstrips in times of war or other emergencies.

Chicago: Next to Warsaw, Chicago has the largest Polish population in the world.

Detroit: Woodward Avenue in Detroit, Michigan, carries the designation M-1, so named because it was the first paved road anywhere.

St. Paul: Minnesota: Was originally called Pig's Eye after a man named Pierre *'Pig's Eye'* Parent who set up the first business there.

Los Angeles: Its full name is: El Pueblo de Nuestra Senora la Reina de Los Angeles de Porciuncula - and can be abbreviated to 3.63% of its size: L.A.

Ohio: There are no natural lakes in the state of Ohio, every one is manmade.

New York City: The term *'The Big Apple'* was coined by touring jazz musicians of the 1930s who used the slang expression *'apple'* for any town or city. Therefore, to play New York City is to play the big time - The Big Apple.

There are more Irish in New York City than in Dublin, Ireland; more Italians in New York City than in Rome, Italy; and more Jews in New York City than in Tel Aviv, Israel.

Damascus, Syria: Was flourishing a couple of thousand years before Rome was founded in 753 BC, making it the oldest continuously inhabited city in existence.

Istanbul, Turkey: Is the only city in the world that's located on two continents.

Pitcairn Island: The smallest island with country status is Pitcairn in Polynesia, at just 1.75 sq. Miles/4.53 sq. Km.

Rome: The first city to reach a population of 1 million people was Rome, Italy in 133 B.C. There is a city called Rome on every continent.

Siberia: Contains more than 25% of the world's forests.

S.M.O.M.: The actual smallest sovereign entity in the world is the Sovereign Military Order of Malta (S.M.O.M). It is located in the city of Rome, Italy; has an area of two tennis courts and, as of 2001, had a population of 80 - 20 less people than the Vatican. It is a sovereign entity under international law, just as the Vatican is.

Sahara Desert: In the Sahara Desert, there is a town named Tidikelt, Algeria, which did not receive a drop of rain for ten years. Technically though, the driest place on Earth is in the valleys of the Antarctic near Ross Island. There has been no rainfall there for two million years.

Spain: Literally means *'the land of rabbits.'*

Roads: Chances that a road is unpaved:

In the U.S.A. = 1%;
In Canada = 75%

Waterfalls: The water of Angel Falls (the world's highest) in Venezuela drops 3,212 feet (979 meters). They are 15 times higher than Niagara Falls.

Unusual Interesting Facts

1. The longest one-syllable word in the English language is *'screeched.'*
2. *'Dreamt'* is the only English word that ends in the letters *'mt.'*
3. Almonds are members of the peach family.
4. The symbol on the *'pound'* key (#) is called an octothorpe.
5. The dot over the letter *'I'* is called a tittle.
6. Ingrown toenails are hereditary.
7. The word *'set'* has more definitions than any other word in the English language.
8. *'Underground'* is the only word in the English language that begins and ends with the letters *'und.'*
9. There are only four words in the English language which end in *'-dous:'* tremendous, horrendous, stupendous and hazardous.
10. The longest word in the English language, according to the Oxford English Dictionary, is pneumonoultramicroscopicsilicovolcanoconiosis.
11. The only other word with the same amount of letters is its plural: pneumonoultramicroscopicsilicovolcanoconioses!
12. The longest place-name still in use is Taumatawhakatangihangakoauauotamateaturipukakapikimaung ahoronukup okaiwe-nuakit natahu, a New Zealand hill.
13. Tigers have striped skin, not just striped fur.
14. Telly Savalas and Louis Armstrong died on their birthdays.
15. Donald Duck's middle name is Fauntleroy.
16. The muzzle of a lion is like a fingerprint - no two lions have the same pattern of whiskers.
17. A pregnant goldfish is called a twit.
18. There is a seven-letter word in the English language that contains ten words without rearranging any of its letters, *'therein:'* the, there, he, in, rein, her, here, ere, therein, herein.
19. Duelling is legal in Paraguay as long as both parties are registered blood donors.
20. A goldfish has a memory span of three seconds.
21. It's impossible to sneeze with your eyes open.

22. Cranberries are sorted for ripeness by bouncing them; a fully ripened cranberry can be dribbled like a basketball.
23. The letters KGB stand for Komitet Gosudarstvennoy Bezopasnosti.
24. *'Stewardesses'* is the longest English word that is typed with only the left hand.
25. The combination *'ought'* can be pronounced in nine different ways; the following sentence contains them all: *'A rough-coated, dough-faced, thoughtful ploughman strode through the streets of Scarborough; after falling into a slough, he coughed and hiccoughed.'*
26. The only 15 letter word that can be spelled without repeating a letter is uncopyrightable.
27. Facetious and abstemious contain all the vowels in the correct order, as does arsenious, meaning *'containing arsenic.'*
28. Emus and kangaroos cannot walk backwards and are on the Australian seal for that reason.
29. Cats have over one hundred vocal sounds, while dogs only have about ten.
30. The word *'Checkmate'* in chess comes from the Persian phrase *'Shah Mat,'* which means *'the king is dead.'*
31. The reason firehouses have circular stairways is from the days of yore when the engines were pulled by horses. The horses were stabled on the ground floor and figured out how to walk up straight staircases.

CHAPTER 2 – FAMOUS QUOTES

The True Origin of the Internet

In ancient Israel, it came to pass that a trader called Abraham of Com did take unto himself a young wife by the name of Dot. And Dot of Com was a comely woman, broad of shoulder and long of leg. Indeed, she had been called *'Amazon Dot Com.'*

And she said unto Abraham, her husband, *'Why dost thou travel far from town to town with thy goods when thou can trade without ever leaving thy tent?'*

And Abraham did look at her as though she were several saddle bags short of a camel load, but simply said, *'How, dear?'*

And Dot replied, *'I will place drums in all the towns and drums in between to send messages saying what you have for sale and they will reply telling you which hath the best price. And the sale can be made on the drums and delivery made by Uriah's Pony Stable (UPS).'*

Abraham thought long and decided he would let Dot have her way with the drums. And the drums rang out and were an immediate success. Abraham sold all the goods he had at the top price, without ever moving from his tent. But this success did arouse envy. A man named Maccabia did secreted (look it up, it means to hide) himself inside Abraham's drum and was accused of insider trading. And the young man did take to Dot Com's trading as doth the greedy horsefly take to camel dung.

They were called Nomadic Ecclesiastical Rich Dominican Siderites or NERDS for short.

And lo, the land was so feverish with joy at the new riches and the deafening sound of drums that no one noticed that the real riches were going to the drum maker, one Brother William of Gates, who bought up every drum company in the land. And indeed did insist on making drums that would work only with Brother Gates' drumheads and drumsticks.

And Dot did say, *'Oh, Abraham, what we have started is being taken over by others.'*

And as Abraham looked out over the Bay of Ezekiel or as it came to be known *'eBay'* he said, *'We need a name that reflects what we are.'*

And Dot replied, *'Young Ambitious Hebrew Owner Operators.'*

'YAHOO!' exclaimed Abraham.

And that is how it all began. Al Gore had absolutely nothing to do with it!

Bob hope in heaven

Tribute to a man who DID make a difference.

On turning 70
'I still chase women, but only downhill.'
On turning 80
'That's the time of your life when even your birthday suit needs pressing.'
On turning 90
'You know you're getting old when the candles cost more than the cake.'
On turning 100
'I don't feel old. In fact, I don't feel anything until noon. Then it's time for my nap.'
On giving up his early career, boxing
'I ruined my hands in the ring. The referee kept stepping on them.'
On never winning an Oscar
'Welcome to the Academy Awards or, as it's called at my home, 'Passover'.
On golf
'Golf is my profession. Show business is just to pay the green fees.'
On presidents
'I have performed for 12 presidents and entertained only six.'
On why he chose showbiz for his career
'When I was born, the doctor said to my mother, 'Congratulations, you have an eight pound ham.'
On receiving the congressional gold medal
'I feel very humble, but I think I have the strength of character to fight it.'
On his family's early poverty
'Four of us slept in the one bed. When it got cold, mother threw on another brother.'
On his six brothers
'That's how I learned to dance. Waiting for the bathroom.'
On his early failures
'I would not have had anything to eat if it wasn't for the stuff the audience threw at me.'

On going to heaven

'I've done benefits for ALL religions. I'd hate to blow the hereafter on a technicality.'

One of Andy Rooney's [60 minutes ideas:]

Send an ad for your local chimney cleaner to American Express. Send a pizza coupon to Citibank. If you didn't get anything else that day, then just send them their blank application back! If you want to remain anonymous, just make sure your name isn't on anything you send them.

You can even send the envelope back empty if you want to just to keep them guessing! It still costs them 44 cents. The banks and credit card companies are currently getting a lot of their own junk back in the mail, but folks, we need to overwhelm them. Let's let them know what it's like to get lots of junk mail and best of all they're paying for it ... Twice!

Let's help keep our postal service busy since they are saying that e-mail is cutting into their business profits and that's why they need to increase postage costs again. You get the idea!

If enough people follow these tips, it will work. I have been doing this for years and I get very little junk mail any more.

A glass of wine

To my friends who enjoy a glass of wine; and those who don't and are always seen with a bottle of water in their hand:
As Ben Franklin said:
In wine there is wisdom,
In beer there is freedom,
In water there is bacteria.
In a number of carefully controlled trials, scientists have demonstrated that if we drink 1 litre of water each day, at the end of the year we would have absorbed more than 1 kilo of Escherichia coli, (E. Coli) – bacteria found in faeces. In other words, we are consuming 1 kilo of poop.

However, we do NOT run that risk when drinking wine and beer (or tequila, rum, whiskey or other liquor) because alcohol has to go through a purification process of boiling, filtering and/or fermenting.
Remember:
Water = Poop,
Wine = Health.

Therefore, it's better to drink wine and talk stupid, than to drink water and be full of $hit.

There is no need to thank me for this valuable information: I'm doing it as a public service

Confucius Say:

- Woman asks: *'If I sleep with 3 men, everyone calls me a bad woman. But when a man sleeps with 8 girls, everyone calls him a real man. How come?'*
  Man replies: *'It's very simple. Confucius say: When one lock can be opened by 3 different keys, it's a bad lock. But when one key can open 8 different locks, we call it a master key.'*
- *'A lion will not cheat on his wife, but a Tiger Wood!'*
- *'Virginity like bubble, one prick, all gone.'*
- *'Man with hand in pocket feel cocky all day.'*
- *'Foolish man give wife grand piano, wise man give wife upright organ.'*
- *'Man with one chopstick go hungry.'*
- *'Man who scratch ass should not bite fingernails.'*
- *'Man who eat many prunes get good run for money.'*
- *'Baseball is wrong: man with four balls cannot walk.'*
- *'Wife who put husband in doghouse soon find him in cathouse.'*
- *'Man who fight with wife all day get no piece at night.'*
- *'Man who drive like hell, bound to get there.'*
- *'Man who stand on toilet is high on pot.'*
- *'Man who fart in church sit in own pew.'*
- *'Crowded elevator smell different to midget.'*
- *'Sharp tongue can cut own throat?'*
- *'Man who wants pretty nurse, must be patient.'*
- *'Passionate kiss, like spider web, leads to undoing of fly.'*
- *'Better to be pissed off than pissed on.'*
- *'Lady who goes camping must beware of evil intent.'*
- *'Squirrel who runs up woman's leg will not find nuts.'*
- *'Man who leaps off cliff jumps to conclusion.'*
- *'Man who runs in front of car gets tired, man who runs behind car gets exhausted.'*
- *'It takes many nails to build a crib, but one screw to fill it.'*
- *'Man who live in glass house, should change clothes in basement.'*
- *'Man who fish in other man's well, often catch crabs.'*

Twenty-one things to remember

1. Give people more than they expect and do it cheerfully.
2. Marry a man/woman you love to talk to. As you get older, their conversational skills will be as important as any other.
3. Don't believe all you hear, spend all you have or sleep all you want.
4. When you say, *'I love you,'* mean it.
5. When you say, *'I'm sorry,'* look the person in the eye.
6. Be engaged at least six months before you get married.
7. Believe in love at first sight.
8. Never laugh at anyone's dreams. People who don't have dreams don't have much.
9. Love deeply and passionately. You might get hurt but it's the only way to live life completely.
10. In disagreements, fight fairly. No name calling.
11. Don't judge people by their relatives.
12. Talk slowly but think quickly.
13. When someone asks you a question you don't want to answer, smile and ask, *'Why do you want to know?'*
14. Remember that great love and great achievements involve great risk.
15. Say *'bless you'* when you hear someone sneeze.
16. When you lose, don't lose the lesson.
17. Remember the three R's:
    Respect for self;
    Respect for others; and
    Responsibility for all your actions.
18. Don't let a little dispute injure a great friendship.
19. When you realise you've made a mistake, take immediate steps to correct it.
20. Smile when you pick up the phone. The caller will hear it in your voice.
21. Spend some time alone.

Socrates

Keep this in mind the next time you are about to repeat a rumour.

In ancient Greece (469 - 399 BC), Socrates was widely lauded for his wisdom. One day, an acquaintance ran up to him excitedly and said, *'Socrates, do you know what I just heard about Plato, one of your students?'*

'*Wait a moment,*' Socrates replied, '*Before you tell me I'd like you to pass a little test. It's called the Triple Filter Test.*'

'*Triple filter?*' asked the acquaintance.

'*That's right,*' Socrates continued. '*Before you talk to me about my student let's take a moment to filter what you're going to say. The first filter is Truth. Have you made absolutely sure that what you are about to tell me is True?*'

'*No,*' the man said, '*actually I just heard about it.*'

'*All right,*' said Socrates. '*So you don't really know if it's True or not ... Now let's try the second filter, the filter of Goodness. Is what you are about to tell me about my student something Good?*'

'*No, on the contrary ....*'

'*So,*' Socrates continued, '*you want to tell me something bad about him, even though you're not certain it's true?*'

The man shrugged, a little embarrassed.

Socrates continued. '*You may still pass the test though, because there is a third filter - the filter of Usefulness. Is what you want to tell me about my student going to be Useful to me?*'

'*No, not really ...*'

'*Well,*' concluded Socrates, '*if what you want to tell me is neither True nor Good nor even Useful, why tell it to me at all?*'

The man was defeated and ashamed. This is the reason Socrates was a great philosopher and held in such high esteem.

It also explains why he never found out that Plato was shagging his missus.

Family Tree of Vincent Van Gogh:

His dizzy aunt	Verti Gogh
The brother who ate prunes	Gotta Gogh
The brother at a convenience store	Stop N Gogh
The grandfather from Yugoslavia	U Gogh
His magician uncle	Where-diddy Gogh
His Mexican cousin	A Mee Gogh
The nephew who drove a stage coach	Wells-far Gogh
The constipated uncle	Can't Gogh
The ballroom dancing aunt	Tang Gogh
The bird lover uncle	Flamin Gogh
The fruit-loving cousin	Man Gogh
A sister who loved disco	Go Gogh
And his niece who travels in an RV	Winnie Bay Gogh
I saw you smiling	There ya Gogh

Hollywood Squares:

These great questions and answers are from the days when 'Hollywood Squares' game show responses were spontaneous, not scripted, as they are now. Peter Marshall was the host asking the questions, of course.

Q. Paul, what is a good reason for pounding meat?
   A. Paul Lynde (About fifteen minutes later): Loneliness!
   And the audience laughed for another 10 to 15 minutes.
Q. Do female frogs croak?
   A. Paul Lynde: If you hold their little heads under water long enough.
Q. If you're going to make a parachute jump, at least how high should you be?
   A. Charley Weaver: Three days of steady drinking should do it.
Q. True or False, a pea can last as long as 5,000 years.
   A. George Gobel: Boy, it sure seems that way sometimes.
Q. You've been having trouble going to sleep. Are you probably a man or a woman?
   A. Don Knotts: That's what's been keeping me awake.
Q. According to Cosmopolitan, if you meet a stranger at a party and you think that he is attractive, is it okay to come out and ask him if he's married.
   A. Rose Marie: No wait until morning.
Q. Which of your five senses tends to diminish as you get older?
   A. Charley Weaver: My sense of decency.
Q. In Hawaii, does it take more than three words to say *'I Love You?'*
   A. Vincent Price: No, you can say it with a pineapple and a twenty.
Q. What are *'Do It,' 'I Can Help,'* and *'I Can't Get Enough?''*
   A. George Gobel: I don't know, but it's coming from the next apartment.
Q. As you grow older, do you tend to gesture more or less with your hands while talking?
   A. Rose Marie: You ask me one more growing old question Peter and I'll give you a gesture you'll never forget.
Q. Paul, why do Hell's Angels wear leather?
   A. Paul Lynde: Because chiffon wrinkles too easily.

Q. Charley, you've just decided to grow strawberries. Are you going to get any during the first year?
A. Charley Weaver: Of course not, I'm too busy growing strawberries.
Q. In bowling, what's a perfect score?
A. Rose Marie: Ralph, the pin boy.
Q. It is considered in bad taste to discuss two subjects at nudist camps. One is politics, what is the other?
A. Paul Lynde: Tape measures.
Q. During a tornado, are you safer in the bedroom or in the closet?
A. Rose Marie: Unfortunately Peter, I'm always safe in the bedroom.
Q. Can boys join the Camp Fire Girls?
A. Marty Allen: Only after lights out.
Q. When you pat a dog on its head he will wag his tail. What will a goose do?
A. Paul Lynde: Make him bark?
Q. If you were pregnant for two years, what would you give birth to?
A. Paul Lynde: Whatever it is, it would never be afraid of the dark.
Q. According to Ann Landers, is there anything wrong with getting into the habit of kissing a lot of people?
A. Charley Weaver: It got me out of the army.
Q. It is the most abused and neglected part of your body, what is it?
A. Paul Lynde: Mine may be abused, but it certainly isn't neglected.
Q. Back in the old days, when Great Grandpa put horseradish on his head, what was he trying to do?
A. George Gobel: Get it in his mouth. [I really laughed at this one.]
Q. Who stays pregnant for a longer period of time, your wife or your elephant?
A. Paul Lynde: Who told you about my elephant?
Q. When a couple have a baby, who is responsible for its sex?
A. Charley Weaver: I'll lend him the car, the rest is up to him.
Q. Jackie Gleason revealed that he firmly believes in them and has actually seen them on at least two occasions. What are they?
A. Charley Weaver: His feet.
Q. According to Ann Landers, what are two things you should never do in bed?

A. Paul Lynde: Point and laugh.

Churchill on Islam

This is amazing. And even more amazing is that this hasn't been published long before now. Unbelievable, but the speech below was written in 1899! [Check Wikipedia - The River War.]

This short speech from Winston Churchill was delivered by him in 1899 when he was a young soldier and journalist. It probably sets out the current views of many, but expressed in the wonderful Churchillian turn of phrase and use of the English language, of which he was a master. Sir Winston Churchill was, without doubt, one of the greatest men of the late 19th and 20th centuries.

He was a brave young soldier, a brilliant journalist, an extraordinary politician and statesman, a great war leader and Prime Minister, to whom the Western world must be forever in his debt. He was a prophet in his own time. He died on 24 January 1965, at the grand old age of 90 and, after a lifetime of service to his country and was accorded a State funeral.

Here is the speech:

'How dreadful are the curses which Mohammedanism lays on its votaries! Besides the fanatical frenzy, which is as dangerous in a man as hydrophobia in a dog, there is this fearful fatalistic apathy. The effects are apparent in many countries, improvident habits, slovenly systems of agriculture, sluggish methods of commerce and insecurity of property exist wherever the followers of the Prophet rule or live.

A degraded sensualism deprives this life of its grace and refinement, the next of its dignity and sanctity. The fact that in Mohammedan law every woman must belong to some man as his absolute property, either as a child, a wife or a concubine, must delay the final extinction of slavery until the faith of Islam has ceased to be a great power among men.

Individual Muslims may show splendid qualities, but the influence of the religion paralyses the social development of those who follow it.

No stronger retrograde force exists in the world. Far from being moribund, Mohammedanism is a militant and proselytising faith. It has already spread throughout Central Africa, raising fearless warriors at every step and were it not that Christianity is

sheltered in the strong arms of science, the science against which it had vainly struggled, the civilisation of modern Europe might fall, as fell the civilisation of ancient Rome.'
Sir Winston Churchill;

[Source: The River War, first edition, Vol. II, pages 248-50 London) Churchill saw it coming ...]

The current plight of the Costa Concordia recalls a comment made by Churchill.

After his retirement he was cruising the Mediterranean on an Italian cruise liner and some Italian journalists asked why an ex British Prime Minister should choose an Italian ship.

There are three things I like about being on an Italian cruise ship said Churchill. *'First their cuisine is unsurpassed. Second their service is superb. And then, in time of emergency, there is none of this nonsense about women and children first.'*

Maya Angelou Said

Maya Angelou was interviewed by Oprah on her 70+ birthday. Oprah asked her what she thought of growing older.

I've learned that:
- *'No matter what happens or how bad it seems today, life does go on and it will be better tomorrow.'*
- *'You can tell a lot about a person by the way s/he handles these three things: a rainy day, lost luggage and tangled Christmas tree lights.'*
- *'Regardless of your relationship with your parents, you'll miss them when they're gone from your life.'*
- *'Making a living' is not the same thing as 'making a life.'*
- *'Life sometimes gives you a second chance.'*
- *'You shouldn't go through life with a catcher's mitt on both hands; you need to be able to throw some things back.'*
- *'Whenever I decide something with an open heart, I usually make the right decision.'*
- *'Even when I have pains, I don't have to be one.'*
- *'Every day you should reach out and touch someone. People love a warm hug or just a friendly pat on the back.'*
- *'I still have a lot to learn.'*
- *'People will forget what you said, people will forget what you did, but people will never forget how you made them feel.'*

Written By Regina Brett, 90 years old, of The Plain Dealer, Cleveland, Ohio

'To celebrate growing older, I once wrote the 45 lessons life taught me. It is the most-requested column I've ever written. My odometer rolled over to 90 in August, so here is the column once more.'

1. Life isn't fair, but it's still good.
2. When in doubt, just take the next small step.
3. Life is too short to waste time hating anyone.
4. Your job won't take care of you when you are sick. Your friends and parents will. Stay in touch.
5. Pay off your credit cards every month.
6. You don't have to win every argument. Agree to disagree.
7. Cry with someone. It's more healing than crying alone.
8. It's okay to get angry.
9. Save for retirement starting with your first paycheque.
10. When it comes to chocolate; resistance is futile.
11. Make peace with your past so it won't screw up the present.
12. It's okay to let your children see you cry.
13. Don't compare your life to others. You have no idea what their journey is all about.
14. If a relationship has to be a secret, you shouldn't be in it.
15. Everything can change in the blink of an eye. But don't worry; God never blinks.
16. Take a deep breath. It calms the mind.
17. Get rid of anything that isn't useful, beautiful or joyful.
18. Whatever doesn't kill you really does make you stronger.
19. It's never too late to have a happy childhood. But the second one is up to you and no one else.
20. Over-prepare, then go with the flow.
21. Be eccentric now. Don't wait for old age to wear purple.
22. The most important sex organ is the brain.
23. When it comes to going after what you love in life, don't take no for an answer.
24. Burn the candles, use the nice sheets and wear the fancy lingerie. Don't save it for a special occasion. Today is special.
25. No one is in charge of your happiness but you.
26. Frame every so-called disaster with these words, *'In five years, will this matter?'*

27. Always choose life.
28. Forgive everyone everything.
29. What other people think of you is none of your business.
30. Time heals almost everything. Give time, time.
31. However good or bad a situation is, it will change.
32. Don't take yourself so seriously. No one else does.
33. Believe in miracles.
34. God loves you because of who God is, not because of anything you did or didn't do.
35. Don't audit life. Show up and make the most of it now.
36. Growing old beats the alternative - dying young.
37. Your children get only one childhood.
38. All that truly matters in the end is that you loved.
39. Get outside every day. Miracles are waiting everywhere.
40. If we all threw our problems in a pile and saw everyone else's, we'd grab ours back.
41. Envy is a waste of time. You already have all you need.
42. The best is yet to come ...
43. No matter how you feel, get up, dress up and show up.
44. Yield.
45. Life isn't tied with a bow, but it's still a gift.

Talk by Bill Cosby

'They're standing on the corner and they can't speak English I can't even talk the way these people talk:

> *Why you ain't,*
> *Where you is,*
> *What he drive,*
> *Where he stay,*
> *Where he work,*
> *Who you be ...*

And I blamed the kid until I heard the mother talk. And then I heard the father talk. Everybody knows it's important to speak English except these knuckleheads. You can't be a doctor with that kind of crap coming out of your mouth. In fact you will never get any kind of job making a decent living

People marched and were hit in the face with rocks to get an Education and now we've got these knuckleheads walking around. The lower economic people are not holding up their end in this deal. These people are not parenting. They are buying things for kids.

$500 sneakers for what? And they won't spend $200 for Hooked on Phonics.

I am talking about these people who cry when their son is standing there in an orange suit.

Where were you when he was 2?

Where were you when he was 12?

Where were you when he was 18 and how come you didn't know that he had a pistol?

And where is the father? Or who is his father?

People putting their clothes on backward: Isn't that a sign of something gone wrong? People with their hats on backward, pants down around the crack, isn't that a sign of something? Or are you waiting for Jesus to pull his pants up?

Isn't it a sign of something when she has her dress all the way up and got all type of needles [piercing] going through her body? What part of Africa did this come from? We are not Africans. Those people are not Africans; they don't know a thing about Africa. I say this all of the time. It would be like white people saying they are European-American. That is totally stupid.

I was born here and so were my parents and grandparents and, very likely my great grandparents. I don't have any connection to Africa, no more than white Americans have to Germany, Scotland, England, Ireland or the Netherlands. The same applies to 99 percent of all the black Americans as regards to Africa. So stop, already!

With names like Shaniqua, Taliqua and Mohammed and all of that crap ... and all of them are in jail. Brown or black versus the Board of Education is no longer the white person's problem. We have got to take the neighbourhood back.

People used to be ashamed. Today a woman has eight children with eight different 'husbands' - or men or whatever you call them now. We have millionaire football players who cannot read. We have million-dollar basketball players who can't write two paragraphs. We, as black folks have to do a better job. Someone working at Wal-Mart with seven kids, you are hurting us. We have to start holding each other to a higher standard.

We cannot blame the white people any longer.'

Dr. William Henry *'Bill'* Cosby, Jr. Ed.D.

Comments written by Andy Rooney

I've learned:

- That the best classroom in the world is at the feet of an elderly person.
- That when you're in love, it shows.
- That just one person saying to me, *'You've made my day!'* makes my day.
- That having a child fall asleep in your arms is one of the most peaceful feelings in the world.
- That being kind is more important than being right.
- That you should never say no to a gift from a child.
- That I can always pray for someone when I don't have the strength to help him in some other way.
- That no matter how serious your life requires you to be, everyone needs a friend to act goofy with.
- That sometimes all a person needs is a hand to hold and a heart to understand.
- That simple walks with my father around the block on summer nights when I was a child did wonders for me as an adult.
- That life is like a roll of toilet paper. The closer it gets to the end, the faster it goes.
- That we should be glad God doesn't give us everything we ask for.
- That money doesn't buy class.
- That it's those small daily happenings that make life so spectacular.
- That under everyone's hard shell is someone who wants to be appreciated and loved.
- That to ignore the facts does not change the facts.
- That when you plan to get even with someone, you are only letting that person continue to hurt you.
- That love, not time, heals all wounds.
- That the easiest way for me to grow as a person is to surround myself with people smarter than I am.
- That everyone you meet deserves to be greeted with a smile.
- That no one is perfect until you fall in love with them.
- That life is tough, but I'm tougher.
- That opportunities are never lost; someone will take the ones you miss.
- That when you harbor bitterness, happiness will dock elsewhere.
- That a smile is an inexpensive way to improve your looks.

- That I wish I could have told my Mom that I love her one more time before she passed away.
- That one should keep his words both soft and tender, because tomorrow he may have to eat them.
- That when your newly born grandchild holds your little finger in his little fist, that you're hooked for life.
- That everyone wants to live on top of the mountain, but all the happiness and growth occurs while you're climbing it.
- That the less time I have to work with, the more things I get done.

Alerts to threats in 2012 Europe

By John Cleese [British writer, actor and tall person:]

The English are feeling the pinch in relation to recent events in Syria and have therefore raised their security level from *'Miffed'* to *'Peeved.'* Soon, though, security levels may be raised yet again to *'Irritated'* or even *'A Bit Cross.'* The English have not been *'A Bit Cross'* since the blitz in 1940 when tea supplies nearly ran out. Terrorists have been re-categorised from *'Tiresome'* to *'A Bloody Nuisance.'* The last time the British issued a *'Bloody Nuisance'* warning level was in 1588, when threatened by the Spanish Armada.

The Scots have raised their threat level from *'Pissed Off'* to *'Let's get the Bastards.'* They don't have any other levels. This is the reason they have been used on the front line of the British army for the last 300 years.

The French government announced yesterday that it has raised its terror alert level from *'Run'* to *'Hide.'* The only two higher levels in France are *'Collaborate'* and *'Surrender.'* The rise was precipitated by a recent fire that destroyed France's white flag factory, effectively paralysing the country's military capability.

Italy has increased the alert level from *'Shout Loudly and Excitedly'* to *'Elaborate Military Posturing.'* Two more levels remain: *'Ineffective Combat Operations'* and *'Change Sides.'*

The Germans have increased their alert state from *'Disdainful Arrogance'* to *'Dress in Uniform and Sing Marching Songs.'* They also have two higher levels: *'Invade a Neighbour'* and *'Lose.'*

Belgians, on the other hand, are all on holiday as usual; the only threat they are worried about is NATO pulling out of Brussels.

The Spanish are all excited to see their new submarines ready to deploy. These beautifully designed subs have glass bottoms so the new Spanish navy can get a really good look at the old Spanish navy.

Australia meanwhile, has raised its security level from *'No worries'* to *'She'll be all right, Mate.'* Two more escalation levels remain: *'Crikey! I think we'll need to cancel the barbie this weekend!'* and *'The barbie is cancelled.'* So far no situation has ever warranted use of the last final escalation level.

A final thought - Greece is collapsing, the Iranians are getting aggressive and Rome is in disarray. Welcome back to 430 BC.

Old favourites

Some of the artists of the 60's are revising their hits with new lyrics to accommodate aging baby boomers. They include:

- ✓ Bobby Darin: *Splish Splash, I Was Having' a Flash.*
- ✓ Herman's Hermits: *Mrs. Brown, You've got a Lovely Walker.*
- ✓ Ringo Starr: *I Get By With a Little Help From Depends.*
- ✓ The Bee Gees: *How Can You Mend a Broken Hip?*
- ✓ Roberta Flack: *The First Time Ever I Forgot Your Face.*
- ✓ Johnny Nash: *I Can't See Clearly Now.*
- ✓ Paul Simon: *Fifty Ways to Lose Your Liver*
- ✓ The Commodores: *Once, Twice, Three Times to the Bathroom.*
- ✓ Marvin Gaye: *Heard It Through the Grape Nuts.*
- ✓ Procol Harem: *A Whiter Shade of Hair.*
- ✓ Leo Sayer: *You Make Me Feel Like Napping.*
- ✓ The Temptations: *Papa's Got a Kidney Stone.*
- ✓ Abba: *Denture Queen.*
- ✓ Tony Orlando: *Knock 3 Times On The Ceiling If You Hear Me Fall.*
- ✓ Helen Reddy: *I Am Woman, Hear Me Snore.*
- ✓ Leslie Gore: *It's My Procedure and I'll Cry If I Want To.*

And Last but not least:
- ✓ Willie Nelson: *On the Commode Again*

John Glenn's true hero

For half a century, the world has applauded John Glenn as a heart-stirring American hero. He lifted the nation's spirits when, as one of the original Mercury 7 astronauts, he was blasted alone into orbit around the Earth. The enduring affection for him is so powerful that even now people find themselves misting up at the sight of his face or the sound of his voice.

But for all these years, Glenn has had a hero of his own; someone who he has seen display endless courage of a different kind: Annie Glenn.

They have been married for 69 years. We are being reminded that, half a century down the line, he remains America's unforgettable hero. He has never really bought that.

Because the heroism he most cherishes is of a sort that is seldom cheered. It belongs to the person he has known longer than he has known anyone else in the world. John Glenn and Annie Castor first knew each other when - literally - they shared a playpen. In New Concord, Ohio, his parents and hers were friends. When the families got together, their children played.

John - the future Marine fighter pilot, the future test-pilot ace, the future astronaut - was pure gold from the start. He would end up having what it took to rise to the absolute pinnacle of American regard during the space race; imagine what it meant to be the young John Glenn in the small confines of New Concord.

Three-sport varsity athlete, most admired boy in town, Mr. Everything. Annie Castor was bright, was caring, was talented, was generous of spirit, but she could talk only with the most excruciating of difficulty. It haunted her. Her stuttering was so severe that it was categorised as an '85%' disability - 85% of the time, she could not manage to make words come out.

When she tried to recite a poem in elementary school, she was laughed at. She was not able to speak on the telephone. She could not have a regular conversation with a friend. And John Glenn loved her. Even as a boy he was wise enough to understand that people who could not see past her stutter were missing out on knowing a rare and wonderful girl.

They married on April 6, 1943. As a military wife, she found that life as she and John moved around the country could be quite hurtful. She has written: *'I can remember some very painful experiences - especially the ridicule.'*

In department stores, she would wander unfamiliar aisles trying to find the right section, embarrassed to attempt to ask the salesclerks for help. In taxis, she would have to write requests to the driver, because she couldn't speak the destination out loud. In restaurants, she would point to the items on the menu.

A fine musician, Annie, in every community where she and John moved, would play the organ in church as a way to make new friends. She and John had two children; she has written: *'Can you imagine living in the modern world and being afraid to use the telephone? 'Hello' used to be so hard for me to say. I worried that my children would be injured and need a doctor. Could I somehow find the words to get the information across on the phone?'*

John, as a Marine aviator, flew 59 combat missions in World War II and 90 during the Korean War. Every time he was deployed, he and Annie said goodbye the same way. His last words to her before leaving were: *'I'm just going down to the corner store to get a pack of gum.'*

And, with just the two of them there, she was able to always reply: *'Don't be long.'*

On that February day in 1962 when the world held its breath and the Atlas rocket was about to propel him toward space, those were their words, once again. And in 1998, when, at 77, he went back to space aboard the shuttle Discovery, it was an understandably tense time for them. What if something happened to end their life together?

She knew what he would say to her before boarding the shuttle. He did - and this time he gave her a present to hold onto: A pack of gum. She carried it in a pocket next to her heart until he was safely home.

Many times in her life she attempted various treatments to cure her stutter. None worked.

But in 1973, she found a doctor in Virginia who ran an intensive program she and John hoped would help her. She travelled there to enrole and to give it her best effort. The miracle she and John had always waited for at last, as miracles will do, arrived. At age 53, she was able to talk fluidly and not in brief, anxiety-ridden, agonising bursts.

John has said that on the first day he heard her speak to him with confidence and clarity, he dropped to his knees to offer a prayer of gratitude.

He has written: *'I saw Annie's perseverance and strength through the years and it just made me admire her and love her even more.'* He has heard roaring ovations in countries around the globe for his own valour, but his awe is reserved for Annie and what she accomplished: *'I don't know if I would have had the courage.'*

Her voice is so clear and steady now that she regularly gives public talks. If you are lucky enough to know the Glenns; the sight and sound of them bantering and joking with each other and playfully finishing each others' sentences is something that warms you and makes you thankful just to be in the same room.

But if you ever find yourself at an event where the Glenns are appearing and you want to see someone so brimming with pride and love that you may feel your own tears start to well up, wait until the moment that Annie stands to say a few words to the audience. And as she begins, take a look at her husband's eyes.

They Teach This at Stanford

In an evening class at Stanford, the last lecture was on the mind-body connection - the relationship between stress and disease. The speaker [head of psychiatry at Stanford] said, among other things, that one of the best things that a man could do for his health is to be married to a woman, whereas for a woman, one of the best things she could do for her health was to nurture her relationships with her girlfriends. At first everyone laughed, but he was serious.

Women connect with each other differently and provide support systems that help each other to deal with stress and difficult life experiences. Physically this quality 'girlfriend time' helps us to create more serotonin - a neurotransmitter that helps combat depression and can create a general feeling of well being.

Women share feelings whereas men often form relationships around activities. They rarely sit down with a buddy and talk about how they feel about certain things or how their personal lives are going. Jobs? Yes. Sports? Yes. Cars? Yes. Fishing, hunting, golf? Yes, but their feelings? Rarely.

Women do it all of the time. We share from our souls with our sisters/mothers and evidently that is very good for our health. He said that spending time with a friend is just as important to our general health as jogging or working out at a gym.

There's a tendency to think that when we are 'exercising' we are doing something good for our bodies, but when we are hanging out with friends, we are wasting our time and should be more productively engaged - not true. In fact, he said that failure to create and maintain quality personal relationships with other humans is as dangerous to our physical health as smoking!

So every time you hang out to schmooze with a gal pal, just pat yourself on the back and congratulate yourself for doing something good for your health!

December, '09 update on Sheriff Joe Arpaio

You all remember Sheriff Joe Arpaio of Arizona, who painted the jail cells pink and made the inmates wear pink prison garb. Well ... he's at it again!

Maricopa County was spending approximately $18 million dollars a year on stray animals, like cats and dogs. Sheriff Joe offered to take the department over and the County Supervisors said okay. The animal shelters are now all staffed and operated by prisoners. They feed and care for the strays. Every animal in his care is taken out and walked twice daily. He now has prisoners who are experts in animal nutrition and behaviour. They give great classes for anyone who'd like to adopt an animal. He has literally taken stray dogs off the street, given them to the care of prisoners and had them place in dog shows.

The best part? His budget for the entire department is now under $3 million. Teresa and I adopted a Weimaraner from a Maricopa County shelter two years ago. He was neutered and current on all shots, in great health and even had a microchip inserted the day we got him. The cost: $78.00

The prisoners get the benefit of about $0.28 an hour for working, but most would work for free, just to be out of their cells for the day. Most of his budget is for utilities, building maintenance, etc. He pays the prisoners out of the fees collected for adopted animals.

I have long wondered when the rest of the country would take a look at the way he runs the jail system and copy some of his ideas. He has a huge farm, donated to the county years ago, where inmates can work and they grow most of their own fresh vegetables and food, doing all the work and harvesting by hand.

He has a pretty good sized hog farm, which provides meat and fertilizer. It fertilizes the Christmas tree nursery, where prisoners work and you can buy a living Christmas tree for $6.00 to $8.00 for the holidays and plant it later. We have six trees in our yard from the Prison.

Yup, he was re-elected last year with 83% of the vote. Now he's in trouble with the ACLU again. He painted all his buses and vehicles with a mural that has a special hotline phone number painted on it, where you can call and report suspected illegal aliens. Immigrations and Customs Enforcement wasn't doing enough in his eyes, so he had 40 deputies trained specifically for enforcing immigration laws, started up his hotline and bought four new buses just for hauling folks back to the border. He's kind of a *'Git-R Dun'* kind of Sheriff.

To those of you not familiar with Joe Arpaio he is the Maricopa, Arizona county sheriff and he keeps getting elected over and over and this is one of the reasons why:

He created the *'Tent City Jail:'* He has jail meals down to 40 cents a serving and charges the inmates for them. He stopped smoking and porno magazines in the jails. He took away their weights; cut off all but *'G'* rated movies. He started chain gangs so the inmates could do free work on county and city projects. Then he started chain gangs for women so he wouldn't get sued for discrimination.

He took away cable TV until he found out there was a Federal Court Order that required cable TV for jails so he hooked up the cable TV again; only let in the Disney Channel and the Weather Channel. When asked why the Weather Channel he replied, *'So they will know how hot it's gonna be while they are working on my Chain Gangs.'*

He cut off coffee since it has zero nutritional value. When the inmates complained, he told them *'This isn't the Ritz/Carlton ... if you don't like it, don't come back!'*

More on the Arizona Sheriff: With temperatures being even hotter than usual in Phoenix (116 F degrees just set a new record) the Associated Press reports: About 2,000 inmates living in a barbed-wire-surrounded tent encampment at the Maricopa County Jail have been given permission to strip down to their government-issued pink boxer shorts. On Wednesday, hundreds of men wearing boxers were either curled up on their bunk beds or chatted in the tents, which reached 138 F degrees inside the week before. Many were also swathed in wet, pink towels as sweat collected on their chests and dripped down to their pink socks.

'It feels like we are in a furnace,' said James Zanzot, an inmate who has lived in the tents for one year. *'It's inhumane.'*

Joe Arpaio, the tough-guy sheriff who created the tent city and long ago started making his prisoners wear pink and eat bologna sandwiches, is not one bit sympathetic. He said Wednesday that he told all of the inmates: *'It's 120 F degrees in Iraq and our soldiers are living in tents too and they have to wear full battle gear, but they didn't commit any crimes, so shut your mouths!'*

Way to go, Sheriff! Maybe if all prisons were like this one there would be a lot less crime and/or repeat offenders. Criminals should be punished for their crimes - not live in luxury until it's time for their parole, only to go out and commit another crime so they can get back in to live on taxpayers money and enjoy things taxpayers can't afford to have for themselves.

Polk County Florida Sheriff Grady Judd

An illegal alien in Polk County Florida who got pulled over in a routine traffic stop ended up 'executing' the deputy who stopped him. The deputy was shot eight times, including once behind his right ear at close range. Another deputy was wounded and a police dog was killed.

A state-wide manhunt ensued. The murderer was found hiding in a wooded area with his gun. After he shot at them, SWAT team officers open fired and hit him 68 times.

Now here's the kicker: Naturally, the liberal media went nuts and asked why they shot the poor undocumented immigrant 68 times. Sheriff Grady Judd told the Orlando Sentinel: [Talk about an all-time classic answer.]

'Because that's all the ammunition we had.'

Famous Quotes:

➢ *'Bisexuality immediately doubles your chances for a date on Saturday night.'* - Rodney Dangerfield

➢ *'There are a number of mechanical devices which increase sexual arousal, in women. Chief among these is the Mercedes-Benz 380SL.'* - Lynn Lavner

➢ *'Sex at age 90 is like trying to shoot pool with a rope.'* - Camille Paglia

➢ *'Sex is one of the nine reasons for incarnation. The other eight are unimportant.'* - George Burns

➢ *'Women might be able to fake orgasms, but men can fake a whole relationship.'* - Sharon Stone

➢ *'Hockey is a sport for white men. Basketball is a sport for black men. Golf is a sport for white men dressed like black pimps.'* - Tiger Woods

➢ *'My mother never saw the irony in calling me a son-of-a-bitch.'* - Jack Nicholson

➢ *'Clinton lied. A man might forget where he parks or where he lives, but he never forgets oral sex, no matter how bad it is.'* - Barbara Bush Former US First Lady. [And you didn't think Barbara had a sense of humour?]

- *'Women need a reason to have sex. Men just need a place.'* - Billy Crystal
- *'According to a new survey, women say they feel more comfortable undressing in front of men than they do undressing in front of other women. They say that women are too judgmental, where, of course, men are just grateful.'* - Robert De Niro
- *'There's a new medical crisis. Doctors are reporting that many men are having allergic reaction to latex condoms. They say they cause severe swelling. So what's the problem?'* - Dustin Hoffman
- *'There's very little advice in men's magazines, because men think, 'I know what I'm doing - Just show me somebody naked'.'* - Jerry Seinfeld
- *'See, the problem is that God gives men a brain and a penis and only enough blood to run one at a time.'* - Robin Williams
- *'It's been so long since I've had sex, I've forgotten who ties up whom.'* - Joan Rivers
- *'Sex is one of the most wholesome, beautiful and natural experiences money can buy.'* - Steve Martin
- *'You don't appreciate a lot of stuff in school until you get older. Little things like being spanked every day by a middle-aged woman. Stuff you pay good money for in later life.'* - Elmo Phillips
- *'Bigamy is having one spouse too many. Monogamy is the same.'* - Oscar Wilde;
- *'It isn't premarital sex if you have no intention of getting married.'* George Burns
- *'Sometimes, when I look at my children, I say to myself, 'Lillian, you should have remained a virgin.'* - Lillian Carter [mother of Jimmy Carter.]
- *'I had a rose named after me and I was very flattered. But I was not pleased to read the description in the catalogue: - 'No good in a bed, but fine against a wall.'* - Eleanor Roosevelt
- *'Last week, I stated this woman was the ugliest woman I had ever seen. I have since been visited by her sister and now wish to withdraw that statement.'* - Mark Twain
- *'The secret of a good sermon is to have a good beginning and a good ending; and to have the two as close together as possible '* - George Burns
- *'Santa Claus has the right idea. Visit people only once a year.'* - Victor Borge

➤ *'Be careful about reading health books. You may die of a misprint.'* - Mark Twain

➤ *'By all means, marry. If you get a good wife, you'll become happy; if you get a bad one, you'll become a philosopher.'* - Socrates

➤ *'I was married by a judge. I should have asked for a jury.'* - Groucho Marx

➤ *'My wife has a slight impediment in her speech. Every now and then she stops to breathe.'* - Jimmy Durante

➤ *'I have never hated a man enough to give his diamonds back.'* - Zsa Zsa Gabor

➤ *'Only Irish coffee provides in a single glass all four essential food groups: alcohol, caffeine, sugar and fat.'* - Alex Levine

➤ *'My luck is so bad that if I bought a cemetery, people would stop dying.'* - Rodney Dangerfield

➤ *'Money can't buy you happiness ... but it does bring you a more pleasant form of misery.'* - Spike Milligan

➤ *'Until I was thirteen, I thought my name was SHUT UP.'* - Joe Namath

➤ *'I don't feel old. I don't feel anything until noon. Then it's time for my nap.'* - Bob Hope

➤ *'I never drink water because of the disgusting things that fish do in it.'* - W. C. Fields

➤ *'We could certainly slow the aging process down if it had to work its way through Congress.'* - Will Rogers

➤ *'Don't worry about avoiding temptation. As you grow older, it will avoid you.'* - Winston Churchill

➤ *'Maybe it's true that life begins at fifty, but everything else starts to wear out, fall out or spread out.'* - Phyllis Diller

➤ *'By the time a man is wise enough to watch his step, he's too old to go anywhere.'* - Billy Crystal

➤ And finally ...The cardiologist's diet: - *'If it tastes good spit it out.'*

Forrest Gump goes to Heaven

The day finally arrived. Forrest Gump dies and goes to Heaven. He is at the Pearly Gates, met by St. Peter himself. However, the gates are closed and Forrest approaches the gatekeeper.

St. Peter said, *'Well, Forrest, it is certainly good to see you. We have heard a lot about you. I must tell you though, that the place is filling up fast and we have been administering an entrance examination for everyone. The test is short, but you have to pass it before you can get into Heaven.'*

Forrest responds, *'It sure is good to be here, St. Peter, sir. But nobody ever told me about any entrance exam. I sure hope that the test ain't too hard. Life was a big enough test as it was.'*

St. Peter continued, *'Yes, I know, Forrest, but the test is only three questions.*

First: What two days of the week begin with the letter T? Second: How many seconds are there in a year? Third: What is God's first name?'

Forrest leaves to think the questions over. He returns the next day and sees St. Peter, who waves to him and says, *'Now that you have had a chance to think the questions over, tell me your answers.'*

Forrest replied, *'Well, the first one - which two days in the week begins with the letter 'T?' Shucks, that one is easy. That would be Today and Tomorrow.'*

The Saint's eyes opened wide and he exclaimed, *'Forrest, that is not what I was thinking, but you do have a point and I guess I did not specify, so I will give you credit for that answer. How about the next one?'* asked St. Peter.

'How many seconds in a year? Now that one is harder,' replied Forrest, *'but I thought and thought about that and I guess the only answer can be twelve.'*

Astounded, St. Peter said, *'Twelve? Twelve? Forrest, how in Heaven's name could you come up with twelve seconds in a year?'*

Forrest replied, *'Shucks, there's got to be twelve: January 2nd, February 2nd, March 2nd ... '*

'Hold it,' interrupts St. Peter. *'I see where you are going with this and I see your point, though that was not quite what I had in mind ... but I will have to give you credit for that one, too. Let us go on with the third and final question. Can you tell me God's first name?'*

'Sure,' Forrest replied, *'it's Andy.'*

'Andy?' exclaimed an exasperated and frustrated St Peter. *'Okay, I can understand how you came up with your answers to my first two questions, but just how in the world did you come up with the name Andy as the first name of God?'*

'Shucks, that was the easiest one of all,' Forrest replied. *'I learnt it from the song Andy walks with me Andy talks with me Andy tells me I am his own.'*

St. Peter opened the Pearly Gates and said: *'Run, Forrest, Run.'*

Why do cops harass people

A North Island [Australian] police station received this question from a resident through the feedback section of a local Police website: *'I would like to know how it is possible for police officers to continually harass people and get away with it?'* In response, a sergeant posted this reply:

Beginner's guide to police harassment:

First of all, let me tell you this ... it's not easy. In the Palmerston North and rural area we average one cop for every 505 people. Only about 60 per cent of those cops are on general duty [or what you might refer to as 'general patrols'] where we do most of our harassing. The rest are in non-harassing units that do not allow them contact with the day-to-day innocents. At any given moment, only one-fifth of the 60 per cent of general patrols are on duty and available for harassing people while the rest are off duty.

So, roughly, one cop is responsible for harassing about 6,000 residents. When you toss in the commercial business and tourist locations that attract people from other areas, sometimes you have a situation where a single cop is responsible for harassing 15,000 or more people a day.

Now, your average eight-hour shift runs 28,800 seconds long. This gives a cop two-thirds of a second to harass a person and then only another third of a second to drink a Massey iced coffee and then find a new person to harass.

This is not an easy task. To be honest, most cops are not up to the challenge day in and day out. It is just too tiring. What we do is utilise some tools to help us narrow down those people we can realistically harass.

Phone: People will call us up and point out things that cause us to focus on a person for special harassment. *'My neighbour is beating his wife'* is a code phrase used often. This means we'll come out and give somebody some special harassment. Another popular one is, *'There's a guy breaking into a house.'* The harassment team is then put into action.

Cars: We have special cops assigned to harass people who drive. They like to harass the drivers of fast cars, cars with no insurance or drivers with no licences and the like. It's lots of fun when you pick them out of traffic for nothing more obvious than running a red light. Sometimes you get to really heap the harassment on when you find they have drugs in the car, they are drunk or have an outstanding warrant on file.

Laws: When we don't have phone or cars and have nothing better to do, there are actually books that give us ideas for reasons to harass folks. They are called 'statutes.' These include the Crimes Act, Summary Offences Act, Land Transport Act and a whole bunch of others ... They spell out all sorts of things for which you can really mess with people. After you read the law, you can just drive around for a while until you find someone violating one of these listed offences and harass them.

Just last week I saw a guy trying to steal a car. Well, the book says that's not allowed. That meant I had permission to harass this guy.

It is a really cool system that we have set up and it works pretty well. We seem to have a never-ending supply of folks to harass. And we get away with it. Why? Because, for the good citizens who pay the tab, we try to keep the streets safe for them and they pay us to 'harass' some people.

Next time you are in Palmerston North, give me the old *'single finger wave.'* That's another one of those codes. It means, *'You can harass me.'* It's one of our favourites.

CHAPTER 3 - REMEMBER WHEN?

To all the kids who survived the 1930's 40's, 50's, 60's and 70's!!

First, we survived being born to mothers who smoked and/or drank while they were pregnant. They took aspirin, ate blue cheese dressing, tuna from a can and didn't get tested for diabetes.

Then after that trauma, we were put to sleep on our tummies in baby cribs covered with bright coloured lead-based paints. We had no childproof lids on medicine bottles, doors or cabinets and when we rode our bikes, we had no helmets, not to mention, the risks we took hitchhiking.

As infants and children, we would ride in cars with no car seats, booster seats, seat belts or air bags. Riding in the back of a pick up on a warm day was always a special treat.

We drank water from the garden hose and NOT from a bottle. We shared one soft drink with four friends, from one bottle and NO ONE actually died from this. We ate cupcakes, white bread and real butter and drank koolade made with sugar, but we weren't overweight because WE WERE ALWAYS OUTSIDE PLAYING! We would leave home in the morning and play all day, as long as we were back when the streetlights came on. No one was able to reach us all day. And we were okay.

We would spend hours building our go-carts out of scraps and then ride down the hill, only to find out we forgot the brakes. After running into the bushes a few times, we learned to solve the problem.

We did not have Playstations, Nintendo's, X-boxes, no video games at all, no 150 channels on cable, no video movies or DVD's, no surround-sound or CD's, no cell phones, no personal computers, no Internet or chat rooms ... WE HAD FRIENDS and we went outside and found them!

We fell out of trees, got cut, broke bones and teeth and there were no lawsuits from these accidents. We ate worms and mud pies made from dirt and the worms did not live in us forever. We made up games with sticks and tennis balls and, although we were told it would happen, we did not put out very many eyes. We rode bikes or walked to a friend's house and knocked on the door or rang the bell or just walked in and talked to them!

Little League had tryouts and not everyone made the team. Those who didn't had to learn to deal with disappointment. Imagine that!! The idea of a parent bailing us out if we broke the law was unheard of. They actually sided with the law!

Televisions - you could hardly see for all the snow; Spread the rabbit ears as far as they go. Pull a chair up to the TV set, *'Good Night, David. Good Night, Chet.'*

My Mom used to defrost hamburger on the counter and I used to eat it raw sometimes, too. Our school sandwiches were wrapped in wax paper in a brown paper bag, not in ice pack coolers, but I can't remember getting e.coli. Maybe being allowed to say the Lord's Prayer saved us from food poisoning.

Almost all of us would have rather gone swimming in the lake instead of a pristine pool [talk about boring] no beach closures then. The term cell phone would have conjured up a phone in a jail cell and a pager was the school PA system.

We all took gym, not PE ... and risked permanent injury with a pair of high top Ked's [only worn in gym] instead of having cross-training athletic shoes with air cushion soles and built in light reflectors. I can't recall any injuries but they must have happened because they tell us how much safer we are now.

Flunking gym was not an option ... even for stupid kids! I guess PE must be much harder than gym.

Speaking of school, we all said prayers and sang the national anthem and staying in detention after school caught all sorts of negative attention.

We must have had horribly damaged psyches. What an archaic health system we had then. Remember school nurses? Ours wore a hat and everything.

I thought that I was supposed to accomplish something before I was allowed to be proud of myself.

I just can't recall how bored we were without computers, Play Station, Nintendo, X-box or 270 digital TV cable stations.

Oh yeah ... and where was the Benadryl and sterilisation kit when I got that bee sting? I could have been killed!

We played *'king of the hill'* on piles of gravel left on vacant construction sites and when we got hurt, Mom pulled out the 48-cent bottle of mercurochrome [kids liked it better because it didn't sting like iodine did] and then we got our butt spanked.

Now it's a trip to the emergency room, followed by a 10-day dose of a $49 bottle of antibiotics and then Mom calls the attorney to sue the contractor for leaving a horribly vicious pile of gravel where it was such a threat.

We didn't act up in church or at the neighbour's house either; because if we did we got our butt spanked there and then we got our butt spanked again when we got home.

I recall the kid who lived next door coming over and doing his hand balancing tricks on our front stoop railing, just before he fell off. Little did his mom know that she could have owned our house. Instead, she picked him up and swatted him for being such a goof. It was a neighbourhood run amuck.

Not a single person I knew had ever been told that they were from a dysfunctional family. How could we possibly have known that we needed to get into group therapy and anger management classes?

And I don't remember one child that had cancer.

We were obviously so duped by so many societal ills, that we didn't even notice that the entire country wasn't taking Prozac or medication for ADDD! How did we ever survive?

These generations have produced some of the best risk-takers, problem solvers and inventors ever! The past 50 years have been an explosion of innovation and new ideas.

We had freedom, failure, success and responsibility and we learned HOW TO DEAL WITH IT ALL!

The Aussie Version of Creation

In the beginning God created day and night.

He created day for footy matches, going to the beach ... and BBQ's.

He created night for going prawning, sleeping and BBQ's and God saw that it was good.

On the Second Day, God created water ... for surfing, swimming and BBQ's on the beach and God saw that it was good.

On the Third Day God created the Earth to bring forth plants to provide malt and yeast for beer and wood for BBQs and God saw that it was good ...

On the Fourth Day God created animals and crustaceans, chops, sausages, steak and prawns for BBQ's and God saw that it was good.

On the Fifth day God created a Bloke to make use of all these wondrous creations - go to the footy, enjoy the beach, drink the beer and eat the meat and prawns at BBQ's and God saw that it was good.

On the Sixth Day God saw that the Bloke was lonely and needed someone to go to the footy, surf, drink beer, eat and stand around the barbie with. So God created Mates and God saw that they were good Blokes and God saw that it was good.

On the Seventh Day God looked around at the twinkling barbie fires, heard the hiss of opening beer cans and the raucous laughter of all the Blokes. He smelled the aroma of grilled chops and sizzling prawns and God saw that it was good

Well ... Almost good ... He saw that the Blokes were too tired to clean up and needed a rest. So God created Sheilas to clean the house, to bear children, to wash, to cook and to clean the Barbie and then God saw that it was not just good ... It was better than that ... It was BLOODY AWESOME ...!!! IT WAS AUSTRALIA ...!!!!!

Here are some statistics for the Year 1909:

- The average life expectancy was 47 years. [Imagine being middle-aged at 24?]
- Only 14 percent of the homes had a bathtub.
- Only 8 percent of the homes had a telephone.
- There were only 8,000 cars and only 144 miles of paved roads.
- The maximum speed limit in most cities was 10 mph.
- The tallest structure in the world was the Eiffel Tower.
- The average wage in 1909 was 22 cents per hour.
- The average worker made between $200 and $400 per year.
- A competent accountant could expect to earn $2,000 per year; A dentist $2,500 per year; a veterinarian between $1,500 and $4,000 per year; and a mechanical engineer about $5,000 per year.
- More than 95 percent of all births took place at HOME.
- Ninety percent of all doctors had no college education! Instead, they attended so-called medical schools, many of which were condemned in the press and the government as 'substandard. '
- Sugar cost four cents a pound; Eggs were fourteen cents a dozen; Coffee was fifteen cents a pound.
- Most women only washed their hair once a month and used Borax or egg yolks for shampoo.
- Canada passed a law that prohibited poor people from entering into their country for any reason.
- Five leading causes of death were:
  1. Pneumonia and influenza
  2. Tuberculosis
  3. Diarrhea

4. Heart disease

5. Stroke

- The American flag had 45 stars.
- The population of Las Vegas, Nevada, was only 30!
- Crossword puzzles, canned beer and ice tea hadn't been invented yet.
- There was no Mother's or Father's Day.'
- Two out of every 10 adults couldn't read or write. [It seems that is still the case!]
- Only 6 percent of all Americans had graduated from high school.
- Marijuana, heroin and morphine were all available over the counter at the local corner drugstores. Back then pharmacists said, *'Heroin clears the complexion, gives buoyancy to the mind, regulates the stomach and bowels and is, in fact, a perfect guardian of health.'* [Shocking!]
- Eighteen percent of households had at least one full-time servant or domestic help. [We could use more of that now with 2-career families.]
- There were about 230 a year reported murders in the entire U.S.A.!

Comments made in the year 1955:

- *'I'll tell you one thing, if things keep going the way they are, it's going to be impossible to buy a week's groceries for $20.'*
- *'Have you seen the new cars coming out next year? It won't be long before $2000 will only buy a used one.'*
- *'If cigarettes keep going up in price, I'm going to quit. A quarter a pack is ridiculous.'*
- *'Did you hear the post office is thinking about charging a dime just to mail a letter?'*
- *'If they raise the minimum wage to $1, nobody will be able to hire outside help at the store.'*
- *'When I first started driving, who would have thought gas would someday cost 29 cents a gallon. Guess we'd be better off leaving the car in the garage.'*
- *'I never thought I'd see the day all our kitchen appliances would be electric. They re even making electric typewriters now.'*
- *'It's too bad things are so tough nowadays. I see where a few married women have to work to make ends meet.'*

- *'It won't be long before young couples are going to have to hire someone to watch their kids so they can both work.'*
- *'Kids today are impossible. Those duck tail haircuts make it impossible to stay groomed. Next thing you know, boys will be wearing their hair as long as the girls.'*
- *'I'm afraid to send my kids to the movies any more. Ever since they let Clark Gable get by with saying 'damn' in 'Gone With The Wind,' it seems every new movie has either 'hell' or 'damn' in it.'*
- *'I read the other day where some scientist thinks it's possible to put a man on the moon by the end of the century. They even have some fellows they call astronauts preparing for it down in Texas.'*
- *'Did you see where some baseball player just signed a contract for $75,000 a year just to play ball? It wouldn't surprise me if someday they'll be making more than the president.'*
- *'Marriage doesn't mean a thing any more; those Hollywood stars seem to be getting divorced at the drop of a hat.'*
- *'I'm just afraid the Volkswagen car is going to open the door to a whole lot of foreign business.'*
- *'Thank goodness I won't live to see the day when the Government takes half our income in taxes. I sometimes wonder if we are electing the best people to congress.'*
- *'The drive-in restaurant is convenient in nice weather, but I seriously doubt they will ever catch on.'*
- *'There is no sense going to another state any more for a weekend. It costs nearly $15 a night to stay in a hotel.'*
- *'No one can afford to be sick any more; $35 a day in the hospital is too rich for my blood.'*
- *'If they think I'll pay 50 cents for a haircut; forget it.'*

1950's version of an E-Mail

I have no idea who put this together, but it is good

> Long ago and far away, in a land that time forgot,
> Before the days of Dylan or the dawn of Camelot.
> There lived a race of innocents and they were you and me,
> For Ike was in the White House in that land where we were born,
> Where navels were for oranges and Peyton Place was porn.
> We longed for love and romance and waited for our Prince,
> Eddie Fisher married Liz and no one's seen him since.

We danced to *'Little Darlin,'* and sang to *'Stagger Lee'*
And cried for Buddy Holly in the Land That Made Me, Me.
Only girls wore earrings then and 3 was one too many,
And only boys wore flat-top cuts, except for Jean McKinney.
And only in our wildest dreams did we expect to see
A boy named George with Lipstick, in the Land That Made Me, Me.
We fell for Frankie Avalon, Annette was oh, so nice,
And when they made a movie, they never made it twice.
We didn't have a Star Trek Five or Psycho Two and Three,
Or Rocky-Rambo Twenty in the Land That Made Me, Me.
Miss Kitty had a heart of gold and Chester had a limp,
And Reagan was a Democrat whose co-star was a chimp.
We had a Mr. Wizard, but not a Mr. T,
And Oprah couldn't talk yet, in the Land That Made Me, Me.
We had our share of heroes; we never thought they'd go,
At least not Bobby Darin or Marilyn Monroe.
For youth was still eternal and life was yet to be,
And Elvis was forever in the Land That Made Me, Me.
We'd never seen the rock band that was Grateful to be Dead,
And Airplanes weren't named Jefferson and Zeppelins were not Led.
And Beatles lived in gardens then and Monkeys lived in trees,
Madonna was Mary in the Land That Made Me, Me.
We'd never heard of microwaves or telephones in cars,
And babies might be bottle-fed, but they were not grown in jars.
And pumping iron got wrinkles out and 'gay' meant fancy-free,
And dorms were never co-Ed in the Land That Made Me, Me.
We hadn't seen enough of jets to talk about the lag,
And microchips were what was left at the bottom of the bag.
And hardware was a box of nails and bytes came from a flea,
And rocket ships were fiction in the Land That Made Me, Me.
T-Birds came with portholes and side shows came with freaks,
And bathing suits came big enough to cover both your cheeks.
And Coke came just in bottles and skirts below the knee,
And Castro came to power near the Land That Made Me, Me.
We had no Crest with Fluoride; we had no Hill Street Blues,
We had no patterned pantyhose or Lipton herbal tea
Or prime-time ads for those dysfunctions in the Land That Made
Me, Me.
There were no golden arches, no Perrier to chill,
And fish were not called Wanda and cats were not called Bill
And middle-aged was 35 and old was forty-three,
And ancient were our parents in the Land That Made Me, Me.

93

But all things have a season or so we've heard them say,
And now instead of Maybelline we swear by Retin-A.
They send us invitations to join AARP,
We've come a long way baby, from the Land That Made Me, Me.
So now we face a brave new world in slightly larger jeans,
And wonder why they're using smaller print in magazines.
And we tell our children's children of the way it used to be,
Long ago and far away in the Land That Made Me, Me.
If you didn't grow up in the fifty's, you missed the greatest time in
history.

Green Thing

In the line at the store, the cashier told an older woman that she should bring her own grocery bags because plastic bags weren't good for the environment.

The woman apologised to him and explained, *'We didn't have the green thing back in my day.'*

The clerk responded, *'That's our problem today. Your generation did not care enough to save our environment.'*

He was right - our generation didn't have the green thing in its day. Back then, we returned milk bottles, soda bottles and beer bottles to the store. The store sent them back to the plant to be washed and sterilised and refilled, so it could use the same bottles over and over. So they really were recycled.

But we didn't have the green thing back in our day.

We walked up stairs because we didn't have an escalator in every store and office building. We walked to the grocery store and didn't climb into a 300-horsepower machine every time we had to go two blocks.

But she was right. We didn't have the green thing back in our day.

Back then, we washed the baby's diapers because we didn't have the throw-away kind. We dried clothes on a line, not in energy gobbling machine burning up 220 volts - wind and solar power really did dry the clothes. Kids got hand-me-down clothes from their brothers or sisters, not always brand-new clothing. But that lady is right; we didn't have the green thing back in our day.

Back then, we had one TV or radio, in the house - not a TV in every room. And the TV had a small screen the size of a handkerchief [remember them?] not a screen the size of the state of

94

Montana. In the kitchen, we blended and stirred by hand because we didn't have electric machines to do everything for us.

When we packaged a fragile item to send in the mail, we used a wadded up old newspaper to cushion it, not Styrofoam or plastic bubble wrap. Back then, we didn't fire up an engine and burn gasoline just to cut the lawn. We used a push mower that ran on human power. We exercised by working so we didn't need to go to a health club to run on treadmills that operate on electricity.

But she's right; we didn't have the green thing back then.

We drank from a fountain when we were thirsty instead of using a cup or a plastic bottle every time we had a drink of water. We refilled writing pens with ink instead of buying a new pen and we replaced the razor blades in a razor instead of throwing away the whole razor just because the blade got dull.

But we didn't have the green thing back then.

Back then, people took the streetcar or a bus and kids rode their bikes to school or walked instead of turning their moms into a 24-hour taxi service. We had one electrical outlet in a room, not an entire bank of sockets to power a dozen appliances. And we didn't need a computerised gadget to receive a signal beamed from satellites 2,000 miles out in space in order to find the nearest pizza joint.

But isn't it sad the current generation laments how wasteful we old folks were just because we didn't have the *green thing* back then?

If you are 40 or younger you will think this is hilarious!!

When I was a kid, adults used to bore me to tears with their tedious diatribes about how hard things were when they were growing up; what with walking twenty-five miles to school every morning ... uphill BOTH ways ... through year 'round blizzards. Carrying their younger siblings on their backs ... to their one-room schoolhouse, where they maintained a straight-A average, despite their full-time, after-school job at the local textile mill where they worked for 35 cents an hour just to help keep their family from starving to death!

And I remember promising myself that when I grew up, there was no way in hell I was going to lay a bunch of crap like that on kids about how hard I had it and how easy they've got it!

But now that I'm over the ripe old age of forty, I can't help but look around and notice the youth of today. You've got it so easy! I mean, compared to my childhood, you live in a damn Utopia! And I hate to say it but you kids today you don't know how good you've got it! I mean, when I was a kid we didn't have The Internet. If we wanted to know something, we had to go to the damned library and look it up ourselves, in the card catalogue!!

Child Protective services didn't care if our parents beat us. As a matter of fact, the parents of all my friends also had permission to kick our ass! Nowhere was safe.

There was no email! We had to actually write somebody a letter ... with a pen! Then you had to walk all the way across the street and put it in the mailbox and it would take like a week to get there!

There were no MP3's or CD's or DVD's! You wanted to steal music, you had to hitchhike to the damned record store and shoplift! Or you had to wait around all day to tape it off the radio and the DJ would usually talk over the beginning and mess it all up. There were no CD players - we had tape decks in our car. We'd play our favourite tape and eject it when it was finished and the tape would come undone rendering it useless.

We didn't have fancy crap like Call Waiting! If you were on the phone and somebody else called they got a busy signal, that's it! And we didn't have fancy Caller ID Boxes either! When the phone rang, you had no idea who it was! It could be your school, your mom, your boss, your bookie, your drug dealer, a collections agent, you just didn't know!!! You had to pick it up and take your chances, mister!

There weren't any freaking' cell phones either. If you left the house, you just didn't make a damned call or receive one. You actually had to be out of touch with your friends. Oh my gosh! Think of the horror - not being in touch with someone 24/7. And then there's texting. Yeah, right. Please! You kids have no idea how annoying you are.

We didn't have any fancy video games with high-resolution 3-D graphics! We had the Atari 2600! With games like *'Space Invaders'* and 'Asteroids' and the graphics sucked! Your guy was a little square! You actually had to use your imagination! And there were no multiple levels or screens - it was just one screen forever! And you could never win. The game just kept getting harder and harder and faster and faster until you died! ... Just like LIFE!

You had to use a little book called a TV Guide to find out what was on! You had to get off your ass and walk over to the TV to change the channel. No remotes. Oh, no, what's the world coming to?

When you went to the movie theatre there was no such thing as stadium seating! All the seats were the same height! If a tall guy or some old broad with a hat sat in front of you and you couldn't see, you were just screwed!

Sure, we had cable television, but back then that was only like 15 channels and there was no onscreen menu and no remote control! You had to use a little book called a TV Guide to find out what was on! You were screwed when it came to channel surfing! You had to get off your ass and walk over to the TV to change the channel and there was no Cartoon Network either! You could only get cartoons on Saturday morning. Do you hear what I'm saying!?! We had to wait ALL WEEK for cartoons, you spoiled little bastards!

And our parents told us to stay outside and play - all day long. No electronics to soothe and comfort. And if you came back inside - you had to do chores.

And car seats - oh please! Mom threw you in the back seat and you hung on. If you were lucky, you got the safety arm across the chest at the last moment if she had to stop suddenly and if your head hit the dashboard, well that was your fault for riding shot gun.

And we didn't have microwaves; if we wanted to heat something up ... we had to use the stove or go build a frigging fire. Imagine that! If we wanted popcorn, we had to use that stupid Jiffy Pop thing and shake it over the stove forever like an idiot. That's exactly what I'm talking about! You kids today have got it too easy. You're spoiled.

You guys wouldn't have lasted five minutes back in 1970!

Just bringing back old memories

A kid asked the other day, *'What was your favourite fast food when you were growing up?'*

'We didn't have fast food when I was growing up,' I informed him. *'All the food was slow.'*

'C'mon, seriously. Where did you eat?'

'It was a place called home,' I explained!

'Mom cooked every day and when Dad got home from work, we sat down together at the dining room table and if I didn't like what she put on my plate I was allowed to sit there until I did like it.'

By this time, the kid was laughing so hard I was afraid he was going to suffer serious internal damage, so I didn't tell him the part about how I had to have permission to leave the table. But here are some other things I would have told him about my childhood if I figured his system could have handled it:

Some parents NEVER owned their own house, wore Levis, set foot on a golf course, travelled out of the country or had a credit card.

My parents never drove me to school. I had a bicycle that weighed probably 50 pounds and only had one speed, [slow]. We didn't have a television in our house until I was 19. It was, of course, black and white and the station went off the air at midnight, after playing the national anthem and a poem about God; it came back on the air at about 6 am and there was usually a locally produced news and farm show on, featuring local people.

I never had a telephone in my room. The only phone was on a party line. Before you could dial, you had to listen and make sure some people you didn't know weren't already using the line.

Pizzas were not delivered to our home. But milk was. All newspapers were delivered by boys and all boys delivered newspapers - my brother delivered a newspaper, six days a week. He had to get up at 6 am every morning.

Movie stars kissed with their mouths shut. At least, they did in the movies. There were no movie ratings because all movies were responsibly produced for everyone to enjoy viewing, without profanity or violence or most anything offensive.

If you grew up in a generation before there was fast food, you may want to share some of these memories with your children or grandchildren. Just don't blame me if they bust a gut laughing. Growing up isn't what it used to be, is it?

These Ads actually existed!

Your kids and grandkids will never believe there was a time when these ads were in every paper and magazine.

- A Lucky Strike ad showing Santa smoking a cigarette!
- An ad encouraging mothers to buy Coca Cola and 7-Up for their babies!
- *'More doctors smoke Camels than any other cigarette!'*
- *'Blow smoke in her face and she will follow you anywhere!*
- Advertising a blender: *'The Chef does everything but cook — that's what wives are for!'*
- Advertisement for vitamins: *'So the harder the wife works, the cuter she looks.'*

Sun, Moon and Stars

In the primitive days of the human race, people didn't understand how the sun, moon and stars worked. A caveman always saw the sun go down but when he woke up and stepped out of the cave, the sun was already in the sky and he wondered how it got up there. So one night he camped outside the cave and forced himself to stay up all night.

Hours and hours went by in the dark and all the while he wondered how the sun worked ... and then ... all of a sudden ... it dawned on him.

Man's age, as determined by a trip to Bunnings

You are in the middle of some kind of project around the house - mowing the lawn, putting in a new fence, painting the living room or whatever. You are hot and sweaty, covered in dust, lawn clippings, dirt or paint. You have your old work clothes on. You know the outfit - shorts with the hole in the crotch, old T-shirt with a stain from who-knows what and an old pair of tennis shoes.

Right in the middle of this great home improvement project you realise you need to run to Bunnings to get something to help complete the job.

Depending on your age you might do the following:

In your 20's:
Stop what you are doing. Shave, take a shower, blow dry your hair, brush your teeth, floss and put on clean clothes.

Check yourself in the mirror and flex. Add a dab of your favourite cologne because you never know, you just might meet some hot chick while standing in the checkout lane. And you went to school with the pretty girl running the register.

In your 30's:
Stop what you are doing, put on clean shorts and shirt. Change shoes. You married the hot chick so no need for much else. Wash your hands and comb your hair. Check yourself in the mirror. You've still got it! Add a shot of your favourite cologne to cover the smell. The cute girl running the register is the kid sister to someone you went to school with.

In your 40's:
Stop what you're doing. Put on a sweatshirt that is long enough to cover the hole in the crotch of your shorts.

Put on different shoes and a hat. Wash your hands. Your bottle of Brute Cologne is almost empty so you don't want to waste any of it on a trip to Bunnings. Check yourself in the mirror and do more sucking in than flexing. The hot young thing running the register is your daughter's age and you feel weird thinking she is hot.

In your 50's:

Stop what you are doing. Put on a hat; wipe the dirt off your hands onto your shirt. Change shoes because you don't want to get dog crap in your new sports car. Check yourself in the mirror and you swear not to wear that shirt anymore because it makes you look fat. The cutie running the register smiles when she sees you coming and you think you've still got it. Then you remember the hat you have on is from Bubba's Bait and Beer Bar and it says, *'I Got Worms.'*

In your 60's:

Stop what you're doing. No need for a hat anymore. Hose the dog crap off your shoes. The mirror was shattered when you were in your 50's. You hope you have underwear on so nothing hangs out the hole in your pants. The girl running the register may be cute, but you don't have your glasses on so you're not sure.

In your 70's:

Stop what you're doing. Wait to go to Bunnings until the drug store has your prescriptions ready, too. Don't even notice the dog crap on your shoes. The young thing at the register stares at you and you realise your balls are hanging out the hole in your crotch.

In your 80's:

Stop what you're doing. Start again. Then stop again. Now you remember. You need to go to Bunnings. Go to Big W instead and wander around trying to think what it is you are looking for. Fart out loud and you think someone called out your name. You went to school with the old lady who greeted you at the front door.

In your 90's and beyond:

What am I here for? Is it something for my garden? Where am I? Who am I? Who farted?

Sharing

The old man placed an order for one hamburger, French fries and a drink. He unwrapped the plain hamburger and carefully cut it in half, placing one half in front of his wife. He then carefully counted out the French fries, dividing them into two piles and neatly placed one pile in front of his wife.

He took a sip of the drink; his wife took a sip and then set the cup down between them. As he began to eat his few bites of hamburger, the people around them were looking over and whispering.

Obviously, they were thinking, *'That poor old couple - all they can afford is one meal for the two of them.'*

As the man began to eat his fries a young man came to the table and politely offered to buy another meal for the old couple. The old man said that they were just fine - they were used to sharing everything.

People closer to the table noticed the little old lady hadn't eaten a bite. She sat there watching her husband eat and occasionally taking turns sipping the drink.

Again, the young man came over and begged them to let him buy another meal for them. This time the old woman said, *'No, thank you; we are used to sharing everything.'*

Finally, as the old man finished and was wiping his face neatly with the napkin, the young man again came over to the little old lady who had yet to eat a single bite of food and asked, *'What is it you are waiting for?'*

She answered, *'The teeth!'*

Kitchen Wisdom

Martha Stewart: Stuff a miniature marshmallow in the bottom of an ice cream cone to prevent ice cream drips.

Ethel: Just suck the ice cream out of the bottom of the cone, for Pete's sake! You are probably lying on the couch with your feet up eating it anyway!

Martha: To keep potatoes from budding, place an apple in the bag with the potatoes.

Ethel: Buy Hungry Jack mashed potato mix. Keeps in the pantry for up to a year.

Martha: Wrap celery in aluminum foil when putting in the refrigerator and it will keep for weeks.

Ethel: Celery? Never heard of it!

Martha: When a cake recipe calls for flouring the baking pan, use a bit of the dry cake mix instead and there won't be any white mess on the outside of the cake.

Ethel: Go to the bakery! Hell, they'll even decorate it for you!

Martha: Brush some beaten egg white over pie crust before baking to yield a beautiful glossy finish.

Ethel: The Mrs. Smith frozen pie directions do not include brushing egg whites over the crust, so I don't.

Martha: If you accidentally over-salt a dish while it's still cooking, drop in a peeled potato and it will absorb the excess salt for an instant 'fix-me-up.'

Ethel: If you over-salt a dish while you are cooking, that's too bad. Please recite with me the real woman's motto: *'I made it, you will eat it and I don't care how bad it tastes!'*

Martha: Cure for headaches: take a lime, cut it in half and rub it on your forehead. The throbbing will go away.

Ethel: Take a lime, mix it with tequila, chill and drink! All your pains go away!

Martha: If you have a problem opening jars, try using latex dish washing gloves. They give a non-slip grip that makes opening jars easy.

Ethel: Go ask that very cute neighbour if he can open it for you.

The history of words

I know some of you will not understand this message, but I bet you know someone who might.

I came across this phrase yesterday **Fender skirts.** A term I haven't heard in a long time and thinking about fender skirts started me thinking about other words that quietly disappear from our language with hardly a notice like **curb feelers** and **steering knobs. (AKA) suicide knob, necker's knobs.**

Since I'd been thinking of cars, my mind naturally went that direction first. Any kids will probably have to find some elderly person over 50 to explain some of these terms to you.

Remember **Continental kits?** They were rear bumper extenders and spare tire covers that were supposed to make any car as cool as a Lincoln Continental.

When did we quit calling them **emergency brakes?** At some point **parking brake** became the proper term. But I miss the hint of drama that went with 'emergency brake.'

I'm sad, too, that almost all the old folks are gone who would call the accelerator the **foot feed.** Many today do not even know what a **clutch** is or that the **dimmer switch** used to be on the floor.

Didn't you ever wait at the street for your daddy to come home, so you could ride the **running board** up to the house?

Here's a phrase I heard all the time in my youth but never any more - **store-bought.** Of course, just about everything is store-bought these days. But once it was bragging material to have a store-bought dress or a store-bought bag of candy.

Coast to coast is a phrase that once held all sorts of excitement and now means almost nothing. Now we take the term **worldwide** for granted. This floors me.

On a smaller scale, **wall-to-wall** was once a magical term in our homes. In the '50s, everyone covered his or her hardwood floors with, wow, **wall-to-wall carpeting!** Today, everyone replaces their wall-to-wall carpeting with hardwood floors. Go figure.

When's the last time you heard the quaint phrase **in a family way**? It's hard to imagine that the word **pregnant** was once considered a little too graphic, a little too clinical for use in polite company, so we had all that talk about **stork visits** and **being in a family way** or simply **expecting.**

Apparently **brassiere** is a word no longer in usage. I said it the other day and my daughter cracked up. I guess it's just **bra** now. **Unmentionables** they probably wouldn't understood at all.

I always loved going to the **picture show,** but I considered calling it a **movie** an affectation.

Most of these words go back to the '50s, but here's a pure '60s word I came across the other day - **rat fink.** Ooh, what a nasty put-down!

Here's a word I miss - **percolator.** That was just a fun word to say. And what was it replaced with? **Coffee maker.** How dull. Mr. Coffee, I blame you for this.

I miss those made-up marketing words that were meant to sound so modern and now sound so retro. Words like **DynaFlow** and **Electrolux.** Introducing the 1963 Admiral TV, now with **SpectraVision!**

Food for thought - Was there a telethon that wiped out **lumbago**? Nobody complains of that anymore. Maybe that's what **castor oil** cured, because I never hear mothers threatening kids with castor oil any more.

Some words aren't gone, but are definitely on the endangered list. The one that grieves me most, is **supper.** Now everybody says **dinner.** Save a great word. Invite someone to supper. Discuss fender skirts.

My travels

I have been in many places, but I've never been in **Cahoots**. Apparently, you can't go alone. You have to be in Cahoots with someone.

I've also never been in **Cognito**. I hear no one recognises you there.

I have, however, been in **Sane**. They don't have an airport; you have to be driven there. I have made several trips there, thanks to my friends, family and work.

I would like to go to **Conclusions**, but you have to jump and I'm not too much on physical activity any more.

I have also been in **Doubt**. That is a sad place to go and I try not to visit there too often.

I've been in **Flexible**, but only when it was very important to stand firm.

Sometimes I'm in **Capable** and I go there more often as I'm getting older.

One of my favourite places to be is in **Suspense**! It really gets the adrenalin flowing and pumps up the old heart! At my age I need all the stimuli I can get!

I may have been in **Continent** and I don't remember what country I was in. It's an age thing.

Things Mom would never say

- ✓ *'How on earth can you see the TV sitting so far back?'*
- ✓ *'Yeah, I used to skip school a lot too.'*
- ✓ *'Just leave all the lights on ... it makes the house look more cheery.'*
- ✓ *'Let me smell that shirt. Yeah, it's good for another week.'*
- ✓ *'Go ahead and keep that stray dog honey. I'll be glad to feed and walk him every day.'*
- ✓ *'Well, if Paul's mom says it's okay, that's good enough for me.'*
- ✓ *'The curfew is just a general time to shoot for. It's not like I'm running a prison around here.'*
- ✓ *'I don't have a tissue with me ... just use your sleeve.'*
- ✓ *'Don't bother wearing a jacket – the wind-chill is bound to improve.'*

Automotive repair advertisement in 1928 sent on a penny postcard

Dear Sir,

We're writing this letter to you today because we want to help you get your money out of your Model T. It's still as good a car as it was the day the new Model A Ford was announced and there's no need to sacrifice it. The Model T Ford is still used by more people than any other automobile. Eight million are in active service right now and many of them can be driven one, two, three and five years and even longer.

Bring your car to us and let us look it over. You'll be surprised to see how little it costs to put it in tip-top shape.

New fenders, for instance, cost from $3.50 to $5.00 each, with a labour charge of $1.00 to $2.50. Tuning up the motor and replacing commutator case, brush and vibrator points costs only $1.00, with a small charge for material. Brake shoes can be installed and emergency brakes equalised for a labour charge of only $1.25. A labour charge of $4.00 to $5.00 will cover the overhauling of the front axle, rebushing springs and spring perches and straightening, aligning and adjusting wheels.

The labour charge for overhauling the average rear axle runs from $5.75 to $7.00. Grinding valves and cleaning carbon can be done for $3.00 to $4.00.

A set of four new pistons and rings cost only $7.00. For labour charge of $20.00 to $25.00, you can have your motor and transmission completely overhauled. Parts are extra.

Very truly yours,

C.R. Gleason Co., Bottineau N. Dakota

Memories

My Dad was cleaning out my grandmother's house [she died in December] and he brought me an old Royal Crown Cola bottle. In the bottle top was a stopper with a bunch of holes in it. I knew immediately what it was, but my daughter had no idea. She thought they had tried to make it a salt shaker or something. I knew it as the bottle that sat on the end of the ironing board to 'sprinkle' clothes with because we didn't have steam irons. Man, I'm old.

'I don't like to be the one to have to tell you this Sadie, but there's a rumour going around that your husband Max is chasing women. And him over 80!'

'Yeah! So he's 82, so what? Let him chase girls. Dogs chase cars, but when they catch one, can they drive?'

Middle age is when your old classmates are so gray and wrinkled and bald they don't recognise you.

You know you're over the hill when the only whistles you get are from the tea kettle.

My granddaughter asked me what it was like to be old. So I told her, *'Put cotton in your ears and pebbles in your shoes. Pull on rubber gloves, smear Vaseline over your glasses and there you have it: instant old age.'*

How many do you remember:

- ✓ Head lights dimmer switches on the floor?
- ✓ Ignition switches on the dashboard?
- ✓ Pant leg clips for bicycles without chain guards?
- ✓ Soldering irons you heat on a gas burner?
- ✓ Using hand signals for cars without turn signals?
- ✓ Candy cigarettes?
- ✓ Coffee shops with tableside juke boxes?
- ✓ Home milk delivery in glass bottles?
- ✓ Party lines on the telephone?
- ✓ Newsreels before the movie?
- ✓ TV test patterns that came on at night after the last show and were there until TV shows started again in the morning? [there were only 3 channels.]
- ✓ Peashooters?
- ✓ Howdy Doody?
- ✓ 45 RPM records?
- ✓ Hi-fi's?
- ✓ Metal ice trays with lever?
- ✓ Blue flashbulb on cameras?
- ✓ Cork popguns?
- ✓ Studebakers?
- ✓ Wash tub wringers?

I might be older than dirt but those memories are some of the best parts of my life.

- ✓ Forg: An army or colony of frogs
- ✓ Geese: A flock, gaggle or skein (in flight) of geese
- ✓ Hare: A down or husk of hares
- ✓ Hawk: A cast or kettle of hawks.
- ✓ Hog: A drift or parcel of hogs
- ✓ Hound: A pack, mute or cry of hounds.
- ✓ Jellyfish: A smack of jellyfish
- ✓ Loepard: A leap (leep) of leopards
- ✓ Magpie: A tidint of magpies
- ✓ Owl: A parliament of owls
- ✓ Partridge: A covey of partridges
- ✓ Peacock: A muster or ostentatio of peacocks
- ✓ Plover: A wig or congregation of plovers
- ✓ Rattlesnake: A rhumba of rattlesnakes
- ✓ Swan: A bevy, herd, lamentation or wedge of swans.
- ✓ Toad: A knot of toads
- ✓ Trout: A hover of trout
- ✓ Turkey: A rafter of turkeys
- ✓ Turtledove: A pitying or dule of turtledoves
- ✓ Turte: A bale of turtles
- ✓ Woodpecker: A descent of woodpeckers

Eonverye taht can raed tihs rsaie yuor hnad.

Only great minds can read this. It's weird, but interesting!

Fi yuo cna raed tihs, yuo hvae a sgtrane mnid too. Cna yuo raed tihs? Olny 55 plepoe out of 100 can.

I cdnuolt blveiee taht I cluod aulaclty uesdnatnrd waht I was rdanieg. The phaonmneal pweor of the hmuan mnid, aoccdrnig to a rscheearch at Cmabrigde Uinervtisy, it dseno't mtaetr in waht oerdr the ltteres in a wrod are, the olny iproamtnt tihng is taht the frsit and lsat ltteer be in the rghit pclae. The rset can be a taotl mses and you can sitll raed it whotuit a pboerlm. Tihs is bcuseae the huamn mnid deos not raed ervey lteter by istlef, but the wrod as a wlohe. Azanmig huh? Yaeh and I awlyas tghuhot slpeling was ipmorantt!

Male or Female?

You might not have known this, but a lot of non-living objects are actually either male or female. Here are some examples:

- ❖ Freezer bags: These are male, because they hold everything in, but you can see right through them.

- ❖ Photocopiers: These are female, because once turned off; it takes a while to warm them up again. They are an effective reproductive device if the right buttons are pushed, but can also wreak havoc if you push the wrong buttons.
- ❖ Tyres: Tyres are male, because they go bald easily and are often over inflated.
- ❖ Hot air balloons: Also a male object, because to get them to go anywhere, you have to light a fire under their butt.
- ❖ Sponges: These are female, because they are soft, squeezable and retain water.
- ❖ Web pages: Female, because they're constantly being looked at and frequently getting hit on.
- ❖ Trains: Definitely male, because they always use the same old lines for picking up people.
- ❖ Egg timers: Egg timers are female because, over time, all the weight shifts to the bottom.
- ❖ Hammers: Male, because in the last 5,000 years, they've hardly changed at all and are occasionally handy to have around.
- ❖ The remote control: Female. Ha! You probably thought it would be male, but consider this: It easily gives a man pleasure, he'd be lost without it and while he doesn't always know which buttons to push, he just keeps trying.

English Signs from Around the World

- In a Bangkok temple: It is forbidden to enter a woman, even a foreigner, if dressed as a man.
- Doctor's office, Rome: Specialist in women and other diseases.
- Dry cleaners, Bangkok: Drop your trousers here for the best results.
- In a Nairobi restaurant: Customers who find our waitresses rude ought to see the manager.
- On the main road to Mombasa, leaving Nairobi: Take notice: when this sign is under water, this road is impassable.
- On a poster at Kencom: Are you an adult that cannot read? If so we can help.
- In a City restaurant: Open seven days a week and weekends.
- In a cemetery: Persons are prohibited from picking flowers from any but their own graves.
- Tokyo hotel's rules and regulations: Guests are requested not to smoke or do other disgusting behaviours in bed.
- On the menu of a Swiss restaurant: Our wines leave you nothing to hope for.

- In a Tokyo bar: Special cocktails for the ladies with nuts.
- Hotel, Yugoslavia: The flattening of underwear with pleasure is the job of the chambermaid.
- Hotel: Japan: You are invited to take advantage of the chambermaid.
- In the lobby of a Moscow hotel across from a Russian Orthodox monastery: You are welcome to visit the cemetery where famous Russian and Soviet composers, artists and writers are buried daily except Thursday.
- A sign posted in Germany's Black Forest: It is strictly forbidden on our black forest camping site that people of different sex, for instance, men and women, live together in one tent unless they are married with each other for this purpose.
- Hotel, Zurich: Because of the impropriety of entertaining guests of the opposite sex in the bedroom, it is suggested that the lobby be used for this purpose.
- Advertisement for donkey rides, Thailand: Would you like to ride on your own ass?
- Airline ticket office, Copenhagen: We take your bags and send them in all directions.

Mixed Words:

The following are exceptionally clever. Someone out there either has far too much time on his or her hands or they're not so good at Scrabble. When you re-arrange the letters:

Dormitory = Dirty Room
Evangelist = Evil's Agent
Desperation = A rope ends it
The Morse Code = Here come dots
Slot Machines = Cash lost in 'em
Animosity = Is no amity
Presbyterian = best in prayer.
Astronomer = moon starer.
Desperation = a rope ends it.
The eyes = they see.
George bush = he bugs gore.
The Morse code = here come dots.
Dormitory = dirty room.
Slot machines = cash lost in me.
Animosity = is no amity.
Election results = lies - let's recount.

Snooze alarms = alas! No more Z's.
A decimal point = I'm a dot in place.
The earthquakes = that queer shake.
Eleven plus two = twelve plus one.
Mother-in-law = woman Hitler.
Snooze Alarms = Atlas! No more Z's
Alec Guinness = Genuine Class
Semolina = Is no meal
The Public Art Galleries = large picture halls, I bet
A Decimal Point - = I'm a Dot in place
The Earthquakes = That Queer Shake
Eleven plus Two = Twelve plus one
Contradiction = Accord not in it
And for the grand finale:
President Clinton of the USA = To copulate he finds interns

Oxymorons:

An oxymoron is a figure of speech that uses two words that contradict each other, such as *'a serious joke'* or *'the deafening silence.'* However the word *oxymoron* is itself an oxymoron! The Greek word *oxy* means *'sharp'* and *moron* means *'dull.'*

1. Is it good if a vacuum really sucks?
2. Why is the third hand on a watch called the second hand?
3. If a word is misspelled in the dictionary, how would we ever know?
4. If Webster wrote the first dictionary, where did he find the words?
5. Why do we say something is out of whack? What is a whack?
6. Why does *'slow down'* and *'slow up'* mean the same thing?
7. Why does *'fat chance'* and *'slim chance'* mean the same thing?
8. Why do *'tug'* boats push their barges?
9. Why do we sing *'Take me out to the ball game'* when we are already there?
10. Why are they called *'stands'* when they are made for sitting?
11. Why is it called *'after dark'* when it is really *'after light?'*
12. Doesn't *'expecting the unexpected'* make the unexpected expected?
13. Why are a *'wise man'* and a *'wise guy'* opposites?
14. Why do *'overlook'* and *'oversee'* mean opposite things?
15. Why is *'phonics'* not spelled the way it sounds?
16. If work is so terrific, why do they have to pay you to do it?

17. If all the world is a stage, where is the audience sitting?
18. If love is blind, why is lingerie so popular?
19. If you are cross-eyed and have dyslexia, can you read all right?
20. Why is bra singular and panties plural?
21. Why do you press harder on the buttons of a remote control when you know the batteries are dead?
22. Why do we put suits in garment bags and garments in a suitcase?
23. How come abbreviated is such a long word?
24. Why do we wash bath towels? Aren't we clean when we use them?
25. Why doesn't glue stick to the inside of the bottle?
26. Why do they call it a TV set when you only have one?
27. Christmas - What other time of year do you sit in front of a dead tree and eat candy out of your socks?
28. Then there's:
    Military intelligence.
    Jumbo shrimp.
    Postal worker.
    Student teacher. and
    Civil war.

Doesn't anyone proof-read anymore?

The year's best [actual] headlines of 2005:

a) Is There a ring of debris around Uranus? [Not if I wipe thoroughly!]
b) Panda mating fails; Veterinarian takes over [What a guy!!]
c) Crack found on governor's daughter [Yea, kids *are* wearing those low-rider pants ...]
d) Man kills self before shooting wife and daughter. [This one I caught in the SGV Tribune the other day and called the Editorial Room and asked who wrote this. It took two or three readings before the editor realised that what he was reading was impossible!!! They put in a correction the next day.]
e) Something went wrong in jet crash, expert says. [No crap, really?]
f) Police begin campaign to run down jaywalkers. [Now that's taking things a bit far!]
g) Miners refuse to work after death. [No-good-for-nothing' lazy so-and-so's!]

h) If strike isn't settled quickly, it may last a while [Really?]
i) Juvenile court to try shooting defendant. [See if that works any better than a fair trial.]
j) War dims hope for peace [I can see where it might have that effect!]
k) Cold wave linked to temperatures [Who would have thought!]
l) Enfield [London] couple slain; Police suspect homicide. [They may be on to something!]
m) Red tape holds up new bridges [You mean there's something stronger than duct tape?]
n) Man struck by lightning: faces battery charge [He probably IS the battery charge!]
o) New study of obesity looks for larger test group. [Weren't the first group fat enough?]
p) Astronaut takes blame for gas in spacecraft. [That's what he gets for eating those beans!]
q) Kids make nutritious snacks. [Do they taste like chicken?]
r) Local high school dropouts cut in half. [Chainsaw Massacre all over again!]
s) Hospitals are sued by 7 foot doctors. [Boy, are they tall!]

And the winner is ...
t) Typhoon rips through cemetery; hundreds dead. [Did I read that right?]

Consumer bloopers

In case you needed further proof that the human race is doomed through stupidity, here are some actual label instructions on consumer goods:

- On Tesco's Tiramisu dessert [printed on bottom] - *'Do not turn upside down.'* [Well ... duh, a bit late!]
- On Sainsbury's peanuts - *'Warning: contains nuts.'* (Talk about a news flash)
- On Boot's Children Cough Medicine - *'Do not drive a car or operate machinery after taking this medication.'* [We could do a lot to reduce the rate of construction accidents if we could just get those 5 year-olds with head-colds off those bulldozers.]
- On Marks &Spencer Bread Pudding - *'Product will be hot after heating.'* [And you thought it would be cold?]
- On a Sears hairdryer - *'Do not use while sleeping.'* [Aw shucks. That's the only time I have to work on my hair.]

- On a bag of Doritos - *'You could be a winner! No purchase necessary. Details inside.'* [The shoplifter special?]
- On a bar of Dial soap - *'Directions: Use like regular soap.'* [And that would be?]
- On some Swanson frozen dinners - *'Serving suggestion: Defrost.'* [But, it's just a suggestion.]
- On packaging for a Rowenta iron - *'Do not iron clothes on body.'* [but wouldn't this save me time?]
- On Nytol Sleep Aid - *'Warning: May cause drowsiness.'* [I'm taking this because?]
- On most brands of Christmas lights - *'For indoor or outdoor use only.'* [As opposed to ...?]
- On a Japanese food processor - *'Not to be used for the other use.'* [Now, somebody out there, help me on this. I'm a bit curious.]
- On an American Airlines packet of nuts - *'Instructions: Open packet, eat nuts.'* [Step 3?]
- On a child's Superman costume - *'Wearing of this garment does not enable you to fly.'* [I don't blame the company. I blame the parents for this one.]
- On a Swedish Chainsaw – *'Do not attempt to stop chain with your hands or genitals.'* [Oh my God ... was there a lot of this happening somewhere?]
- House for Sale by owner - because my neighbour is an asshole!

Poetry

These are entries to a Washington post competition asking for a two-line rhyme with the most romantic first line and the least romantic second line:

1. My darling, my lover, my beautiful wife; marrying you has screwed up my life.
2. My love, you take my breath away. What have you stepped in to smell this way?
3. Kind, intelligent, loving and hot; this describes everything you're not.
4. Love may be beautiful, love may be bliss; but I only slept with you 'cause I was pissed.
5. I thought that I could love no other; that is until I met your brother.

6. Roses are red, violets are blue, sugar is sweet and so are you; but the roses are wilting, the violets are dead, the sugar bowl's empty and so is your head.
7. I want to feel your sweet embrace; but don't take that paper bag off your face.
8. I love your smile, your face and your eyes; damn, I'm good at telling lies!
9. I see your face when I am dreaming; that's why I always wake up screaming.
10. My feelings for you no words can tell; except for maybe *'Go to hell.'*
11. What inspired this amorous rhyme? Two parts vodka, one part lime.

Who said poetry is boring?

From the Bristol Evening Post

Outside Bristol Zoo is the car park, with spaces for 150 cars and 8 coaches. It has been manned 6 days a week for 23 years by the same charming and very polite car park attendant with the ticket machine. The charges are £1 per car and £5 per coach.

On Monday 1 June, he did not turn up for work. Bristol Zoo management phoned Bristol City Council to ask them to send a replacement parking attendant.

The Council said *'That car park is your responsibility.'*

The Zoo said *'The attendant was employed by the City Council ... wasn't he?'*

The Council said, *'What attendant?'*

Gone missing from his home is a man who has been taking the daily car park fees amounting to about £400 per day for the last 23 years ... total sum just short £2.9 million! Some retirement fund!

The English Language

One reason I do not teach English. You think English is easy? Read to the end ... a new twist.

1) The bandage was wound around the wound.
2) The farm was used to produce produce.
3) The dump was so full that it had to refuse more refuse.
4) We must polish the Polish furniture.
5) He could lead if he would get the lead out of his shoes.
6) The soldier decided to desert his dessert in the desert.

7) Since there is no time like the present, he thought it was time to present the present.
8) A bass was painted on the head of the bass drum.
9) When shot at, the dove dove into the bushes.
10) I did not object to the object.
11) The insurance was invalid for the invalid.
12) There was a row among the oarsmen about how to row.
13) They were too close to the door to close it.
14) The buck does funny things when the does are present.
15) A seamstress and a sewer fell down into a sewer line.
16) To help with planting, the farmer taught his sow to sow.
17) The wind was too strong to wind the sail.
18) Upon seeing the tear in the painting I shed a tear.
19) I had to subject the subject to a series of tests.
20) How can I intimate this to my most intimate friend?

Let's face it - English is a crazy language. Sweetmeats are candies while sweetbreads, which aren't sweet, are meat. If the plural of tooth is teeth, why isn't the plural of booth, beeth? One goose, two geese. So one moose, two meese?

English was invented by people, not computers and it reflects the creativity of the human race, which, of course, is not a race at all That is why, when the stars are out, they are visible, but when the lights are on, they are invisible. And why doesn't *'Buick'* rhyme with *'quick.'* and why doesn't *'dough'* rhyme with *'tough?'*

Rural Australian Computer Terminology [A little bit of Aussie culcha.]

- Log on: Adding wood to make the barbie hotter.
- Log off: Not adding any more wood to the barbie.
- Monitor: Keeping an eye on the barbie.
- Download: Getting the firewood off the Ute.
- Hard drive: Making the trip back home without any cold tinnies.
- Keyboard: Where you hang the Ute keys.
- Window: What you shut when the weather's cold.
- Screen: What you shut in mozzie season.
- Byte: What mozzies do.
- Megabyte: What Townsville mozzies do.
- Chip: A bar snack.

- Microchip: What's left in the bag after you've eaten the chips.
- Modem: What you did to the lawns.
- Laptop: Where the cat sleeps.
- Software: Plastic knives and forks you get at Red Rooster.
- Hardware: Stainless steel knives and forks - from K-Mart.
- Mouse: The small rodent that eats the grain in the shed.
- Mainframe: What holds the shed up.
- Web: What spiders make.
- Website: Usually in the shed or under the veranda.
- Search engine: What you do when the Ute won't go.
- Cursor: What you say when the Ute won't go.
- YAHOO: What you say when the Ute does go.
- Upgrade: A steep hill.
- Server: The person at the pub who brings out the counter lunch.
- Mail server: The bloke who delivers our mail.
- User: The neighbour who keeps borrowing things.
- Network: What you do when you need to repair the fishing net.
- Internet: Where you want the fish to go.
- Netscape: What the fish do when they discover a hole in the net.
- Online: Where you hang the washing.
- Offline: Where the washing ends up when the pegs aren't strong enough.

Ambiguity

For those who love the philosophy of ambiguity, as well as the idiosyncrasies of English: Please enjoy and understand the following:

1. One tequila, two tequila, three tequila, floor.
2. Atheism is a non-prophet organisation.
3. The main reason that Santa is so jolly is because he knows where all the bad girls live.
4. I went to a bookstore and asked the saleswoman, *'Where's the self- help section?'* she said if she told me, it would defeat the purpose.
5. What if there were no hypothetical questions?
6. If a deaf child signs swear words, does his mother wash his hands with soap?
7. Can an atheist get insurance against acts of god?

8. If someone with multiple personalities threatens to kill himself, is it considered a hostage situation?
9. Is there another word for synonym?
10. Where do forest rangers go to 'get away from it all?'
11. What do you do when you see an endangered animal eating an endangered plant?
12. If a parsley farmer is sued, can they garnish his wages?
13. Would a fly without wings be called a walk?
14. Why do they lock petrol station bathrooms? Are they afraid someone will break-in and clean them?
15. If a turtle doesn't have a shell, is he homeless or naked?
16. Can vegetarians eat animal crackers?
17. If the police arrest a mute, do they tell him he has the right to remain silent?
18. Why do they put Braille on the drive-through bank machines?
19. How do they get deer to cross the road only at those yellow road signs?
20. What was the best thing before sliced bread?
21. One nice thing about egotists: they don't talk about other people.
22. Does the little mermaid wear an algebra?
23. Do infants enjoy infancy as much as adults enjoy adultery?
24. How is it possible to have a civil war?
25. If one synchronised swimmer drowns, do the rest drown too?
26. If you ate both pasta and antipasto, would you still be hungry?
27. If you try to fail and succeed, which have you done?
28. Why is there an expiration date on sour cream?
29. Why are haemorrhoids called 'haemorrhoids' instead of 'assteroids'?
30. Why is it called tourist season if we can't shoot at them?

Language Problem

A refuse collector is driving along a street picking up the wheelie bins and emptying them into his compactor.

He went to one house where the bin hadn't been left out and in the spirit of kindness and after having a quick look about for the bin, he gets out of his truck, goes to the front door and knocks. There's no answer.

Being a kindly and conscientious bloke, he knocks again - much harder. Eventually a Japanese man comes to the door.

'Harro!' says the Japanese man.

'Gidday, mate! Where's ya bin?' asks the collector.

'I bin on toiret,' explains the Japanese bloke, a bit perplexed.

Realising the little foreign fellow had misunderstood him, the bin man smiles and tries again. *'No! No! Mate, where's your dust bin?'*

'I dust been to toiret, I toll you!'' says the Japanese man, still perplexed.

'Listen,' says the collector. *'You're misunderstanding me. Where's your 'wheelie' bin?'*

'Okay, okay.' replies the Japanese man with a sheepish grin and whispers in the collector's ear. *'I wheelie bin having sex wirra wife's sista!'*

Lexiphiles

- ✓ To write with a broken pencil is pointless.
- ✓ When fish are in schools they sometimes take debate.
- ✓ A thief who stole a calendar got twelve months.
- ✓ When the smog lifts in Los Angeles, U.C.L.A.
- ✓ The professor discovered that her theory of earthquakes was on shaky ground.
- ✓ The batteries were given out free of charge.
- ✓ A dentist and a manicurist married. They fought tooth and nail.
- ✓ If you don't pay your exorcist you can get repossessed.
- ✓ With her marriage, she got a new name and a dress.
- ✓ Show me a piano falling down a mineshaft and I'll show you A-flat miner.
- ✓ You are stuck with your debt if you can't budge it.
- ✓ Local Area Network in Australia: The LAN down under.
- ✓ A boiled egg is hard to beat.
- ✓ When you've seen one shopping centre you've seen a mall.
- ✓ Police were called to a day care where a three-year-old was resisting a rest.
- ✓ Did you hear about the fellow whose whole left side was cut off? He's all right now.
- ✓ If you take a laptop computer for a run you could jog your memory.
- ✓ A bicycle can't stand alone; it is two tired.
- ✓ In a democracy it's your vote that counts; in feudalism, it's your Count that votes.
- ✓ When a clock is hungry it goes back four seconds.

- ✓ The guy who fell onto an upholstery machine was fully recovered.
- ✓ He had a photographic memory which was never developed.
- ✓ Those who get too big for their britches will be exposed in the end.
- ✓ When she saw her first strands of gray hair, she thought she'd dye.
- ✓ Acupuncture: a jab well done.
- ✓ Those who jump off a bridge in Paris are in Seine.
- ✓ A man's home is his castle, in a manor of speaking.
- ✓ Dijon vu - the same mustard as before.
- ✓ Practice safe eating - always use condiments.
- ✓ Shotgun wedding - A case of wife or death.
- ✓ A man needs a mistress just to break the monogamy.
- ✓ A hangover is the wrath of grapes.
- ✓ Dancing cheek-to-cheek is really a form of floor play.
- ✓ Does the name Pavlov ring a bell?
- ✓ Condoms should be used on every conceivable occasion.
- ✓ Reading while sunbathing makes you well red.
- ✓ When two egotists meet, it's an I for an I.
- ✓ What's the definition of a will? It's a dead give-away.
- ✓ Time flies like an arrow. Fruit flies like a banana.
- ✓ She was engaged to a boyfriend with a wooden leg but broke it off.
- ✓ A chicken crossing the road is poultry in motion.
- ✓ Every calendar's days are numbered.
- ✓ A lot of money is tainted. T'aint yours and t'aint mine.
- ✓ A midget fortune-teller who escapes from prison is a small medium at large.
- ✓ Bakers trade bread recipes on a knead-to-know basis.
- ✓ Santa's helpers are subordinate clauses.

Service

I became confused when I heard the word *'Service'* used with these agencies:

Internal Revenue *'Service'*
Canada Post 'S*ervice'*
Cable TV *'Service'*
Civil *'Service'* [Also known as the *'Silly Service'*]
Provincial, City, County and Public *'Service'*
Customer *'Service'*

This is not what I thought *'Service'* meant, but today, I overheard two farmers talking and one of them said he had hired a bull to *'Service'* a few cows. All of a sudden - it all came into focus. Now I understand what all those agencies are doing to us. Now you are as enlightened as I am.

Coloured folks

When I was born, I was BLACK,
When I grew up, I was BLACK,
When I went in the sun, I stayed BLACK,
When I got cold, I was BLACK,
When I was scared, I was BLACK,
When I was sick, I was BLACK,
And when I die, I'll still be BLACK.

NOW, you 'white' folks ...

When you're born, you're PINK,
When you grow-up, you're WHITE,
When you go in the sun, you get RED,
When you're cold, you turn BLUE,
When you're scared, you're YELLOW,
When you get sick, you're GREEN,
When you bruise, you turn PURPLE,
And when you die, you look GRAY.

So who y'all callin' COLORED Folks?

How to say I Love You in Eleven Languages

English - I Love You
French - Je T'aime
Italian - Ti Amo
Chinese - Wo Ai Nin
Spanish – Te Amo
German – Ich Liebe Dich
Japanese – Ai Shite Imasu
Swedish – Jag Alskar Dig
Lithuanian – As TaveMeliu
Newfoundland - Nice arse, get in the truck
Australia – Nice tits, get in the ute

An ode of English plurals

We'll begin with a box and the plural is boxes,
But the plural of ox becomes oxen, not oxes.
One fowl is a goose, but two are called geese,
Yet the plural of moose should never be meese.
You may find a lone mouse or a nest full of mice,
Yet the plural of house is houses, not hice.
If the plural of man is always called men,
Why shouldn't the plural of pan be called pen?
If I speak of my foot and show you my feet,
And I give you a boot, would a pair be called beet?
If one is a tooth and a whole set are teeth,
Why shouldn't the plural of booth be called beeth?
Then one may be that and three would be those,
Yet hat in the plural would never be hose,
And the plural of cat is cats, not cose.
We speak of a brother and also of brethren,
But though we say mother, we never say methren.
Then the masculine pronouns are he, his and him,
But imagine the feminine: she, shis and shim!
Let's face it - English is a crazy language.
There is no egg in eggplant nor ham in hamburger;
Neither apple nor pine in pineapple.
English muffins weren't invented in England ...
We take English for granted, but if we explore its paradoxes,
We find that quicksand can work slowly, boxing rings are square,
And a guinea pig is neither from Guinea nor is it a pig.
And why is it that writers write but fingers don't fing,
Grocers don't groce and hammers don't ham?
Doesn't it seem crazy that you can make amends but not one amend.
If you have a bunch of odds and ends and
get rid of all but one of them, what do you call it?
If teachers taught, why didn't preachers praught?
If a vegetarian eats vegetables, what does a humanitarian eat?
Sometimes I think all the folks who grew up speaking English
Should be committed to an asylum for the verbally insane.
In what other language do people recite at a play and play at a
recital?
We ship by truck but send cargo by ship.
We have noses that run and feet that smell.
We park in a driveway and drive in a parkway.

123

And how can a slim chance and a fat chance be the same,
While a wise man and a wise guy are opposites?
You have to marvel at the unique lunacy of a language
In which your house can burn up as it burns down,
In which you fill in a form by filling it out and
In which an alarm goes off by going on.
And in closing, if Father is Pop, how come Mother's not Mop?

Grounds for divorce

A judge was interviewing a woman regarding her pending divorce and asked, *'What are the grounds for your divorce?'*

She replied, *'About four acres and a nice little home in the middle of the property with a stream running by.'*

'No,' he said, *'I mean what is the foundation of this case?'*

'It is made of concrete, brick and mortar,' she responded.

'I mean,' he continued, *'What are your relations like?'*

'I have an aunt and uncle living here in town and so do my husband's parents.'

He said, *'Do you have a real grudge?'*

'No,' she replied, *'We have a two-car carport and have never really needed one.'*

'Please,' he tried again, *'is there any infidelity in your marriage?'*

'Yes, both my son and daughter have stereo sets. We don't necessarily like the music, but the answer to your questions is yes.'

'Ma'am, does your husband ever beat you up?'

'Yes,' she responded, *'about twice a week he gets up earlier than I do.'*

Finally, in frustration, the judge asked, *'Lady, why do you want a divorce?'*

'Oh, I don't want a divorce,' she replied. *'I've never wanted a divorce. My husband does. He said he can't communicate with me!'*

Ever notice how all of women's problems start with MEN?

Woman has Man in it;
Mrs. Has Mr. in it;
Female has Male in it;
She has He in it;
Madam has Adam in it;

Women can get:
  MENtal illness!
  MENstrual cramps
  MENtal breakdown
  MENopause
  GUYnecologist and
When we have REAL trouble, it's a ... HISterectomy?

Okay, Okay, it all makes sense now ... I never looked at it that way before.

Tenjooberrymuds

By the time you read through this you will understand *'tenjooberrymuds.'*

In order to continue getting-by in our home land, we all need to learn the NEW English language! Practice by reading the following conversation until you are able to understand the term *'Tenjooberrymuds.'* With a little patience, you'll be able to fit right in. Now, here goes ...

The following is a telephone exchange between you (a hotel guest) and a room service employee.

Room Service : *'Morrin. Roon sirbees.'*

Guest : *'Sorry, I thought I dialled room-service.'*

Room Service: *'Rye . Roon sirbees ... morrin! Joow ish to oddor sunteen???'*

Guest: *'Uh ... Yes, I'd like to order bacon and eggs.'*

Room Service: *'Ow July den?'*

Guest: *'... What??'*

Room Service: *'Ow July den?!?... pryed, boyud, poochd?'*

Guest: *'Oh, the eggs! How do I like them? Sorry ... scrambled, please.'*

Room Service: *'Ow July dee baykem? Crease?'*

Guest: *'Crisp will be fine.'*

Room Service: *'Hokay. An Sahn toes?'*

Guest: *'What?'*

Room Service: *'An toes. July Sahn toes?'*

Guest: *'I ... don't think so.'*

RoomService: *'No? Judo wan sahn toes???'*

Guest: *'I feel really bad about this, but I don't know what 'judo wan sahn toes' means.'*

RoomService: *'Toes! Toes...! Why Joo don Juan toes? Ow bow Anglish moppin we bodder?'*

Guest: *'Oh, English muffin!!! I've got it! You were saying 'toast'... Fine ... Yes, an English muffin will be fine.'*

RoomService: *'We bodder?'*

Guest: *'No, just put the bodder on dee side.'*

RoomService: *'Wad?!?'*

Guest: *'I mean butter ... just put the butter on the side.'*

RoomService: *'Copy?'*

Guest: *'Excuse me?'*

RoomService: *'Copy ... tea ... meel?'*

Guest: *'Yes. Coffee, please ... and that's everything.'*

RoomService: *'One Minnie. Scramah egg, crease baykem, Anglish moppin, we bodder on sigh and copy ... rye??'*

Guest: *'Whatever you say.'*

RoomService: *'Tenjooberrymuds.'*

Guest: *'You're welcome.'*

Remember I said 'that by the time you read through this you would understand *'tenjooberrymuds.'*... and you do, don't you?' And you thought you didn't speak a foreign language!!

Politically Correct

30 Politically Correct ways to say someone is stupid:

1. Not the sharpest knife in the drawer.
2. A few clowns short of a circus.
3. A few fries short of a Happy Meal.
4. An experiment in artificial stupidity.
5. A few beers short of a six-pack.
6. A few peas short of a casserole.
7. Doesn't have all his cornflakes in one box.
8. One Fruit Loop shy of a full bowl.
9. One taco short of a combination plate.
10. A few feathers short of a whole duck.
11. All foam, no beer.
12. The cheese slid off his cracker.
13. Body by Fisher, brains by Mattel.
14. Warning: Objects in mirror are dumber than they appear.
15. Couldn't pour water out of a boot with instructions on the heel.
16. He fell out of the Stupid tree and hit every branch on the way down.
17. An intellect rivalled only by garden tools.
18. Chimney's clogged.
19. Doesn't know much but leads the league in nostril hair.

20. Elevator doesn't go all the way to the top floor.
21. Her sewing machine's out of thread.
22. His antenna doesn't pick up all the channels.
23. His belt doesn't go through all the loops.
24. Missing a few buttons on his remote control.
25. No grain in the silo.
26. Proof that evolution **can** go in reverse.
27. Receiver is off the hook.
28. Several cards short of a full deck.
29. Skylight leaks a little.
30. Too much yardage between the goal posts.

Signs of the Times:

❖ Sign over a Gynaecologist's Office: Dr. Jones, at your cervix.
❖ In a Podiatrist's office: Time wounds all heels.
❖ On a Septic Tank Truck: Yesterday's Meals on Wheels.
❖ On a Plumber's truck: We repair what your husband fixed.
❖ On another Plumber's truck: Don't sleep with a drip. Call your plumber.
❖ On a Church's billboard: 7 days without God makes one weak.
❖ At a Tyre Store: Invite us to your next blowout.
❖ On an Electrician's truck: Let us remove your shorts.
❖ In a Non-smoking Area: If we see smoke, we will assume you are on fire and take appropriate action.
❖ On a Maternity Room door: Push. Push. Push.
❖ At an Optometrist's Office: If you don't see what you're looking for, you've come to the right place.
❖ On a Taxidermist's window: We really know our stuff.
❖ On a Fence: Salesmen welcome! Dog food is expensive!
❖ At a Car Dealership: The best way to get back on your feet - miss a car payment.
❖ Outside a Car Exhaust Store: No appointment necessary. We hear you coming.
❖ In a Vets waiting room: Be back in 5 minutes. Sit! Stay!
❖ In a Restaurant window: Don't stand there and be hungry; come on in and get fed up.
❖ In the front yard of a Funeral Home: Drive carefully. We'll wait.
❖ And don't forget the sign at a Radiator Shop: Best place in town to take a leak.
❖ Sign on the back of a Septic Tank Truck; We are in the number 2 business.

❖ Sign on the back of yet another Septic Tank Truck: Caution - This Truck is full of Political Promises.

Southern Slang: (Most effective if said out loud)

Heidi - howdy or hi
Hire yew - how are you
Bard - borrowed
Jawjah - Georgia
Birminhayum Bammer - Birmingham, Alabama
Munts - months
Thank - think
Bare - beer
Ignernt - ignorant
Ranch - wrench
All - oil
Far - fire
Tar - tire
Retard - retired
Fat - fight
Rats - rights
Farn - foreign
Ear - air
Bob war - barbed wire
Jew here - did you hear
Haze -he's
Seed - to see
View - have you
Gubmint - government

What's the difference between a northern fairytale and a southern fairytale?

A northern fairytale begins, _'Once upon a time ...'_

A southern fairytale begins, _'Y'all ain't gonna believe this s**t!'_

CHAPTER 5 - THE ELDERLY

I'm kinder to myself

As I've aged, I've become kinder to myself and less critical of myself. I've become my own friend.

I have seen too many dear friends leave this world, too soon; before they understood the great freedom that comes with aging.

Whose business is it, if I choose to read or play on the computer until 4 am or sleep until noon? I will dance with myself to those wonderful tunes of the 50, 60 and 70's and if I, at the same time, wish to weep over a lost love, I will.

I will walk the beach, in a swim suit that is stretched over a bulging body and will dive into the waves with abandon if I choose to, despite the pitying glances from the jet set. They, too, will get old.

I know I am sometimes forgetful. But there again, some of life is just as well forgotten. And, I eventually remember the important things.

Sure, over the years, my heart has been broken. How can your heart not break, when you lose a loved one or when a child suffers or even when somebody's beloved pet gets hit by a car? But, broken hearts are what give us strength, understanding and compassion. A heart never broken is pristine and sterile and will never know the joy of being imperfect.

I am so blessed to have lived long enough to have my hair turning gray and to have my youthful laughs be forever etched into deep grooves on my face. So many have never laughed and so many have died before their hair could turn silver.

As you get older, it is easier to be positive. You care less about what other people think. I don't question myself any more. I've even earned the right to be wrong.

So, to answer your question, I like being old. It has set me free. I like the person I have become. I am not going to live forever, but while I am still here, I will not waste time lamenting what could have been or worrying about what will be. And I shall eat dessert every single day [if I feel like it.]

When asked by a young patrol officer *'Do you know you were speeding?'* this 83-year-old woman talked herself out of a ticket by stating, *'Yes, but I had to get there before I forgot where in the hell I was going.'*

What is Success?

At 3 - not pooping your pants
At 12 - having friends
At 18 - having a drivers licence
At 20 - having sex
At 35 - having money
At 50 - having money
At 60 - having sex
At 70 - having a drivers licence
At 75 - having friends
At 80 - not pooping your pants

Claude the Hypnotist

It was entertainment night at the Old Folks home. Claude the hypnotist exclaimed: *'I'm here to put you into a trance; I intend to hypnotise each and every member of the audience.'*

The excitement was almost electric as Claude withdrew a beautiful antique pocket watch from his coat. *'I want you each to keep your eye on this antique watch. It's a very special watch. It's been in my family for six generations'*

He began to swing the watch gently back and forth while quietly chanting, *'Watch the watch, watch the watch and watch the watch ...'*

The crowd became mesmerised as the watch swayed back and forth, light gleaming off its polished surface. Hundreds of pairs of eyes followed the swaying watch, until suddenly, it slipped from the hypnotist's fingers and fell to the floor, breaking into a hundred pieces.

'SHIT!' said the hypnotist.

It took three days to clean up the Old Folks home

The meeting place

A group of 40 year-old buddies discuss and discuss where they should meet for dinner. Finally it is agreed upon that they should meet at the Gausthof zum Lowen restaurant because the waitresses there have low cut blouses and nice breasts.

Ten years later, at 50 years of age, the group meets and once again they discuss and discuss where they should meet. Finally it is agreed upon that they should meet at the Gausthof zum Lowen because the food there is very good and the wine selection is good also.

Ten years later at 60 years of age, the group meets and once again they discuss and discuss where they should meet. Finally it is agreed upon that they should meet at the Gausthof zum Lowen because they can eat there in peace and quiet and the restaurant is smoke free.

Ten years later, at 70 years of age, the group meets and once again they discuss and discuss where they should meet. Finally it is agreed upon that they should meet at the Gausthof zum Lowen because the restaurant is wheel chair accessible and they even have an elevator.

Ten years later, at 80 years of age, the group meets and once again they discuss and discuss where they should meet. Finally it is agreed upon that they should meet at the Gausthof zum Lowen because that would be a great idea as they have never been there before.

Older Driver

A friend of a friend of mine was sitting on a lawn sunning and reading, when he was startled by a fairly late model car crashing through a hedge and coming to rest on his lawn. He helped the elderly driver out and sat him on a lawn chair.

'My goodness' he exclaimed, *'you are quite old to be driving!'*

'Yes' he replied, *'I am old enough that I don't need a licence. The last time I went to my doctor he examined me and asked if I had a driving licence. I told him yes and handed it to him. He took scissors out of a drawer, cut the licence into pieces and threw them in the wastebasket.*

'You won't be needing this any more,' he said. *'So I thanked him and left.'*

A trip to Aldi

Yesterday I was at my local Aldi buying a large bag of Purina dog chow for my loyal pet Dog and was in the checkout line when a woman behind me asked if I had a dog. What did she think I had - an elephant? So since I'm retired and have little to do, on impulse I told her that no, I didn't have a dog, I was starting the Purina Diet again. I added that I probably shouldn't, because I ended up in the hospital last time, but that I'd lost 50 pounds before I awakened in an intensive care ward with tubes coming out of most of my orifices and IVs in both arms.

I told her that it was essentially a perfect diet and that the way that it works is to load your pants pockets with Purina nuggets and simply eat one or two every time you feel hungry. The food is nutritionally complete so it works well and I was going to try it again. [I have to mention here that practically everyone in line was now enthralled with my story.]

Horrified, she asked if I ended up in intensive care because the dog food poisoned me. I told her no, I stepped off a curb to sniff an Irish Setter's ass and a car hit us both.

I thought the guy behind her was going to have a heart attack he was laughing so hard. Aldi won't let me shop there any more.

Better watch what you ask retired people. They have all the time in the world to think of crazy things to say.

My promise to my children as long as I live:

I am your parent first, your friend second. I will stalk you, flip out on you, lecture you, drive you insane, be your worst nightmare and hunt you down like a bloodhound when needed because I love you! When you understand that, I will know you are a responsible adult. You will NEVER find someone who loves, prays, cares and worries about you more than I do! If you don't hate me once in your life – I'm not doing my job properly.

Should I Really Join Facebook?

When we bought my Blackberry or is it a Gooseberry, I thought about the 30-year business I ran with 1,800 employees, all without a cell phone that plays music, takes videos, pictures and communicates with Facebook and Twitter. I signed up under duress for Twitter and Facebook, so my seven kids, their spouses, 13 grand kids and 2 great grand kids could communicate with me in the modern way. I figured I could handle something as simple as Twitter with only 140 characters of space.

That was before one of my grandkids hooked me up for Tweeter, Tweetree, Twhirl, Twitterfon, Tweetie and Twittererific Tweetdeck, Twitpix and something that sends every message to my cell phone and every other program within the texting World.

My phone was beeping every three minutes with the details of everything except the bowel movements of the entire next generation. I am not ready to live like this. I keep my cell phone in the garage in my golf bag.

The kids bought me a GPS for my last birthday because they say I get lost every now and then going over to the grocery store or library. I keep that in a box under my tool bench with the Blue tooth [it's red] phone I am supposed to use when I drive. I wore it once and was standing in line at Barnes and Noble talking to my wife and everyone in the nearest 50 yards was glaring at me. I had to take my hearing aid out to use it and I got a little loud.

I mean the GPS looked pretty smart on my dash board, but the lady inside that gadget was the most annoying, rudest person I had run into in a long time. Every 10 minutes, she would sarcastically say, *'Re-calc-u-lating.'* You would think that she could be nicer. It was like she could barely tolerate me. She would let go with a deep sigh and then tell me to make a U-turn at the next light. Then if I made a right turn instead, well, it was not a good relationship ...When I get really lost now, I call my wife and tell her the name of the cross streets and while she is starting to develop the same tone as Gypsy, the GPS lady, at least she loves me.

To be perfectly frank, I am still trying to learn how to use the cordless phones in our house. We have had them for 4 years, but I still haven't figured out how I can lose three phones all at once and have to run around digging under chair cushions and checking bathrooms and the dirty laundry baskets when the phone rings.

The world is just getting too complex for me. They even mess me up every time I go to the grocery store. You would think they could settle on something themselves but this sudden *'Paper or Plastic?'* every time I check out just knocks me for a loop. I bought some of those cloth reusable bags to avoid looking confused, but I never remember to take them in with me.

Now I toss it back to them. When they ask me, *'Paper or Plastic?'* I just say, *'Doesn't matter to me. I am bi-sacksual.'* Then it's their turn to stare at me with a blank look.

Us senior citizens don't need any more gadgets. The TV remote and the garage door remote are about all we can handle.

Smart retort

Two businessmen were sitting down for a break in their soon-to-be opened store. As yet, the store wasn't ready, with only a few shelves set up. One man said to the other, *'I bet any minute now some senior*

133

is going to walk by, put his face to the window and ask what we're selling.'

No sooner were the words out of his mouth when, sure enough, a curious senior walked to the window, had a peek and in a soft voice asked, *'What are you selling' here?'*

One of the men replied sarcastically, *'We're selling ass-holes.'*

Without skipping a beat, the old timer said, *'Must be doing well ... Only two left.'*

Seniors - don't mess with them!

We're Rich!

We finally made it. O.M.G. we're rich!

Silver in the hair; gold in the teeth; crystals in the kidneys; sugar in the blood; iron in the arteries and an inexhaustible supply of natural gas. I never thought we would accumulate such wealth!

Life is short. Live it to the fullest because it has an expiration date.

The expensive hotel

Lucille decided to give herself a big treat for her 70th birthday by staying overnight in a really nice hotel. When she checked out the next morning, the desk clerk handed her a bill for $250.00.

She demanded to know why the charge was so high. *'I agree it's a nice hotel, but the rooms aren't worth $250.00 for just an overnight stay - I didn't even have breakfast!'*

The clerk told her that $250.00 is the 'standard rate,' and breakfast had been included had she wanted it. She insisted on speaking to the Manager. The Manager appeared and, forewarned by the desk clerk, announced: *'This hotel has an Olympic-sized pool and a huge conference centre which are available for use.'*

'But I didn't use them'

"Well, they are here and you could have'

He went on to explain that she could also have seen one of the in-hotel shows for which they were so famous. *'We have the best entertainers from the world over performing here'*

'But I didn't go to any of those shows'

'Well, we have them and you could have'

No matter what amenity the Manager mentioned, she replied, *'But I didn't use it!'* and the Manager countered with his standard response.

After several minute's discussion and with the Manager still unmoved, she decided to pay, wrote a check and gave it to him.

The Manager was surprised when he looked at the amount of the cheque. *'This cheque is for only $50.00.'*

'That's correct' she replied. *'I charged you $200.00 for sleeping with me'*

'But I didn't!'

'Well, too bad, I was here and you could have'

Don't mess with seniors!

Forgetter Be Forgotten?

My forgetter's getting better,
but my rememberer is broke.
To you that may seem funny,
but, to me, that is no joke

For when I'm 'here' I'm wondering
if I really should be 'there.'
And, when I try to think it through,
I haven't got a prayer!

Oft times I walk into a room,
say 'what am I here for?'
I wrack my brain, but all in vain!
A zero, is my score.

At times I put something away
where it is safe, but, Gee!
The person it is safest from
is, generally, me!

When shopping I may see someone,
say *'Hi'* and have a chat,
Then, when the person walks away
I ask myself, *'Who the hell was that?*

Yes, my forgetter's getting better
While my rememberer is broke
and it's driving me plumb crazy
And that isn't any joke.

This is not a hoax!

You've heard about people who have been abducted and had their kidneys removed by black-market organ thieves.

135

My thighs were stolen from me during the night a few years ago. I went to sleep and woke up with someone else's thighs. It was just that quick. The replacements had the texture of cooked oatmeal. Whose thighs were these and what happened to mine? I spent the entire summer looking for my thighs. Finally, hurt and angry, I resigned myself to living out my life in jeans. And then the thieves struck again.

My butt was next. I knew it was the same gang, because they took pains to match my new rear-end to the thighs they had stuck me with earlier. But my new butt was attached at least three inches lower than my original! I realised I'd have to give up my jeans in favour of long skirts.

Two years ago I realised my arms had been switched. One morning I was fixing my hair and was horrified to see the flesh of my upper arm swing to and fro with the motion of the hairbrush. This was really getting scary - my body was being replaced one section at a time. What could they do to me next?

When my poor neck suddenly disappeared and was replaced with a turkey neck, I decided to tell my story. Women of the world, wake up and smell the coffee! Those 'plastic' surgeons are using REAL replacement body parts - stolen from you and me! The next time someone you know has something 'lifted', look again - was it lifted from you?

This is not a hoax. This is happening to women everywhere every night. Warn your friends!

P. S. Last year I thought someone had stolen my boobs. I was lying in bed and they were gone! But when I jumped out of bed, I was relieved to see that they had just been hiding in my armpits as I slept. Now I keep them hidden in my waistband.

These same thieves come in my closet and shrink my clothes! How do they do it??

I thought this was too 'important' not to pass on

White Lies

Have you ever told a white lie? You are going to love this – especially all of the ladies who bake for church events:

Alice Grayson was to bake a cake for the Baptist Church ladies' group Bake sale in Tuscaloosa, but she forgot to do it until the last minute. She remembered it the morning of the bake sale and after rummaging through cabinets she found an angel food cake mix and quickly made it while drying her hair and dressing and helping her son Bryan pack up for Scout camp. But when Alice took the cake from the oven, the centre had dropped flat and the cake was horribly disfigured. She said, *'Oh dear, there's no time to bake another cake.'*

This cake was so important to Alice because she did so want to fit in at her new church and in her new community of new friends. So, being inventive, she looked around the house for something to build up the centre of the cake. Alice found it in the bathroom - a roll of toilet paper. She plunked it in and then covered it with icing. Not only did the finished product look beautiful, it looked perfect!

Before she left the house to drop the cake by the church and head for work, Alice woke her daughter Amanda and gave her some money and specific instructions to be at the bake sale the minute it opened at 9:30 and to buy that cake and bring it home. When the daughter arrived at the sale, she found that the attractive perfect cake had already been sold. Amanda grabbed her cell phone and called her Mom.

Alice was horrified she was beside herself. Everyone would know, what would they think?

'Oh, my' she wailed! She would be ostracised!! ... talked about!! ... ridiculed!! All night Alice lay awake in bed thinking about people pointing their fingers at her and talking about her behind her back.

The next day, Alice promised herself that she would try not to think about the cake and she would attend the fancy luncheon/bridal shower at the home of a friend of a friend and try to have a good time. Alice did not really want to attend because the hostess was a snob who more than once had looked down her nose at the fact that Alice was a single parent and not from the founding families of Tuscaloosa, but having already RSVP'd she could not think of a believable excuse to stay home.

The meal was elegant, the company was definitely upper crust old South ... and to Alice's horror, the CAKE in question was presented for dessert. Alice felt the blood drain from her body when she saw the cake, she started, out of her chair to rush to tell her hostess all about it, but before she could get to her feet, the Mayor's wife said, *'What a beautiful cake!'*

Alice, who was still stunned, sat back in her chair when she heard the hostess [who was a prominent church member] say, *'Thank you, I baked it myself.'*

Alice smiled and thought to herself, *'GOD is good"*

Drafting Guys over 60 (Written by a Former Soldier)

Here's how we should defend our country:
I am over 60 and the Armed Forces think I'm too old to track down terrorists. You can't be older than 42 to join the military. They've got the whole thing ass-backwards. Instead of sending 18-year olds off to fight, they ought to take us old guys. You shouldn't be able to join a military unit until you're at least 35.

For starters: Researchers say 18-year-olds think about sex every 10 seconds. Old guys only think about sex a couple of times a day, leaving us more than 28,000 additional seconds per day to concentrate on the enemy.

Young guys haven't lived long enough to be cranky and a cranky soldier is a dangerous soldier. *'My back hurts! I can't sleep, I'm tired and hungry'* We are impatient and maybe letting us kill some asshole that desperately deserves it will make us feel better and shut us up for a while.

An 18-year-old doesn't even like to get up before 10 am. Old guys always get up early to pee so what the hell. Besides, like I said, *'I'm tired and can't sleep and since I'm already up, I may as well be up killing some fanatical s-of-a-b ...'*

If captured, we couldn't spill the beans because we'd forget where we put them. In fact, name, rank and serial number would be a real brainteaser.

Boot camp would be easier for old guys. We're used to getting screamed and yelled at and we're used to soft food. We've also developed an appreciation for guns. We've been using them for years as an excuse to get out there and do some hunting.

They could lighten up on the obstacle course however. I've been in combat and didn't see a single 20-foot wall with rope hanging over the side, nor did I ever do any push-ups after completing basic training.

Actually, the running part is kind of a waste of energy, too. I've never seen anyone outrun a bullet.

An 18-year-old has the whole world ahead of him. He's still learning to shave, to start up a conversation with a pretty girl. He still hasn't figured out that a baseball cap has a brim to shade his eyes, not the back of his head.

These are all great reasons to keep our kids at home to learn a little more about life before sending them off into harm's way.

Let us old guys track down those dirty rotten coward terrorists. The last thing an enemy would want to see is a couple of million pissed off old farts with attitudes and automatic weapons who know that their best years are already behind them.

Or, how about recruiting women with PMS or those going through menopause!!! You think men have attitudes !!! Ohhhh!!!

If nothing else, put us on border patrol ... We will have it secured the first night!

A must read for all Grandparents

At one point during a game, the coach called one of his 9-year-old baseball players aside and asked,

'Do you understand what cooperation is? What a team is?'

The little boy nodded in the affirmative.

'Do you understand that what matters is whether we win or lose together as a team?'

The little boy nodded 'Yes,'

'So' the coach continued, 'I'm sure you know, that when an out is called, you shouldn't argue, curse, attack the umpire or call him a pecker-head.'

'Do you understand all that?'

The little boy nodded 'Yes.' again.

He continued, 'And when I take you out of the game so another boy gets a chance to play, it's NOT good sportsmanship to call your coach 'a dumb ass' is it?'

The little boy shook his head 'No.'

'Good!' said the coach. 'Now go over there and explain all that to your grandmother.'

Get out of the car!

[This is supposedly a true account recorded in the Police Log of Sarasota, Florida.]

An elderly Florida lady did her shopping and, upon returning to her car, found four males in the act of leaving with her vehicle.

She dropped her shopping bags and drew her handgun, proceeding to scream at the top of her lungs, 'I have a gun and I know how to use it! Get out of the car!'

The four men didn't wait for a second threat. They got out and ran like mad.

The lady, somewhat shaken then proceeded to load her shopping bags into the back of the car and got into the driver's seat. She was so shaken that she could not get her key into the ignition.

She tried and tried and then she realised why. It was for the same reason she had wondered why there was a football, a Frisbee and two packs of beer on the front passenger seat.

A few minutes later, she found her own car parked four or five spaces farther down. She loaded her bags into the car and drove to the police station to report her mistake.

The sergeant to whom she told the story couldn't stop laughing. He pointed to the other end of the counter, where four pale men were reporting a car-jacking by a mad, elderly woman describe d as white, less than five feet tall, glasses, curly white hair and carrying a large handgun.

No charges were filed. The moral of the story? If you're going to have a senior moment ... make it memorable!

The original Serenity Prayer:

God grant me the serenity to accept the things I cannot change, the courage to change the things I can and the wisdom to know the difference.

Guru Eduardo Serenity Prayer:

God grant me the wine to make bearable what I can't change; the beer to make it funny and the wisdom to never get my knickers in a knot because it solves nothing and makes me walk funny.

Here's another one entitled Senility Prayer:

God grant me the senility to forget the people I never liked, the good fortune to run into the ones that I do and the eyesight to tell the difference.

Truths For Mature Humans

1. I think part of a best friend's job should be to immediately clear your computer history within minutes after you die.
2. Nothing sucks more than that moment during an argument when you realise you're wrong.
3. I totally take back all those times I didn't want to nap when I was younger.
4. There is great need for a sarcasm font.
5. How the hell are you supposed to fold a fitted sheet?
6. Map Quest really needs to start their directions on # 5. I'm pretty sure I know how to get out of my neighbourhood.
7. I can't remember the last time I wasn't at least kind of tired.

8. Bad decisions make good stories.
9. Obituaries would be a lot more interesting if they told you how the person died.
10. You never know when it will strike, but there comes a moment at work when you know that you just aren't going to do anything productive for the rest of the day.
11. Can we all just agree to ignore whatever comes after Blue Ray? I don't want to have to restart my collection ... again.
12. I'm always slightly terrified when I exit out of Word and it asks me if I want to save any changes to my ten-page technical report that I swear I did not make any changes to.
13. *'Do not machine wash or tumble dry'* means I will never wash this – ever.
14. I hate when I just miss a call by the last ring (Hello? Hello? Damn it!) But when I immediately call back, it rings nine times and goes to voice mail. What did you do after I didn't answer? Drop the phone and run away?
15. I hate leaving my house, confident and looking good and then not seeing anyone of importance the entire day. What a waste.
16. I keep some people's phone numbers in my phone just so I know not to answer when they call.
17. I think the freezer deserves a light as well.
18. I wish Google Maps had an *'Avoid - You're not safe here'* routing option.
19. Sometimes, I'll watch a movie that I watched when I was younger and suddenly realise I had no idea what the heck was going on when I first saw it.
20. I would rather try to carry 10 over-loaded plastic bags in each hand than take two trips to bring my groceries in.
21. The only time I look forward to a red light is when I'm trying to finish a text. [Before the law passed banning it that is.]
22. I have a hard time deciphering the fine line between boredom and hunger.
23. How many times is it appropriate to say *'What?'* before you just nod and smile because you still didn't hear or understand a word they said?
24. I love the sense of camaraderie when an entire line of cars team up to prevent a jerk from cutting in at the front. Stay strong, brothers and sisters!
25. As a driver I hate pedestrians and as a pedestrian I hate drivers, but no matter what the mode of transportation, I always hate bicyclists.

26. Is it just me or do high school kids get dumber and dumber every year?
27. Sometimes I'll look down at my watch three consecutive times and still not know what time it is.
28. Shirts get dirty. Underwear gets dirty. Pants? Pants never get dirty and you can wear them forever. [Must have been written by a man.]
29. There's no worse feeling than that millisecond you're sure you are going to die after leaning your chair back a little too far.
30. Even under ideal conditions people have trouble locating their car keys in a pocket, finding their cell phone and Pinning the Tail on the Donkey - but I'd bet my ass everyone can find and push the snooze button from three feet away, in about 1.7 seconds, eyes closed, first time, every time!

Six Retired Irishmen

Six retired Irishmen were playing poker in O'Leary's apartment when Murphy lost $500 on a single hand, clutched his chest and drops dead. Showing respect for their fallen brother, the other five continue playing standing up.

Michael O'Conner looks around and asks, *'Oh, me boys, someone's got to tell Paddy's wife. Who will it be?'*

They draw straws. Paul Gallagher picks the short one. They tell him to be discreet, be gentle; don't make a bad situation any worse.

'Discreet? I'm the most discreet Irishman you'll ever meet. Discrfetio is me middle name. Leave it up to me.'

Gallagher goes over to Murphy's house and knocks on the door. Mrs. Murphy answers and asks him what he wants. Gallagher declares, *'Your husband just lost $500 and is afraid to come home.'*

'Tell him to drop dead' says Murphy's wife.

'I'll go tell him,' says Gallagher.

How to Dance in the Rain

It was a busy morning, about 8:30 when an elderly gentleman in his 80's arrived to have stitches removed from his thumb. He said he was in a hurry as he had an appointment at 9:00 am.

I took his vital signs and had him take a seat, knowing it would be over an hour before someone would to able to see him. I saw him looking at his watch and decided, since I was not busy with another patient, I would evaluate his wound. On exam, it was well healed, so

I talked to one of the doctors, got the needed supplies to remove his sutures and redress his wound.

While taking care of his wound, I asked him if he had another doctor's appointment this morning, as he was in such a hurry. The gentleman told me no, that he needed to go to the nursing home to eat breakfast with his wife. I inquired as to her health. He told me that she had been there for a while and that she was a victim of Alzheimer's disease.

As we talked, I asked if she would be upset if he was a bit late. He replied that she no longer knew who he was, that she had not recognised him in five years.

I was surprised and asked him, *'And you still go every morning, even though she doesn't know who you are?'*

He smiled as he patted my hand and said, *'She doesn't know me, but I still know who she is.'*

I had to hold back tears as he left, I had goose bumps on my arm and thought, *'That is the kind of love I want in my life.'*

True love is neither physical, nor romantic. True love is an acceptance of all that is, has been, will be and will not be. With all the jokes and fun that are in e-mails, sometimes there is one that comes along that has an important message.

The happiest people don't necessarily have the best of everything; they just make the best of everything they have. Life isn't about how to survive the storm, but how to dance in the rain.

CHAPTER 6 - MISCELLANEOUS

A Haircut

One day a florist went to a barber for a haircut. After the cut, he asked about his bill and the barber replied, *'I cannot accept money from you; I'm doing community service this week.'* The florist was pleased and left the shop. When the barber went to open his shop the next morning, there was a *'thank you'* card and a dozen roses waiting for him at his door ...

Later, a police officer came in for a haircut and when he tried to pay his bill, the barber again replied, *'I cannot accept money from you; I'm doing community service this week.'* The officer was happy and left the shop. The next morning when the barber went to open up, there were a *'thank you'* card and a dozen doughnuts waiting for him at his door.

Then a Member of Parliament came in for a haircut and when he went to pay his bill, the barber again replied, *'I can't accept money from you. I'm doing community service this week.'* The Member of Parliament was very happy and left the shop. The next morning, when the barber went to open up, there were a dozen other Members of Parliament lined up waiting for a free haircut.

And that, my friends, illustrates the fundamental difference between the citizens of our country and the politicians who run it.

Both, politicians and nappies need to be changed often and for the same reason!

Why fishing is better than making love:

When you go fishing and you catch something - that's good. If you're making love and you catch something - that's bad.

Fish don't compare you to other fishermen and want to know how many other fish you caught.

In fishing, you lie about the one that got away. In loving you lie about the one you caught.

You can catch and release a fish; you don't have to lie and promise to still be friends after you let it go.

You don't have to necessarily change your line to keep catching fish. You can catch a fish on a 20-cent night crawler. If you want to catch a woman you're talking dinner and a movie minimum.

Fish don't mind if you fall asleep in the middle of fishing.

A real friend test!!

- A simple friend, when visiting, acts like a guest. A real friend opens your refrigerator and helps himself.
- A simple friend has never seen you cry. A real friend has shoulders soggy from your tears.
- A simple friend doesn't know your parents' first names. A real friend has their phone numbers in his address book.
- A simple friend brings a bottle of wine to your party. A real friend comes early to help you cook and stays late to help you clean.
- A simple friend hates it when you call after he has gone to bed. A real friend asks you why you took so long to call.
- A simple friend seeks to talk with you about their problems. A real friend seeks to help you with your problems.
- A simple friend wonders about your romantic history. A real friend could blackmail you with it.
- A simple friend thinks the friendship is over when you have an argument. A real friend calls you after you had a fight.
- A simple friend expects you to always be there for them. A real friend expects to always be there for you!

Council Complaints:

- ✓ I want some repairs done to my cooker as it has backfired and burned my knob off.
- ✓ I wish to complain that my father hurt his ankle very badly when he put his foot in the hole in his back passage.
- ✓ Their 18-year-old son is continuously banging his balls against my fence. Not only is this making a hell of a noise, but the fence is now sagging in the middle.
- ✓ This is to let you know there is a smell coming from the man next door.
- ✓ I am writing on behalf of my sink, which is running away from the wall.
- ✓ I wish to report that tiles are missing from the roof of the outside toilet and I think it was bad wind the other night that blew them off.
- ✓ I request your permission to remove my drawers in the kitchen.
- ✓ The toilet is blocked and we cannot bath the children until it is cleared.
- ✓ The toilet seat is cracked. Where do I stand?

- ✓ Will you please send a man to look at my water - it is a funny colour and not fit to drink.
- ✓ Would you please send a man to repair my spout? I am an old-aged pensioner and need it straight away.
- ✓ I want to complain about the farmer across the road. Every morning at 5:30 his cock wakes me up and it's getting too much. It's all right when my husband is on day shift, but when he's on back-shifts or nights, I get it several times a week from Mr. Docherty next door and at my age it's too much.
- ✓ The man next door has a large erection in his back garden, which is unsightly and dangerous.
- ✓ Our kitchen floor is very damp. We have two children and would like a third, so will you please send someone to do something about it.
- ✓ I'm a single woman living in a downstairs flat and would be pleased if you could do something about the noise made by the man I have on top of me every night.
- ✓ Please send a man with clean tools to finish the job and satisfy the wife.
- ✓ Can you send a carpenter to the house? When the woman next door closed the door the other night, she pulled at my knob too hard and now it's ready to fall off.
- ✓ I have had the Clerk of the Works down on the floor six times and still have no satisfaction.

World's easiest quiz!

[Passing requires only 3 correct answers out of 10!]

1) How long did the Hundred Years' War last?
2) Which country makes Panama hats?
3) From which animal do we get cat gut?
4) In which month do Russians celebrate the October Revolution?
5) What is a camel's hair brush made of?
6) The Canary Islands in the Pacific are named after what animal?
7) What was King George VI's first name?
8) What colour is a purple finch?
9) Where are Chinese gooseberries from?
10) What is the colour of the black box in a commercial airplane?

Remember, you need 3 correct answers to pass. Check your answers.

1) How long did the Hundred Years War last? 116 years
2) Which country makes Panama hats? Ecuador
3) From which animal do we get cat gut? Sheep and Horses
4) In which month do Russians celebrate the October Revolution? November
5) What is a camel's hair brush made of? Squirrel fur
6) The Canary Islands in the Pacific are named after what animal? Dogs
7) What was King George VI's first name? Albert
8) What colour is a purple finch? Crimson
9) Where are Chinese gooseberries from? New Zealand
10) What is the colour of the black box in a commercial airplane? Orange (of course!)

What do you mean, you failed?!! Me, too ...!!! [And if you try to tell me you passed, you lie!]

The Kohl's shopping trip

Clutching their Kohl's shopping bags, Ellen and Kay woefully gazed down at a dead cat in the mall parking lot. Obviously a recent hit ... no flies, no smell.

'What business could that poor kitty have had here?' murmured Ellen.

'Come on, Ellen, let's just go.'

But Ellen had already grabbed her shopping bag and was explaining, *'I'll just put my things in your bag and then I'll use this tissue.'*

She dumped her purchases into Kay's bag and then used the tissue paper to cradle and lower the former feline into her own Kohl's bag and cover it. They continued the short trek to the car in silence,

They intended to stash their goods in the trunk, but it occurred to both of them that if they left Ellen's burial bag in the trunk, warmed by the Texas sunshine while they ate, Kay's Lumina would soon lose that new-car smell. They decided to leave the bag on top of the trunk and they headed over to K & W Cafeteria.

After they went through the serving line and sat down at a window table. They had a view of Kay's Chevy with the Kohl's bag still on the trunk. But not for long! As they ate, they noticed a woman in a red gingham shirt stroll by their car. She looked quickly this way and that and then took the Kohl's bag without breaking stride. She quickly walked out of their line of vision. Kay and Ellen shot each other a wide-eyed look of amazement.

It all happened so fast that neither of them could think how to respond. *'Can you imagine?'* finally sputtered Ellen.

'The nerve of that woman!' Kay sympathised with Ellen, but inwardly a laugh was building as she thought about the grand surprise awaiting the female thief. Just when she thought she'd have to giggle into her napkin, she noticed Ellen's eyes freeze in the direction of the serving line. Following her gaze, Kay recognised the woman in the red gingham shirt with The Kohl's bag hanging from her arm. She was brazenly pushing her tray toward the cashier. Helplessly they watched the scene unfold.

After leaving the register, the woman settled at a table across from theirs, put the bag on an empty chair and began to eat. After a few bites of baked whitefish and green beans, she casually lifted the bag into her lap to survey her treasure. Looking from side to side, but not far enough to notice her rapt audience three tables over, she pulled out the tissue paper and peered into the bag.

Her eyes widened and she began to make a sort of gasping noise. The noise grew. The bag slid from her lap as she sank to the floor, wheezing and clutching her upper chest. The beverage cart attendant quickly recognised a customer in trouble and sent the busboy to call 911, while she administered the Heimlich manoeuvre.

A crowd quickly gathered [that did not include Ellen and Kay who remained riveted to their chairs for seven whole minutes until the ambulance arrived.] In a matter of minutes, the woman with the red gingham shirt emerged from the crowd, still gasping and securely strapped on a gurney.

Two well-trained EMS volunteers steered her to the waiting ambulance, while a third scooped up her belongings. The last they saw of the distressed cat-burglar was as she disappeared behind the ambulance doors ... the Kohl's Bag perched on her stomach!!

God does take care of those who do bad things! [And once in a while ... She allows us to witness it!]

Government bureaucracy:

This is something to really laugh about that demonstrates how a bloated government can soon get out of control.

Part of rebuilding New Orleans caused residents often to be challenged with the task of tracing home titles back potentially hundreds of years. With a community rich with history stretching back over two centuries, houses have been passed along through generations of family, sometimes making it quite difficult to establish ownership. [You have to love this lawyer.]

A New Orleans lawyer sought an FHA loan for a client. He was told the loan would be granted if he could prove satisfactory title to a parcel of property being offered as collateral. The title to the property dated back to 1803, which took the lawyer three months to track down. After sending the information to the FHA, he received the following reply:

[Actual reply from FHA]:

'Upon review of your letter adjoining your client's loan application, we note the request is supported by an Abstract of Title. While we compliment the able manner in which you have prepared and presented the application, we must point out you have only cleared title to the proposed collateral property back to 1803. Before final approval can be accorded, it will be necessary to clear the title back to its origin.'

Annoyed, the lawyer responded as follows: [Actual response]:

'Your letter regarding title in Case No.189156 has been received. I note you wish to have title extended further than the 206 years covered by the present application.

I was unaware any educated person in this country, particularly those working in the property area, would not know Louisiana was purchased by the United States from France in 1803, the year of origin identified in our application. For the edification of uninformed FHA bureaucrats, the title to the land prior to U.S. ownership was obtained from France, which had acquired it by Right of Conquest from Spain. The land came into the possession of Spain by Right of Discovery made in the year 1492 by a sea captain named Christopher Columbus, who had been granted the privilege of seeking a new route to India by the Spanish monarch, Queen Isabella.

The good Queen Isabella, being a pious woman and almost as careful about titles as the FHA, took the precaution of securing the blessing of the Pope before she sold her jewels to finance Columbus's expedition. Now the Pope, as I'm sure you may know, is the emissary of Jesus Christ, the Son of God and God, it is commonly accepted, created this world. Therefore, I believe it is safe to presume God also made the part of the world called Louisiana. God, therefore, would be the owner of origin and His origins date back to before the beginning of time, the world as we know it and the

150

FHA. I hope you find God's original claim to be satisfactory. Now, may we have our loan?'

The loan was immediately approved.

Shirley and Marcy

A mother was concerned about her kindergarten son, Timmy, walking to school. He didn't want his mother to walk with him. She wanted to give him the feeling that he had some independence yet know that he was safe. So she had an idea of how to handle it.

She asked a neighbour if she would please follow him to school in the mornings, staying at a distance, so he probably wouldn't notice her. The neighbour said that since she was up early with her toddler anyway, it would be a good way for them to get some exercise as well, so she agreed.

The next school day, the neighbour and her little girl set out following behind Timmy as he walked to school with another neighbour girl he knew. She did this for the whole week.

As the two walked and chatted, kicking stones and twigs, Timmy's little friend noticed the same lady was following them as she seemed to have done all week. Finally she said to Timmy, *'Have you noticed that lady following us to school all week? Do you know her?'*

Timmy nonchalantly replied, *'Yeah, I know who she is.'*

The little girl said, *'Well, who is she?'*

'That's just Shirley Goodnest,' Timmy replied, *'and her daughter Marcy ...'*

'Shirley Goodnest? Who is she and why is she following us?'

'Well,' Timmy explained, *'every night my Mom makes me say the 23rd Psalm with my prayers, 'cuz she worries about me so much. And in the Psalm, it says, 'Shirley Goodnest (surely goodness) and Marcy (mercy) shall follow me all the days of my life,' so I guess I'll just have to get used to it!'*

25 reasons I owe my mother

1. My mother taught me to appreciate a job well done.
   'If you're going to kill each other, do it outside. I just finished cleaning.'
2. My mother taught me religion.
   'You'd better pray that will come out of the carpet.'
3. My mother taught me logic.
   'Because I said so, that's why.'

4. My mother taught me about time travel.
   'If you don't wise up, I'm going to knock you into the middle of next week!'
5. My mother taught me more logic.
   'If you fall out of that swing and break your neck, you're not going shopping with me.'
6. My mother taught me foresight.
   'Make sure you wear clean underwear, in case you're in an accident.'
7. My mother taught me irony.
   'Keep crying and I'll give you something to cry about.'
8. My mother taught me about the science of osmosis.
   'Shut your mouth and eat your dinner.'
9. My mother taught me about contortionism.
   'Will you look at that dirt on the back of your neck!'
10. My mother taught me about stamina.
   'You'll sit there until those vegetables are gone.'
11. My mother taught me about weather.
   'This room of yours looks as if a tornado went through it.'
12. My mother taught me about hypocrisy.
   'If I told you once, I've told you a million times. Don't exaggerate!'
13. My mother taught me the circle of life.
   'I brought you into this world and I can take you out.'
14. My mother taught me about behaviour modification.
   'Stop acting like your father!'
15. My mother taught me about envy.
   'There are millions of less fortunate children in this world who don't have wonderful parents like you do.'
16. My mother taught me about anticipation.
   'Just wait until we get home.'
17. My mother taught me about receiving.
   'You are going to get it when you get home!'
18. My mother taught me medical science.
   'If you don't stop crossing your eyes, they are going to stick that way.'
19. My mother taught me ESP.
   'Put your jumper on; don't you think I know when you are cold?'
20. My mother taught me how to become an adult.
   'If you don't eat your vegetables, you'll never grow up.'

21. My mother taught me humour.
   'When that lawn mower cuts off your toes, don't come running to me.'
22. My mother taught me genetics.
   'You're just like your father.'
23. My mother taught me about my roots.
   'Shut that door behind you. Do you think you were born in a barn?'
24. My mother taught me wisdom.
   'When you get to be my age, you'll understand.'

And my favourite:
25. My mother taught me about justice
   'One day you'll have kids and I hope they turn out just like you .

Eye Patches

It turns out eye patches were not just an evil-looking accessory, they were helpful for living the sea life as well. Pirates wore eye patches to keep one eye accustomed to the darkness below deck. As the sunlight on the ocean is magnified, a sailor could take a few minutes to adjust to the darkness below deck. With an eye patch, all they needed to do was switch the cover over to the other eye, allowing them to see with the eye that had already become accustomed to the dark. Sailors of all kinds used the eye patch for this function.

The Pit crew

The headline read, *'The Holden Racing Team fired their entire pit crew yesterday.'* This announcement followed Holden's decision to take advantage of the Australian government's *'Work for the Dole'* scheme and employ some unemployed youths.

The decision to hire them was brought about by a recent documentary on how unemployed youths from Collingwood were able to remove a set of wheels in less than 6 seconds without proper equipment, whereas Holden's existing crew could only do it in 8 seconds with millions of dollars worth of high tech gear.

It was thought to be an excellent, bold move by the Holden management team as most races are won and lost in the pits, giving Holden an advantage over the Ford team.

However, Holden got more than they bargained for!

At the crew's first practice session, not only was the Magpie pit crew able to change all four wheels of the Holden in under 6 seconds but, within 12 seconds, they had re-sprayed, re-badged and swapped the car for 4 slabs of Foster's Lager, a bag of weed and some photos of Eddie Maquire's wife in the shower.

In my next life

In this life, I'm a woman. In my next life, I'd like to come back as a bear. When you're a bear, you get to hibernate. You do nothing but sleep for six months. I could deal with that.

Before you hibernate, you're supposed to eat yourself stupid. I could deal with that too.

When you're a girl bear, you deliver your children [who are the size of walnuts] while you're sleeping and wake to partially grown, cute, cuddly cubs. I could definitely deal with that.

If you're a mama bear, everyone knows you mean business. You swat anyone who bothers your cubs. If your cubs get out of line, you swat them too. I could deal with that.

If you're a bear, your mate expects you to wake up growling. He expects that you will have hairy legs and excess body fat.

Yup, gonna be a bear.

Stupid questions, smart answers

Boy: *'May I hold your hand?'*
Girl: *'No thanks, it isn't heavy.'*
Girl: *'Say you love me! Say you love me!'*
Boy: *'You love me.'*
Girl: *'If we become engaged will you give me a ring?'*
Boy: *'Sure, what's your phone number?'*
Girl: *'I think the poorest people are the happiest.'*
Boy: *'Then marry me and we'll be the happiest couple.'*
Girl: *'Darling, I want to dance like this forever.'*
Boy: *'Don't you ever want to improve?'*
Boy: *'I love you and I could die for you!'*
Girl: *'How soon?'*
Boy: *'I would go to the end of the world for you!'*
Girl: *'Yes, but would you stay there?'*
Wife: *'You tell a man something; it goes in one ear and comes out of the other.'*
Husband: *'You tell a woman something: It goes in both ears and comes out of the mouth.'*
Mary: *'John says I'm pretty. Andy says I'm ugly. What do you think, Peter?'*

Peter: *'A bit of both. I think you're pretty ugly.'*
Teacher: *'What do you call a person who keeps on talking when people are no longer interested?'*
Pupil: *'A teacher.'*
Teacher: *'Sam, you talk a lot!'*
Sam: *'It's a family tradition.'*
Teacher: *'What do you mean?'*
Sam: *'Sir, my grandpa was a street hawker, my father is a teacher.'*
Teacher: *'What about your mother?'*
Sam: *'She's a woman.'*
Tom: *'How should I convey the news to my father that I've failed?'*
David: *'You just send a telegram: Result declared, past year's performance repeated.'*

Idiots

I am a medical student currently doing a rotation in toxicology at the poison control centre. A woman called in very upset because she caught her little daughter eating ants. I quickly reassured her that the ants are not harmful and there would be no need to bring her daughter into the hospital. She calmed down and at the end of the conversation happened to mention that she gave her daughter some ant poison to eat in order to kill the ants. I told her that she better bring her daughter into the emergency room right away.

Early last year, some Boeing employees on the airfield decided to steal a life raft from one of the 747s. They were successful in getting it out of the plane and home. Shortly after they took it for a float on the river, they noticed a Westpac Rescue Helicopter coming towards them. It turned out that the chopper was homing in on the emergency locator beacon that activated when the raft was inflated. They are no longer employed at Boeing.

A man, wanting to rob a Bank of Queensland, walked into the Branch and wrote *'Put all your muny in this bag.'* While standing in line, waiting to give his note to the teller, he began to worry that someone had seen him write the note and might call the police before he reached the teller's window. So he left the Bank and crossed the street to the NAB Bank.

After waiting a few minutes in line, he handed his note to the teller. She read it and, surmising from his spelling errors that he wasn't the brightest light in the harbour, told him that she could not accept his stickup note because it was written on a Bank of

Queensland deposit slip and that he would either have to fill out a NAB deposit slip or go back to Bank of Queensland ... Looking somewhat defeated, the man said, *'Okay.'* and left. He was arrested a few minutes later, as he was waiting in line back at the Bank of Queensland. It happened in Noosa!

A man walked into a little corner store with a shotgun and demanded all of the cash from the cash drawer. After the cashier put the cash in a bag, the robber saw a bottle of Scotch that he wanted behind the counter on the shelf. He told the cashier to put it in the bag as well, but the cashier refused and said, *'Because I don't believe you are over 21.'* The robber said he was, but the clerk still refused to give it to him because she didn't believe him. At this point, the robber took his driver's licence out of his wallet and gave it to the clerk. The clerk looked it over and agreed that the man was in fact over 21 and she put the Scotch in the bag. The robber then ran from the store with his loot. The cashier promptly called the police and gave the name and address of the robber that she got off the licence. They arrested the robber two hours later.

A pair of robbers entered a record shop nervously waving revolvers. The first one shouted, *'Nobody move!'* When his partner moved, the startled first bandit shot him.

Seems this man wanted some beer pretty badly. He decided that he'd just throw a brick through a liquor store window, grab some booze and run. So he lifted the brick and heaved it over his head at the window. The brick bounced back knocking him unconscious. It seems the liquor store window was made of Flexi-Glass ... The whole event was caught on videotape. Perth WA.

I was at the airport, checking in at the gate when an airport employee asked, *'Has anyone put anything in your baggage without your knowledge?'* To which I replied, *'If it was without my knowledge, how would I know?'* He smiled knowingly and nodded, *'That's why we ask.'* This happened in Melbourne.

My daughter went to a local McDonalds and ordered a burger. She asked the person behind the counter for *'minimal lettuce.'* He said he was sorry, but they only had iceberg. This happened in Surfers Paradise!

When my husband and I arrived at a car dealers to pick up our car, we were told the keys had been locked in it. We went to the service department and found a mechanic working feverishly to unlock the driver's side door. As I watched from the passenger side, I instinctively tried the door handle and discovered that it was unlocked. *'Hey,' I announced to the technician, 'it's open!'* His reply, *'I know - I already done that side.'* This was at the Ford dealership Dubbo.

Who Employs These Idiots - A True Story

A man living in Kandos [near Mudgee in NSW, Australia] received a bill in March for his as yet unused gas line stating that he owed $0.00. He ignored it and threw it away. In April he received another bill and threw that one away too. The following month the gas company sent him a very nasty note stating that they were going to cancel his gas line if he didn't send them $0.00 by return mail.

He called them, talked to them and they said it was a computer error and they would take care of it. The following month he decided that it was about time that he tried out the troublesome gas line figuring that if there was usage on the account it would put an end to this ridiculous predicament. However, when he went to use the gas, it had been cut off.

He called the gas company who apologised for the computer error once again and said that they would take care of it. The next day he got a bill for $0.00 stating that payment was now overdue. Assuming that having spoken to them the previous day the latest bill was yet another mistake, he ignored it, trusting that the company would be as good as their word and sort the problem out.

The next month he got a bill for $0.00. This bill also stated that he had 10 days to pay his account or the company would have to take steps to recover the debt.

Finally, giving in, he thought he would beat the gas company at their own game and mailed them a cheque for $0.00. The computer duly processed his account and returned a statement to the effect that he now owed the gas company nothing at all.

A week later, the manager of the Mudgee branch of the Westpac Banking Corporation called our hapless friend and asked him what he was doing writing cheque for $0.00. After a lengthy explanation the bank manager replied that the $0.00 cheque had caused their cheque processing software to fail. The bank could therefore not process any cheques They had received from any of their customers that day because the cheque for $0.00 had caused the computer to crash.

The following month the man received a letter from the gas company claiming that his cheque had bounced and that he now owed them $ 0.00 and unless he sent a cheque by return mail they would take immediate steps to recover the debt.

At this point, the man decided to file a debt harassment claim against the gas company. It took him nearly two hours to convince the clerks at the local courthouse that he was not joking. They subsequently helped him in the drafting of statements which were considered substantive evidence of the aggravation and difficulties he had been forced to endure during this debacle.

The matter was heard in the Magistrate's Court in Mudgee and the outcome was this:

The gas company was ordered to:

1) Immediately rectify their computerised accounts system or Show Cause, within 10 days, why the matter should not be referred to a higher court for consideration under Company Law.
2) Pay the bank dishonour fees incurred by the man.
3) Pay the bank dishonour fees incurred by all the Westpac clients whose cheques had been bounced on the day our friend's had been processed.
4) Pay the claimant's court costs; and
5) Pay the claimant a total of $1,500 per month for the 5 month period March to July inclusive as compensation for the aggravation they had caused their client to suffer.

And all this over $0.00

The Dunny

They were funny looking buildings, that were once a way of life,
If you couldn't sprint the distance, then you really were in strife.
They were nailed, they were wired, but were mostly falling down,
There was one in every yard, in every house, in every town.

They were given many names, some were even funny,
But to most of us, we knew them as the outhouse or the dunny.
I've seen some of them all gussied up, with painted doors and all,
But it really made no difference; they were just a port of call.

Now my old man would take a bet, he'd lay an even pound,
That you wouldn't make the dunny with them turkeys hangin' round.
They had so many uses, these buildings out the back,
You could even hide from mother, so you wouldn't get the strap.

That's why we had good cricketers, never mind the bumps,
We used the pathway for the wicket and the dunny door for stumps.
Now my old man would sit for hours, the smell would rot your
socks,
He read the daily back to front in that good old thunderbox.

And if by chance that nature called sometime through the night,
You always sent the dog in first, for there was no flamin' light.
And the dunny seemed to be the place where crawlies liked to hide,
But never ever showed themselves until you sat inside.

There was no such thing as Sorbent, no tissues there at all,
Just squares of well read newspaper, a-hangin' on the wall.
If you had some friendly neighbours, as neighbours sometimes are,
You could sit and chat to them, if you left the door ajar.

When suddenly you got the urge and down the track you fled,
Then of course the magpies were there to peck you on your head.
Then the time there was a wet, the rain it never stopped,
If you had an urgent call, you ran between the drops.

The dunny man came once a week, to these buildings out the back,
And he would leave an extra can, if you left for him a zac.
For those of you who've no idea what I mean by a zac,
Then you're too young to have ever had, a dunny out the back.

For it seems today they call them the bathroom or the loo,
If you've never had one out the back, then I feel sorry for you.
For it used to be a way of life, to race along the track,
To answer natures call, at these buildings out the back.

Riddles

This is one of the best five riddles I have seen. The answers are at
the bottom. Riddle #5 is amazing. It sharpens those genes in your
brain and stalls Alzheimer's for years!!

1. A murderer is condemned to death. He has to choose between
   three rooms. The first is full of raging fires, the second is full of
   assassins with loaded guns and the third is full of lions that
   haven't eaten in 3 years. Which room is safest for him?
2. A woman shoots her husband. Then she holds him under water
   for over 5 minutes. Finally, she hangs him. But 5 minutes later
   they both go out together and enjoy a wonderful dinner
   together. How can this be?

159

3. What is black when you buy it, red when you use it and gray when you throw it away?

4. Can you name three consecutive days without using the words Wednesday, Friday or Sunday?

5. This is an unusual paragraph. I'm curious as to just how quickly you can find out what is so unusual about it. It looks so ordinary and plain that you would think nothing was wrong with it. In fact, nothing is wrong with it! It is highly unusual though. Study it and think about it, but you still may not find anything odd. But if you work at it a bit, you might find out. Try to do so without any coaching!

Answers:

1. The third room. Lions that haven't eaten in three years are dead. That one was easy, right?

2. The woman was a photographer. She shot a picture of her husband, developed it and hung it up to dry [shot; held under water; and hung.]

3. Charcoal, as it is used in barbecuing.

4. Sure you can name three consecutive days, yesterday, today and tomorrow!

5. The letter e, which is the most common letter used in the English language, does not appear even once in the paragraph.

How did you do?

Take your Choice:

In Prison: You spend most of your time in a 10 X 10 cell
    At Work: You spend most of your time in a 6 X 6 cubicle
In Prison: You get three meals a day, fully paid for
    At Work: You get a break for one meal and you have to pay for it
In Prison: For good behaviour, you get time off
    At Work: For good behaviour, you get more work
In Prison: The guard locks and unlocks all the doors for you
    At Work: You must carry a security card and open all the doors yourself
In Prison: You can watch TV and play games
    At Work: You could get fired for watching TV and playing games
In Prison: You get your own toilet

At Work: You have to share the toilet with people who pee on the seat

In Prison: They allow your family and friends to visit

At Work: You aren't even supposed to speak to your family

In Prison: All expenses are paid by the taxpayers with no work required

At Work: You must pay all your expenses to go to work and they deduct taxes from your salary to pay for prisoners

In Prison: You spend most of your life inside bars wanting to get out

At Work: You spend most of your time wanting to get out and go inside bars

In Prison: You must deal with sadistic wardens

At Work: They're called 'managers.'

Welfare cheats

1) You cannot legislate the poor into prosperity by legislating the wealthy out of prosperity.
2) What one person receives without working for, another person must work for without receiving.
3) The government cannot give to anybody anything that the government does not first take from somebody else.
4) You cannot multiply wealth by dividing it! and,

When half of the people get the idea that they do not have to work because the other half is going to take care of them and when the other half gets the idea that it does no good to work because somebody else is going to get what they work for, that is the beginning of the end of any nation.

Stella awards:

It's time again for the annual *'Stella Awards!'* For those unfamiliar with these awards, they are named after 81-year-old Stella Liebeck who spilled hot coffee on herself and successfully sued the McDonald's in New Mexico, where she purchased coffee. You remember, she took the lid off the coffee and put it between her knees while she was driving. Who would ever think one could get burned doing that, right? That's right; these are awards for the most outlandish lawsuits and verdicts in the U.S. You know, the kinds of cases that make you scratch your head. So keep your head scratcher handy.

Here are the Stellas for the year - 2010:

Seventh place

Kathleen Robertson of Austin, Texas was awarded $80,000 by a jury of her peers after breaking her ankle tripping over a toddler who was running inside a furniture store. The store owners were understandably surprised by the verdict, considering the running toddler was her own son.

Sixth place

Carl Truman, 19, of Los Angeles, California won $74,000 plus medical expenses when his neighbour ran over his hand with a Honda Accord. Truman apparently didn't notice there was someone at the wheel of the car when he was trying to steal his neighbour's hubcaps.

Fifth place

Terrence Dickson, of Bristol, Pennsylvania, who was leaving a house he had just burglarised by way of the garage. Unfortunately for Dickson, the automatic garage door opener malfunctioned and he could not get the garage door to open. Worse, he couldn't re-enter the house because the door connecting the garage to the house locked when Dickson pulled it shut. Forced to sit for eight, count 'em, EIGHT days and survive on a case of Pepsi and a large bag of dry dog food, he sued the homeowner's insurance company claiming undue mental Anguish. Amazingly, the jury said the insurance company must pay Dickson $500,000 for his anguish. We should all have this kind of anguish.

Fourth place

Jerry Williams, of Little Rock, Arkansas, garnered 4th Place in the Stella's when he was awarded $14,500 plus medical expenses after being bitten on the butt by his next door neighbour's beagle - even though the beagle was on a chain in its owner's fenced yard. Williams did not get as much as he asked for because the jury believed the beagle might have been provoked at the time of the butt bite because Williams had climbed over the fence into the yard and repeatedly shot the dog with a pellet gun.

Third place

Amber Carson of Lancaster, Pennsylvania because a jury ordered a Philadelphia restaurant to pay her $113,500 after she slipped on a spilled soft drink and broke her tailbone. The reason the soft drink was on the floor: Ms. Carson had thrown it at her boyfriend 30 seconds earlier during an argument. Whatever happened to people being responsible for their own actions?

Second place
Kara Walton, of Claymont, Delaware sued the owner of a night club in a nearby city because she fell from the bathroom window to the floor, knocking out her two front teeth. Even though Ms. Walton was trying to sneak through the ladies room window to avoid paying the $3.50 cover charge, the jury said the night club had to pay her $12,000 ... Oh, yeah, plus dental expenses. Go figure.

And First place went to:
This year's runaway First Place Stella Award winner was: Mrs. Merv Grazinski, of Oklahoma City, Oklahoma, who purchased a new 32-foot Winnebago motor home. On her first trip home, from an OU football game, having driven on to the freeway, she set the cruise control at 70 mph and calmly left the driver's seat to go to the back of the Winnebago to make herself a sandwich. Not surprisingly, the motor home left the freeway, crashed and overturned. Also not surprisingly, Mrs. Grazinski sued Winnebago for not putting in the owner's manual that she couldn't actually leave the driver's seat while the cruise control was set. The Oklahoma jury awarded her, are you sitting down?

$1,750,000 PLUS a new motor home. Winnebago actually changed their manuals as a result of this suit, just in case Mrs. Grazinski has any relatives who might also buy a motor home.

Driving School Test

The following are a sampling of REAL answers received on exams given by the California Department of Transportation's driving school.
Q: Do you yield when a blind pedestrian is crossing the road?
A: What for? He can't see my license plate.
Q: Who has the right of way when four cars approach a four-way stop at the same time?
A: The pickup truck with the gun rack and the bumper sticker saying, *'Guns don't kill people. I do.'*
Q: When driving through fog, what should you use?
A: Your car.
Q: How do you deal with heavy traffic?
A: Heavy psychedelics.
Q: What problems would you face if you were arrested for drunk driving?
A: I'd probably lose my buzz a lot faster.

Q: What changes would occur in your lifestyle if you could no longer drive lawfully?

A: I would be forced to drive unlawfully.

Q: What are some points to remember when passing or being passed?

A: Make eye contact and wave 'hello' if s/he is cute.

Q: What is the difference between a flashing red traffic light and a flashing yellow traffic light?

A: The colour.

Q: What can you do to help ease a heavy traffic problem?

A: Carry loaded weapons.

Q: How many cars may pass through an intersection once the light has changed red? [The answers you get to this one are interesting to say the least.]

    a) 2

    b) 3

    c) 0

    d) 5

The Ladies' Washroom

When you have to visit a public washroom, you usually find a line of women, so you smile politely and take your place. Once it's your turn, you check for feet under the cubicle doors. Every cubicle is occupied.

Finally, a door opens and you dash in, nearly knocking down the woman leaving the cubicle. You get in to find the door won't latch. It doesn't matter, the wait has been so long you are about to wet your pants!

The dispenser for the modern 'seat covers' [invented by someone's Mom, no doubt] is handy, but empty. You would hang your bag on the door hook, if there was one, so you carefully, but quickly drape it around your neck, [Mom would turn over in her grave if you put it on the floor!] Then down with your pants and assume 'The Stance.'

In this position, your aging, toneless, thigh muscles begin to shake. You'd love to sit down, but having not taken time to wipe the seat or to lay toilet paper on it, you hold 'The Stance.'

To take your mind off your trembling thighs, you reach for what you discover to be the empty toilet paper dispenser. In your mind, you can hear your mother's voice saying, 'Dear, if you had tried to clean the seat, you would have known there was no toilet paper!' Your thighs shake more.

You remember the tiny tissue that you blew your nose on yesterday - the one that's still in your bag [the bag around your neck, that now you have to hold up trying not to strangle yourself at the same time]. That would have to do, so you crumple it in the puffiest way possible. It's still smaller than your thumbnail.

Someone pushes your door open because the latch doesn't work. The door hits your bag, which is hanging around your neck in front of your chest and you and your bag topple backward against the tank of the toilet.

'Occupied!' you scream, as you reach for the door, dropping your precious, tiny, crumpled tissue in a puddle on the floor, while losing your footing altogether and sliding down directly onto the toilet seat. It is wet of course. You bolt up, knowing all too well that it's too late. Your bare bottom has made contact with every imaginable germ and life form on the uncovered seat because you never laid down toilet paper - not that there was any, even if you had taken time to try.

You know that your mother would be utterly appalled if she knew, because you're certain her bare bottom never touched a public toilet seat because, frankly, dear, *'You just don't know what kind of diseases you could get.'*

By this time, the automatic sensor on the back of the toilet is so confused that it flushes, propelling a stream of water like a fire hose against the inside of the bowl and spraying a fine mist of water that covers your bum and runs down your legs and into your shoes.

The flush somehow sucks everything down with such force and you grab onto the empty toilet paper dispenser for fear of being dragged in too.

At this point, you give up. You're soaked by the spewing water and the wet toilet seat. You're exhausted. You try to wipe with a sweet wrapper you found in your pocket and then slink out inconspicuously to the sinks.

You can't figure out how to operate the taps with the automatic sensors, so you wipe your hands with spit and a dry paper towel and walk past the line of women still waiting. You are no longer able to smile politely to them. A kind soul at the very end of the line points out a piece of toilet paper trailing from your shoe. [Where was that when you needed it?]

You yank the paper from your shoe, plonk it in the woman's hand and tell her warmly, *'Here, you just might need this.'*

As you exit, you spot your hubby, who has long since entered, used and left the men's toilet. Annoyed, he asks, *'What took you so long and why is your bag hanging around your neck?'*

This is dedicated to women everywhere who deal with any public toilets. It finally explains to the men what really does take us so long. It also answers that other commonly asked question about why women go to the toilets in pairs. It's so the other woman can hold the door, hang onto your bag and hand you tissue under the door.

Virgin

Little girl asks her mother, *'Mom, what does virgin mean?'*

'When a mom and a dad love each other very much ... and they want to show how much ...' began her mother.

'The dad gives a gift to the mom?' questioned the girl.

'Dad does a special thing with mom ... takes his special thing and puts it into mom's special place. This makes mom very happy and then dad gets very happy and then there is an explosion. Dad has a lot of seed and these race to see which is first to reach mom's egg ... This is called making love and until you did that, you are called ... a virgin.'

'I see,' said the girl as she looked at the bottle on the table, *'So then what's extra virgin?'*

Spread the Stupidity

❖ Why do drugstores make the sick walk all the way to the back of the store to get their prescriptions while healthy people can buy cigarettes at the front?

❖ Why do people order double cheeseburgers, large fries and a *diet* coke?

❖ Why do banks leave both doors open and then chain the pens to the counters?

❖ Why do we leave cars worth thousands of dollars in the driveway and put our useless junk in the garage?

❖ Why do we buy hot dogs in packages of ten and buns in packages of eight?

Nine Phrases women use:

1. **'Fine:'** This is the word women use to end an argument when they are right and you had better shut up.

2. **'Five minutes:'** If she is getting dressed, she means half an hour. Five minutes is only five minutes, if you have just been given five more minutes to watch the game before helping out around the house.

3. **'Nothing:'** This is the calm before the storm. This means something and you'd better be on your toes. Arguments that begin with 'nothing' usually end in 'fine.'

4. **'Go ahead:'** This is a dare. Do not do it!

5. **Loud sigh:** This is actually a word, but is a non-verbal statement often misunderstood by men. A loud sigh means she thinks you're an idiot and wonders why she is wasting her time standing here and arguing with you about nothing. (Refer to #3 for the definition of 'nothing.')

6. **'That's okay:'** This is one of the most dangerous statements a woman can make to a man. 'That's okay' means you had better think long and hard before deciding how and when you will pay for your mistake.

7. **'Thanks:'** A woman is thanking you. Do not question or faint, just say 'You're welcome.' [I need to add a clause here. This is true unless she says **'Thanks a lot.'** This is pure sarcasm and she is not thanking you at all. Do not say 'You're welcome.' That will bring on a 'Whatever.']

8. **'Whatever:'** Is a woman's way of saying f*** you!

9. **'Don't worry about it – I've got it.'** Another dangerous statement meaning this is something the woman has told you over and over and is now doing it herself. This will result in the man saying 'What's wrong.' The woman responds with #3, 'Nothing.'

Thanks

I want to thank all of you for your educational e-mails over the past year. I am totally screwed up now and have little chance of recovery.

I no longer open a bathroom door without using a paper towel or have the waitress put lemon slices in my ice water without worrying about the bacteria on the lemon peel.

I can't use the remote in a hotel room because I don't know what the last person was doing while flipping through the adult movie channels.

I can't sit down on the hotel bedspread because I can only imagine what has happened on it since it was last washed.

I can't touch any woman's purse for fear she has placed it on the floor of a public bathroom.

I have trouble shaking hands with someone who has been driving because the number one pastime while driving alone is picking one's nose.

Eating a little snack sends me on a guilt trip because I can only imagine how many gallons of trans fats I have consumed over the years.

I must send my special thanks to whoever sent me the one about rat poop in the glue on envelopes because I now have to use a wet sponge with every envelope that needs sealing.

Also, now I have to scrub the top of every can I open for the same reason.

I no longer have any savings because I gave it to a sick girl [Penny Brown] who is about to die for the 1,387,258th time.

I no longer have any money, but that will change once I receive the $15,000 that Bill Gates/Microsoft and AOL are sending me for participating in their special e-mail program.

I no longer worry about my soul because I have 363,214 angels looking out for me and a special novena/TV evangelist has granted my every wish.

I can't have a drink in a bar because I'll wake up in a bathtub full of ice with my kidneys gone.

I can't eat at KFC because their chickens are actually horrible mutant freaks with no eyes, feet or feathers.

I can't use cancer-causing deodorants even though I smell like a water buffalo on a hot day.

Thanks to you, I have learned that my prayers only get answered if I forward an e-mail to seven of my friends and make a wish within five minutes.

Because of your concern, I no longer drink Coca Cola because it can remove toilet stains.

I no longer buy gas [petrol] without taking someone along to watch the car so a serial killer doesn't crawl in my back seat when I'm filling up.

I no longer use Cling Wrap in the microwave because it causes seven different types of cancer.

I no longer drink Pepsi or Fanta since the people who make these products are atheists who refuse to put 'Under God' on their cans.

I no longer go to the movies because I could be pricked with a needle infected with AIDS when I sit down.

I no longer go to shopping malls because someone will drug me with a perfume sample and rob me.

And thanks for letting me know, I can't boil a cup of water in the microwave any more because it will blow up in my face ... and disfiguring me for life.

I no longer receive packages from UPS or Fed Ex since they are actually Al Qaeda agents in disguise. And I no longer answer the phone because someone will ask me to dial a number for which I will get a phone bill with calls to Jamaica, Uganda, Singapore and Uzbekistan

I no longer buy cookies from Neiman-Marcus since I now have their recipe.

Thanks to you, I can't use anyone's toilet but mine because a big black snake could be lurking under the seat and cause me instant death when it bites my butt.

And thanks to your great advice, I can't ever pick up $2.00 coin dropped in the parking lot because it probably was placed there by a sex molester waiting to grab me as I bend over.

I no longer drive my car because buying gas from some companies supports Al Qaeda and buying gas from all the others supports South American dictators.

I can't do any gardening because I'm afraid I'll get bitten by the Violin Spider and my hand will fall off.

If you don't send this e-mail to at least 144,000 people in the next 70 minutes, a large dove with diarrhoea will land on your head at 5:00 pm tomorrow afternoon and the fleas from 120 camels will infest your back, causing you to grow a hairy hump. I know this will occur because it actually happened to a friend of my next door neighbour's ex-mother-in-law's second husband's cousin's best friend's beautician ...

Oh, by the way ...

A German scientist from Argentina, after a lengthy study, has discovered that people with insufficient brain activity read their e-mail with their hand on the mouse.

Don't bother taking it off now, it's too late.

PS: I now keep my toothbrush in the living room, because I was told by e-mail that water splashes over 6 feet out of the toilet.

Enjoy your life – I won't - thanks to you!

Who says religion can't be funny?

Some good Church sign boards:

- Sonny Manuel Pastor: God does not believe in Atheists; therefore atheists do not exist.

- St. Cyril of Alexandria Catholic Church Diocese of Galveston, Houston: Staying in bed shouting 'Oh God!' does not constitute going to church.
- Donelson View Baptist Church: Forgive your enemies – it messes with their heads.
- Goodwood United Church: Free coffee; everlasting life – yes membership has its privileges.
- Glad Tidings assembly: Welcome. Don't be so open minded – your brains will fall out.
- First Christian Church; Disciples of Christ: God so loved the world that he did not send a committee.
- Wyldwood Baptist Church: Read the Bible – it will scare the Hell out of you.
- Oak Grove Baptist Church: Wal Mart is not the only saving place.
- Neighbourhood Christian Center: Artificial Intelligence is no match for natural stupidity.
- Claude Presbyterian Church: There are some questions that can't be answered by Google.

Why some men have dogs and not wives:

1. The later you are, the more excited your dogs are to see you.
2. Dogs don't notice if you call them by another dog's name.
3. Dogs like it if you leave a lot of things on the floor.
4. A dog's parents never visit.
5. Dogs agree that you have to raise your voice to get your point across.
6. You never have to wait for a dog; they're ready to go 24 hours a day.
7. Dogs find you amusing when you're drunk.
8. Dogs like to go hunting and fishing.
9. A dog will not wake you up at night to ask, *'If I died, would you get another dog?'*
10. Dogs like to ride in the back of a pickup truck.
11. If a dog leaves, it won't take half of your stuff.
12. If a dog has babies, you can put an ad in the paper and give them away.
13. A dog will let you put a studded collar on it without calling you a pervert.
14. If a dog smells another dog on you, they don't get mad. They just think it's interesting.

And last, but not least: To test this theory:
15. Lock your wife and your dog in the garage for an hour, then open it and see who's happy to see you.

Student who scored 0% on an exam [I would have given him 100%]

Q1. In which battle did Napoleon die?   His last battle.
Q2. Where was the Declaration of Independence signed?
    At the bottom of the page.
Q3. River Ravi flows in which state? Liquid.
Q4. What is the main reason for divorce? Marriage.
Q5. What is the main reason for failure? Exams.
Q6. What can you never eat for breakfast? Lunch and dinner.
Q7. What looks like half an apple? The other half.
Q8. If you throw a red stone into the blue sea what it will become? It will simply become wet.
Q9. How can a man go eight days without sleeping? No problem, he sleeps at night.
Q10. How can you lift an elephant with one hand? You will never find an elephant that has only one hand ...
Q11. If you had three apples and four oranges in one hand and four apples and three oranges in other hand, what would you have? Very large hands.
Q12. If it took eight men ten hours to build a wall, how long would it take four men to build it? No time at all, the wall is already built.
Q13. How can you drop a raw egg onto a concrete floor without cracking it? Any way you want, concrete floors are very hard to crack.

Is there any hope for the future ...?

The following questions were set in last year's GCSE examination in the U.K. These are genuine answers (from 16 year olds).

Q. Name the four seasons. A. Salt, pepper, mustard and vinegar.
Q. Explain one of the processes by which water can be made safe to drink. A. Flirtation makes water safe to drink because it removes large pollutants like grit, sand, dead sheep and canoeists.
Q. How is dew formed? A. The sun shines down on the leaves and makes them perspire.
Q. What causes the tides in the oceans? A. The tides are a fight between the earth and the moon. All water tends to flow towards the

171

moon, because there is no water on the moon and nature abhors a vacuum. I forget where the sun joins the fight.

Q. What guarantees may a mortgage company insist on? A. If you are buying a house they will insist that you are well endowed.

Q. In a democratic society, how important are elections? A. Very important. Sex can only happen when a male gets an election.

Q. What are steroids? A. Things for keeping carpets still on the stairs. (Shoot yourself now, there's little hope.)

Q. Name a major disease associated with cigarettes? A. Premature death.

Q. What happens to your body as you age? A. When you get old, so do your bowels and you get intercontinental.

Q. What happens to a boy when he reaches puberty? A. He says goodbye to his boyhood and looks forward to his adultery. (So true!)

Q. What is artificial insemination? A. When the farmer does it to the bull instead of the cow.

Q. How can you delay milk turning sour? A. Keep it in the cow. (Simple, but brilliant!)

Q. How are the main 20 parts of the body categorised (e.g. The abdomen)? A. The body is consisted into 3 parts - the brainium, the borax and the abdominal cavity. The brainium contains the brain, the borax contains the heart and lungs and the abdominal cavity contains the five bowels: A, E, I, O and U. (What the *!!*???)

Q. What is the fibula? A. A small lie.

Q. What does 'varicose' mean? A. Nearby.

Q. What is the most common form of birth control? A. Most people prevent contraception by wearing a condominium. [That would work!]

Q. Give the meaning of the term 'Caesarean section.' A. The caesarean section is a district in Rome.

Q. What is a seizure? A. A Roman Emperor. (Julius Seizure, I came, I saw, I had a fit!)

Q. What is a terminal illness? A. When you are sick at the airport. [Irrefutable!]

Q. Give an example of a fungus. What is a characteristic feature? A. Mushrooms. They always grow in damp places and they look like umbrellas.

Q. Use the word 'judicious' in a sentence to show you understand its meaning. A. Hands that judicious can be soft as your face. [OMG!]

Q. What does the word 'benign' mean? A. Benign is what you will be after you be eight.
Q. What is a turbine? A. Something an Arab or Sheik wears on his head.

Two different doctors' offices

Two patients limp into two different medical clinics with the same complaint. Both have trouble walking and appear to require a hip replacement.

The first patient is examined within the hour, is x-rayed the same day and has a time booked for surgery the following week.

The second sees his family doctor after waiting 3 weeks for an appointment, then waits 8 weeks to see a specialist, then gets an x-ray, which isn't reviewed for another week. And finally has his surgery scheduled for a month from then.

Why the different treatment for the two patients?

The first is a Golden Retriever. The second is a Senior Citizen.
Next time take me to a vet!

Five pearls of Scottish wisdom to remember

1) Money cannot buy happiness but somehow, it's more comfortable to cry in a Mercedes Benz than it is on a bicycle.
2) Forgive your enemy but remember the bastard's name.
3) Help a man when he is in trouble and he will remember you when he is in trouble again.
4) Many people are alive only because it's illegal to shoot them.
5) Alcohol does not solve any problem, but then neither does milk.

My wife and I walked past a swanky new restaurant last night.

'Did you smell that food?' she asked. 'Incredible!'

Being the nice guy I am, I thought, 'What the heck, I'll treat her!' So we walked past it again.

Baby it's cold outside!

It was April and the Aboriginals in a remote part of Northern Australia asked their new elder if the coming winter was going to be cold or mild. Since he was an elder in a modern community he had never been taught the old secrets. When he looked at the sky he couldn't tell what the winter was going to be like. Nevertheless, to be on the safe side, he told his tribe that the winter was indeed going to be cold and that the members of the tribe should collect firewood to be prepared.

But being a practical leader, after several days he had an idea. He walked out to the telephone booth on the highway, called the Bureau of Meteorology and asked, *'Is the coming winter in this area going to be cold?'*

The meteorologist responded, *'It looks like this winter is going to be quite cold.'*

So the elder went back to his people and told them to collect even more wood in order to be prepared. A week later he called the Bureau of Meteorology again. *'Does it still look like it is going to be a very cold winter?'*

The meteorologist again replied, *'Yes, it's going to be a very cold winter.'*

The elder again went back to his community and ordered them to collect every scrap of firewood they could find. Two weeks later the elder called the Bureau again. *'Are you absolutely sure that the winter is going to be very cold?'* he asked.

'Absolutely,' the man replied. *'It's looking more and more like it is going to be one of the coldest winters ever.'*

'How can you be so sure?' the elder asked.

The weatherman replied, *'Our satellites have reported that the Aboriginals in the north are collecting firewood like crazy and that's always a sure sign.'*

True Friendship

Are you tired of those sissy 'friendship' poems that always sound good, but never actually come close to reality? Well, here is a series of promises that actually speak of true friendship. You will see no cutesy little smiley faces on this. Just the stone cold truth of great friendships.

1. When you are blue, I will try to dislodge whatever is choking you.
2. When you are sad - I will jump on the person who made you sad like a spider monkey jacked up on Mountain Dew! Or: I will help you get pissed and plot revenge against the bastard who made you sad.
3. When you smile, I will know you're thinking of something that I would probably want to be involved in.

4. When you're scared, I will rag you about it until you're not. Or: I will shake the piss out of ye every chance I get, until you're NOT. Or: When you're scared - we will high-tail it out of there.
5. When you are worried - I will tell you horrible stories about how much worse it could be until you quit whining!
6. When you are confused - I will use little words.
7. When you are sick, stay the Hell away from me until you are well again. I don't want whatever you've got.
8. When you fall - I will laugh my effin head off at you, you clumsy arse, but I'll help you up.

'Why?' you may ask; *'Because you are my friend. Friendship is like pissing your pants, everyone can see it, but only you can feel the true warmth.'*

Express Lane

I was in the ten item express lane at the store quietly fuming. Completely ignoring the sign, the woman ahead of me had slipped into the check-out line pushing a cart piled high with groceries. Imagine my delight when the cashier beckoned the woman to come forward looked into the cart and asked sweetly, *'So which ten items would you like to buy?'*

Smart remarks

- As the elephant looked at the naked man, he asked, *'That's cute. Can you pick up peanuts with it?'*
- As she looked down at her bathroom scales, the obese woman stated, *'Noooooh ... That can't be my weight, it's my telephone number!'*
- I always start my diet on the same day ... tomorrow.
- After eating an entire bull, a mountain lion felt so good he started roaring. He kept it up until a hunter came along and shot him.
  The moral: When you're full of bull, keep your mouth shut!

Are You Smarter Than Your Right Foot?

Just try this. It will boggle your mind and you will keep trying over and over again to see if you can outsmart your right foot, but you can't. It's pre-programmed in your brain.

1) While sitting where you are at your desk, in front of your computer, lift your right foot off the floor and make clockwise circles.
2) Now, while doing this, draw the number '6' in the air with your right hand. Your foot will change direction!

I told you so!!!! And there's nothing you can do about it. You and I both know how stupid it is, but before the day is done, you are going to try it again, if you've not already done so.

Wouldn't it be great if that happened more often?

Things that are difficult to say when drunk:

- Innovative;
- Preliminary;
- Anesthetists;
- Cinnamon;
- Chrysanthemum.

Things that are downright impossible to say when drunk:

- Thanks, but I don't want to have sex.
- Nope, no more booze for me.
- Sorry, but you're not really my type.
- MacDonald's? No thanks. I'm not hungry.
- Good evening officer. Isn't it lovely out tonight?
- Oh, I couldn't. No one wants to hear me sing karaoke.
- I'm not interested in fighting you.
- Thank you, but I don't make any attempt to dance. I have no coordination. I'd hate to look like a fool.
- Where is the nearest toilet? I refuse to hurl in the street.
- I must be going home now as I have to work in the morning.

Fable of the porcupine

It was the coldest winter ever. Many animals died because of the cold. The porcupines, realising the situation, decided to group together. This way they covered and protected themselves; but the quills of each one wounded their closest companions even though they gave off heat to each other. After a while, they decided to distance themselves one from the other and they began to die, alone and frozen.

So they had to make a choice: Either accept the quills of their companions or disappear from the Earth. Wisely, they decided to go back to being together. This way they learned to live with the little wounds that were caused by the close relationship with their companion, but the most important part of it, was the heat that came from the others. This way they were able to survive.

Moral of the story: The best relationship is not the one that brings together perfect people, but the best is when each individual learns to live with the imperfections of others and can admire the other person's good qualities.

Anal Optic Nerve

Did you know that in the human body, there is a nerve that connects the eyeball to the anus? It's called the Anal Optic Nerve and it is responsible for giving people a shitty outlook on life.

If you don't believe it, pull a hair from your ass and see if it doesn't bring a tear to your eye.

Bumper Stickers:

- ✓ Constipated people don't give a shit!!
- ✓ If it has boobs or wheels, it's gonna give you problems.
- ✓ Seen on a biker's vest - If you can read this - my wife fell off.
- ✓ If sex is a pain in the ass, then you're doing it wrong.
- ✓ Fight crime - shoot back!
- ✓ Sarcasm: Is just one more service we offer.
- ✓ Please tell your pants it's not polite to point!
- ✓ He who laughs last, thinks slowest.
- ✓ Everyone has a photographic memory. Some don't have film.
- ✓ A day without sunshine is like, well, night.
- ✓ All stressed out and no one to choke!
- ✓ And your point is?
- ✓ Don't upset me. I'm running out of places to hide the bodies!
- ✓ The sex was so good that even the neighbours had a cigarette.
- ✓ I don't suffer from insanity; I enjoy every minute of it.
- ✓ I work hard because millions on welfare depend on me.
- ✓ Some people are alive only because it's illegal to kill them.
- ✓ I used to have a handle on life, but it broke.
- ✓ Wanted: Meaningful overnight relationship.
- ✓ You're just jealous because the voices talk only to me.
- ✓ Beer: It's not just for breakfast anymore.
- ✓ I got a gun for my wife - best trade I ever made.

- So you're a feminist - isn't that cute!
- Earth is the insane asylum for the universe.
- To all you virgins, thanks for nothing.
- I'm not a complete idiot; some parts are missing.
- My kid had sex with your honour student.
- I'm just driving this way to piss you off.
- As long as there are tests, there will be prayer in public schools.
- I don't have to be dead to donate my organ.
- God must love stupid people, he made so many of them.
- The gene pool could use a little chlorine.
- It is bad what you think and they are out to get you.
- I took an IQ test and the results were negative.
- It's lonely at the top, but you eat better.
- Give me ambiguity or give me something else.
- Elvis is dead and I'm not feeling too good myself.
- Always remember, you're unique, just like everyone else.
- *'Very funny, Scotty. Now beam up my clothes.'*
- Consciousness: that annoying time between naps.
- Ever stop to think and forget to start again?
- Beer - the reason I get up each afternoon.
- I must be a proctologist because I work with assholes.
- I'm out of bed and dressed. What more do you want?
- Remember my name. You'll be screaming it later.
- Welcome to Shit Creek. Sorry, we're out of paddles.
- If you think I'm a bitch, you should have met my mother!
- On the other hand, you have different fingers.
- I just got lost in thought. It was unfamiliar territory.
- When the chips are down, the buffalo is empty.
- Seen it all, done it all, can't remember most of it.
- Those who live by the sword get shot by those who don't.
- I feel like I'm diagonally parked in a parallel universe.
- He's not dead - he's electroencephalographically challenged.
- Honk if you love peace and quiet.
- I'm one of those bad things that happen to good people.
- If they don't have chocolate in Heaven - I ain't going!
- How can I miss you if you won't go away?
- Sorry if I looked interested. I'm not.
- $o many men ... $o few who can afford me!
- If we are what we eat ... I'm fast, cheap and easy.
- Guys have feelings too, but like ... who cares?
- Next mood swing: six minutes.
- Coffee, chocolate, men. Some things are just better rich.

- ✓ Nothing is foolproof to a sufficiently talented fool.
- ✓ Just remember - if the world didn't suck, we'd all fall off.
- ✓ You can't have everything. Where would you put it?
- ✓ Driver carries no cash – he's married.
- ✓ Take your Ex out tonight – one bullet oughtta do it.
- ✓ Can't feed 'em – don't breed 'em!
- ✓ I child-proof my home – but they still get in.
- ✓ The shortest sentence is 'I am.' The longest is 'I do.'
- ✓ Where the Hell is Easy Street?
- ✓ If money is the root of all evil, why do churches beg for it?
- ✓ Keep honking – I'm reloading.
- ✓ Guns don't kill people – drivers with cell phones do! Hang up and drive!
- ✓ Drugs lead nowhere, but it's the scenic route.
- ✓ I'm not an alcoholic. I'm a drunk. Alcoholics go to meetings.
- ✓ Work harder. Millions on welfare depend on you.
- ✓ Jesus is coming. Look busy!

Fridge Magnets

- ❖ The other day, someone told me that I could make ice cubes with leftover wine. I was confused: what leftover wine?
- ❖ I wouldn't need to manage my anger if people could learn how to manage their stupidity.
- ❖ When a woman says, *'What?'* it's not because she didn't hear you. She's giving you a chance to change what you said.
- ❖ The speed at which a woman says, *'Nothing'* when asked *'What's wrong?'* is inversely proportional to the severity of the shit that's coming.
- ❖ Some day when you have your own kids, you will understand why mommy drinks.
- ❖ Women are not moody! We simply have days when we are less inclined to put up with other's shit.
- ❖ A husband is someone who, after taking out the garbage, gives the impression that he's just cleaned the whole house.
- ❖ Men think a woman's biggest dream is to find a perfect man. Every woman's dream is to eat anything she wants without gaining weight.

Greenie revenge!

The chief woman *'Greenie Tree-Hugging Activist,'* who was responsible for getting horses banned from National parks and State

179

forests, was climbing a tree to have a look out over the forest when a Tawny Frogmouth Owl attacked her for invading its nesting site.

In a panic to escape, she slid down the tree, getting a great number of splinters lodged in her crotch area. In considerable pain she hurried to the nearest doctor, told him she was an environmentalist and how she got all the splinters.

The doctor listened with great patience and then told her to go into the examining room and he would see if he could help her. She waited for three hours before he reappeared.

Angry, she asked what took him so long.

'Well ...' replied the doctor, *'I had to get permits from the Environmental Protection Agency; the Forestry Service; the National Parks and Wildlife Service; the Wilderness Society and the Department of Conservation and Land Management before I could remove 'old growth timber' from a 'recreational area' ... I'm sorry but they all turned me down.'*

Answering Machine Messages:

1. *'Hi, This is John. If you are the phone company, I already sent the money. If you are my parents, please send money. If you are my financial aid institution, you didn't lend me enough money. If you are my friends, you owe money. If you are a female, don't worry, I have plenty of money.'*

2. *'Hi. Now you say something.'*

3. *'Hi. I'm not home right now, but my answering machine is, so you can talk to it instead. Wait for the beep.'*

4. *'Hello, I'm David's answering machine. What are you?'*

5. [From Japanese/English person] *'He-lo! This is Sa-to. If you leave message, I call you soon. If you leave *sexy* message, I call sooner!'*

6. *'Hi! John's answering machine is broken. This is his refrigerator. Please speak very slowly and I'll stick your message to myself with one of those magnets.'*

7. *'Hello, this is Sally's microwave. Her answering machine just eloped with her tape deck, so I'm stuck with taking her calls. Say, if you want anything cooked while you leave your message, just hold it up to the phone.'*

8. *'This is not an answering machine - this is a telepathic thought-recording device. After the tone, think about your name, your reason for calling and a number where I can reach you and I'll think about returning your call.'*

9.   *'Hello. I'm home right now, but cannot find the phone. Please leave a message and I will call you as soon as I find it.'*

10. *'I can't come to the phone right now because I have amnesia and feel stupid talking to people I don't remember. I'd appreciate it if you would help me out by leaving my name and telling me something about myself. Thanks.'*

11. *'I can't come to the phone right now because I'm down in the basement printing up a fresh batch of twenty dollar bills. If you need any money or if you just want to check out my handiwork, please leave your name, number and how much cash you need after the tone. If you're from the Department of Treasury, please ignore this message.*

12. *'Hi. I'm probably home, but am just avoiding someone I don't like. Leave me a message and if I don't call back, it's you.'*

13. *'Hello, this is Ron. I'm not home right now, but I can take a message. Hold on a second while I get a pencil.'* (Open a drawer and shuffle stuff around) *'Okay, what would you like me to tell me?'*

14. [Noisy pick-up of phone.] *'Hi, I'm a burglar and I was just about to steal Troy's answering machine. If you give me your name and number I'll ... I'll post it on the fridge where he'll see it. Uh ... By the way, where did you say you live?'*

15. *'Now I lay me down to sleep; leave a message at the beep. If I die before I wake, remember to erase this tape.'*

16. *'How do you leave a message on this thing? I can't understand the instructions. Hello. Testing 1 2 3. I wonder what happens if I touch this ... OW!'*

17. *'Hi, this is George. I'm sorry I can't answer the phone right now. Leave a message and then wait by your phone until I call you back.'*

18. *'If you're a burglar, then we're probably at home cleaning our weapons right now and can't come to the phone. Otherwise, we probably aren't home and it's safe to leave us a message.'*

19. *'You're growing tired. Your eyelids are getting heavy. You feel very sleepy now. You are gradually losing your willpower and your ability to resist suggestions. When you hear the tone, you will feel helplessly compelled to leave your name, number and a message.'*

20. [For telemarketers] *'You have reached the CPX-2000 Voice Blackmail System. Your voice patterns are now being digitally encoded and stored for later use. Once this is done our computers will be able to use the sound of* **YOUR** *voice for*

literally thousands of illegal and immoral purposes. There is no charge for this initial consultation. However our staff of professional extortionists will contact you in the near future to further explain the benefits of our service and to arrange for your schedule of payment. Remember to speak clearly at the sound of the tone. Thank you.'

21. *'Hello, you are talking to a machine. I am capable of receiving messages. My owners do not need siding, windows or a hot tub and their carpets are clean. They give to charity through the office and don't need their picture taken. If you are still with me, leave your name and number and they will get back to you.'*

22. [Very fast] *'Thank you for calling 555-5555. If you wish to speak to Tim, push 1 on your touch-tone phone now. If you wish to speak to Lynn, push 2 on your touch-tone phone now. If you have a wrong number, then press 6 and dial your number. If you want to leave your name and just a message, press star, press 6 for extension 4443, then leave your name and message. If you want to leave your number and the time you called, please press star twice, spin in a circle, press 1 twice, talk loud and ... Beep.'*

23. *'I am not available right now, but thank you for caring enough to call. I am making some changes in my life. Please leave a message after the beep. If I do not return your call, you are one of those changes.'*

Answering Machine

This is the message that the Pacific Palisades High School [California] staff voted unanimously to record on their school telephone answering machine. This is the actual answering machine message for the school. This came about because they implemented a policy requiring students and parents to be responsible for their children's absences and missing homework. The school and teachers are being sued by parents who want their children's failing grades changed to passing grades - even though those children were absent 15-30 times during the semester and did not complete enough schoolwork to pass their classes.

The outgoing message: *'Hello! You have reached the automated answering service of your school. In order to assist you in connecting to the right staff member, please listen to all the options before making a selection:*

1. *To lie about why your child is absent - Press 1*
2. *To make excuses for why your child did not do his work- Press 2.*
3. *To complain about what we do - Press 3.*
4. *To swear at staff members - Press 4.*
5. *To ask why you didn't get information that was already enclosed in your newsletter and several flyers mailed to you - Press 5.*
6. *If you want us to raise your child - Press 6.*
7. *If you want to reach out and touch, slap or hit someone - Press 7.*
8. *To request another teacher, for the third time this year - Press 8.*
9. *To complain about bus transportation - Press 9.*
10. *To complain about school lunches - Press 0.*
11. *If you realise this is the real world and your child must be accountable and responsible for his/her own behaviour, class work, homework and that it's not the teachers' fault for your child's lack of effort: Hang up and have a nice day!*
12. *If you want this in Spanish, you must be in the wrong country.'*

Tips for Handling Telemarketers

Three Little Words That Work!!
(1)The three little words are: *'Hold On, Please ...'*

Saying this, while putting down your phone and walking off [instead of hanging-up immediately] would make each telemarketing call so much more time-consuming that sales would grind to a halt.

Then when you eventually hear the phone company's *'beep-beep*-beep' tone, you know it's time to go back and hang up your handset, which has efficiently completed its task. These three little words will help eliminate telephone soliciting.

(2) Do you ever get those annoying phone calls with no one on the other end?

This is a telemarketing technique where a machine makes phone calls and records the time of day when a person answers the phone. This technique is used to determine the best time of day for a 'real' sales person to call back and get someone at home.

What you can do after answering, if you notice there is no one there, is to immediately start hitting your # button on the phone, 6 or 7 times as quickly as possible. This confuses the machine that dialled the call and it kicks your number out of their system. Gosh, what a shame not to have your name in their system any longer!

(3) Junk Mail Help:

When you get *'ads'* enclosed with your phone or utility bill, return these *'ads'* with your payment. Let the sending companies throw their own junk mail away.

When you get those *'pre-approved'* letters in the mail for everything from credit cards to second mortgages and similar type junk, do not throw away the return envelope.

Most of these come with postage-paid return envelopes, right? It costs them more than the regular postage; if and when they receive them back.

It costs them nothing if you throw them away! The postage is according to the weight. In that case, why not get rid of some of your other junk mail and put it in these cool little, postage-paid return envelopes.

Grandparents' answering machine

Good morning ... At present we are not at home but, please leave your message after you hear the beep ... beeeeeppp ...

1. If you are one of our children, dial 1 and then select the option from 1 to 5 in order of 'arrival' so we know who it is.
2. If you need us to stay with the children, press 2
3. If you want to borrow the car, press 3
4. If you want us to wash your clothes and ironing, press 4
5. If you want the grandchildren to sleep here tonight, press 5
6. If you want us to pick up the kids at school, press 6
7. If you want us to prepare a meal for Sunday or to have it delivered to your home, press 7
8. If you want to come to eat here, press 8
9. If you need money, dial 9
10. If you are going to invite us to dinner or, taking us to the theatre start talking we are listening!!!!

Door Mats

✓ Come back with a warrant.
✓ Our dog is not a biter – it's a humper.
✓ Nice underwear.
✓ Go away – come back with wine.

✓ I'm really glad to see you. But then I lie like a mat.
✓ This is not a joke. If you ever want to see these people again, bring me a two kg roast in a plain brown bag. Signed, *'The Dog.'*
✓ I will not be a doormat. I will not be a doormat. I will not be a doormat. Oh just walk all over me!
✓ Beer gets you in the door.
✓ We love our vacuum. We found God and we gave at the office. Thanks.
✓ Please stay on the mat. Your visit is very important to us. Your knock will be answered in the order in which it was received.
✓ Ask not for whom the dog barks. It barks for thee.
✓ Beware of the cat – roar!
✓ A lovely lady and a grumpy old man live here.
✓ Oh shit! Not you again!

Play on words

- How does Moses make his tea? Hebrews it.
- Venison for dinner again? Oh deer!
- A cartoonist was found dead in his home. Details are sketchy.
- I used to be a banker, but then I lost interest.
- French pancakes give me the crêpes.
- England has no kidney bank, but it does have a Liverpool.
- I tried to catch some fog, but I mist.
- They told me I had type-A blood, but it was a Type-O.
- I changed my iPod's name to Titanic. It's syncing now.
- Jokes about German sausage are the wurst.
- I know a guy who's addicted to brake fluid, but he says he can stop any time.
- I stayed up all night to see where the sun went and then it dawned on me.
- This girl said she recognised me from the vegetarian club, but I'd never met herbivore.
- When chemists die; they barium.
- I'm reading a book about anti-gravity. I just can't put it down.
- I did a theatrical performance about puns. It was a play on words.
- I didn't like my beard at first. Then it grew on me.
- Did you hear about the cross-eyed teacher who lost her job because she couldn't control her pupils?

- Broken pencils are pointless.
- What do you call a dinosaur with an extensive vocabulary? A thesaurus.
- I dropped out of communism class because of lousy Marx.
- All the toilets in New York's police stations have been stolen. The police have nothing to go on.
- I got a job at a bakery because I kneaded dough.
- Velcro - what a rip off!

Voice Mail

Most of us have now learned to live with voice mail as a necessary part of our lives. Have you ever wondered what it would be like if God decided to install voice mail? Imagine praying and hearing the following:

Thank you for calling heaven.

For English press 1

For Spanish press 2

For all other languages, press 3

Please select one of the following options:

Press 1 for request

Press 2 for thanksgiving

Press 3 for complaints

Press 4 for all others

I am sorry, all our Angels and Saints are busy helping other sinners right now. However, your prayer is important to us and we will answer it in the order it was received. Please stay on the line!

If you would like to speak to:

God, press 1

Jesus, press 2

Holy Spirit, press 3

To find a loved one that has been assigned to heaven press 5 and then enter his social security number followed by the pound sign. If you receive a negative response, please hang up and dial area code 666.

CHAPTER 7 - ON THE SERIOUS SIDE

Time management

One day, an expert in time management was speaking to a group of business students and, to drive home a point, used an illustration those students will never forget.

As he stood in front of the group of high-powered overachievers he said,

'Okay, time for a quiz,' and he pulled out a large, wide-mouth jar and set it on the table in front of him. He also produced about a dozen fist-sized rocks and carefully placed them, one at a time, into the jar. When the jar was filled to the top and no more rocks would fit inside, he asked, *'Is this jar full?'*

'Yes,' everyone in the class yelled.

The time management expert replied, *'Really?'* He then reached under the table and pulled out a bucket of gravel. He dumped some gravel in and shook the jar causing pieces of gravel to work themselves down into the spaces between the big rocks. He then asked the group once more, *'Is the jar full?'*

By this time the class was on to him. *'Probably not,'* one of them answered.

'Good!' he replied. He reached under the table and brought out a bucket of sand. He started dumping the sand in the jar and it went into all of the spaces left between the rocks and gravel. Once more, he asked the question, *'Is this jar full?'*

'No?!' the class shouted.

Once again he said, *'Good.'* Then he grabbed a pitcher of water and began to pour it in until the jar was filled to the brim. Then he looked at the class and asked, *'What is the point of this illustration?'*

One eager beaver raised his hand and said, *'The point is, no matter how full your schedule is, if you try really hard you can always fit some more things in it!'*

'No,' the speaker replied, *'That's not the point. The truth this illustration teaches us is: if you don't put the big rocks in first, you'll never get them in at all. What are the 'big rocks' in your life - time with your loved ones, your faith, your education, your dreams, a worthy cause, teaching or mentoring others? Remember to put these big rocks in first or you'll never get them in at all.'*

So tonight or in the morning when you're reflecting on this short story, ask yourself this question: What are the *'big rocks'* in my life? Then put those into your jar first.

Can I Borrow $5?

A woman came home from work late, tired and irritated, to find her 5-year old son waiting for her at the door.

Son: *'Mommy, may I ask you a question?'*

Mom: *'Yeah sure, what it is?'* replied the woman.

Son: *'Mommy, how much do you make an hour?'*

Mom: *'That's none of your business. Why do you ask such a thing?'* the woman said angrily.

Son: *'I just want to know. Please tell me, how much do you make an hour?'*

Mom: *'If you must know, I make $20 an hour.'*

Son: *'Oh,'* the little boy replied, with his head down. *'Mommy, may I please borrow $5?'*

The mother was furious, *'If the only reason you asked that is so you can borrow some money to buy a silly toy or some other nonsense, then you march yourself straight to your room and go to bed. Think about why you are being so selfish. I don't work hard every day for such childish frivolities.'*

The little boy quietly went to his room and shut the door.

The woman sat down and started to get even angrier about the little boy's questions. How dare he ask such questions only to get some money?

After about an hour or so, the woman had calmed down and started to think: Maybe there was something he really needed to buy with that $5 and he really didn't ask for money very often. The woman went to the door of the little boy's room and opened the door.

'Are you asleep, son?' She asked.

'No Mommy, I'm awake,' replied the boy.

'I've been thinking, maybe I was too hard on you earlier' said the woman. *'It's been a long day and I took out my aggravation on you. Here's the $5 you asked for.'*

The little boy sat straight up, smiling. *'Oh, thank you Mummy!'* he yelled. Then, reaching under his pillow he pulled out some crumpled up bills.

The woman saw that the boy already had money, started to get angry again.

The little boy slowly counted out his money and then looked up at his mother.

'Why do you want more money if you already have some?' the mother grumbled.

'Because I didn't have enough, but now I do,' the little boy replied. *'Mommy, I have $20 now. Can I buy an hour of your time? Please come home early tomorrow. I would like to have dinner with you.'*

The mother was crushed. She put her arms around her little son and she begged for his forgiveness.

It's just a short reminder to all of you working so hard in life. We should not let time slip through our fingers without having spent some time with those who really matter to us, those close to our hearts. Do remember to share that $20 worth of your time with someone you love.

If we die tomorrow, the company that we are working for could easily replace us in a matter of hours. But the family and friends we leave behind will feel the loss for the rest of their lives.

Saving for a Special Occasion:

My brother-in-law opened the bottom drawer of my sister's bureau and lifted out a tissue-wrapped package. *'This,'* he said, *'is not a slip. This is lingerie.'*

He discarded the tissue and handed me the slip. It was exquisite; silk, handmade and trimmed with a cobweb of lace. The price tag with the astronomical figure on it was still attached. *'Jan bought this the first time we went to New York, at least eight or nine years ago. She never wore it. She was saving it for a special occasion. Well, I guess this is that occasion.'*

He took the slip from me and put it on the bed with the other clothes we were taking to the mortician. His hands lingered on the soft material for a moment and then he slammed the drawer shut and turned to me. *'Don't ever save anything for a special occasion. Every day you're alive is a special occasion.'*

I remembered those words through the funeral and the days that followed when I helped him and my niece attend to all the sad chores that follow an unexpected death.

I thought about them on the plane returning home from the town where my sister's family lives. I thought about all the things that she hadn't seen or heard or done. I thought about the things that she had done without realising that they were special. I'm still thinking about his words and they've changed my life.

189

I'm reading more and dusting less. I'm sitting on the deck and admiring the view without fussing about the weeds in the garden. I'm spending more time with my family and friends and less time in committee meetings. Whenever possible, life should be a pattern of experience to savour, not endure. I'm trying to recognise these moments now and cherish them. I'm not *'saving'* anything. We use our good china and crystal for every special event such as losing a pound, getting the sink unstopped, the first camellia in blossom.

I wear my good blazer to the market if I like it. My theory is if I look prosperous, I can shell out $28.49 for one small bag of groceries without wincing. I'm not saving my good perfume for special parties; clerks in hardware stores and tellers in banks have noses that function as well as my party-going friends.

'Someday' and *'one of these days'* are losing their grip on my vocabulary. If it's worth seeing or hearing or doing, I want to see and hear and do it now.

I'm not sure what my sister would have done had she known that she wouldn't be here for the tomorrow we all take for granted. I think she would have called family members and a few close friends. She might have called a few former friends to apologise and mend fences or past squabbles. I like to think she would have gone out for Chinese dinner, her favourite food. I'm guessing – I'll never know.

It's those little things left undone that would make me angry if I knew that my hours were limited. Angry because I put off seeing good friends whom I was going to get in touch with - someday. Angry because I hadn't written certain letters that I intended to write - one of these days. Angry and sorry that I didn't tell my husband and daughter often enough how much I truly love them. I'm trying very hard not to put off, hold back or save anything that would add laughter and lustre to our lives. And every morning when I open my eyes, I tell myself that it is special. Every day, every minute, every breath truly is a gift to take advantage of.

The Marine

As I came out of the supermarket that sunny day, pushing my cart of groceries towards my car, I saw an old man with the hood of his car up and a lady sitting inside the car, with the door open. The old man was looking at the engine. I put my groceries away in my car and continued to watch the old gentleman from about twenty five feet away.

I saw a young man in his early twenties with a grocery bag in his arm walking towards the old man. The old gentleman saw him coming too and took a few steps towards him. I saw the old gentleman point to his open hood and say something. The young man put his grocery bag into what looked like a brand new Cadillac Escalade. He then turned back to the old man. I heard him yell at the old gentleman saying, *'You shouldn't even be allowed to drive a car at your age.'* And then with a wave of his hand, he got in his car and peeled rubber out of the parking lot.

I saw the old gentleman pull out his handkerchief and mop his brow as he went back to his car and again looked at the engine. He then went to his wife and spoke with her; he appeared to tell her it would be okay. I had seen enough and I approached the old man. He saw me coming and stood straight and as I got near him I said, *'Looks like you're having a problem.'*

He smiled sheepishly and quietly nodded his head. I looked under the hood myself and knew that whatever the problem was, it was beyond me. Looking around, I saw a gas station up the road and I told the old man that I would be right back. I drove to the station and went inside. I saw three attendants working on cars. I approached one of them and related the problem the old man had with his car. I offered to pay them if they could follow me back down and help him.

The old man had pushed the heavy car under the shade of a tree and appeared to be comforting his wife. When he saw us he straightened up and thanked me for my help. As the mechanics diagnosed the problem [overheated engine] I spoke with the old gentleman. When I shook hands with him earlier, he had noticed my Marine Corps ring and had commented about it, telling me that he had been a Marine too. I nodded and asked the usual question, *'What outfit did you serve with?'*

He said that he served with the first Marine Division at Guadalcanal Pelieliu and Okinawa. He had hit three of the worst ones and retired from the Corps after the war was over. As we talked we heard the car engine come on and saw the mechanics lower the hood. They came over to us as the old man reached for his wallet, but was stopped by me. I told him I would just put the bill on my AAA card.

He still reached for the wallet and handed me a card that I assumed had his name and address on it and I stuck it in my pocket. We all shook hands all around again and I said my goodbye's to his wife.

I then told the two mechanics that I would follow them back up to the station. Once at the station, I told them that they had interrupted their own jobs to come along with me and help the old man. I said I wanted to pay for the help, but they refused to charge me.

One of them pulled out a card from his pocket, looking exactly like the card the old man had given to me. Both of the men told me then that they were Marine Corps Reserves. Once again we shook hands all around and as I was leaving, one of them told me I should look at the card the old man had given to me. I said I would and drove off.

For some reason I had gone about two blocks, when I pulled over and took the card out of my pocket and looked at it for a long, long time. The name of the old gentleman was on the card in golden leaf and under his name was written: *'Congressional Medal of Honour Society.'*

I sat there motionless, looking at the card and reading it over and over. I looked up from the card and smiled to no one but myself and marvelled that on this day, four Marines had all come together because one of us needed help. He was an old man all right, but it felt good to have stood next to greatness and courage and an honour to have been in his presence.

Two Stories – both true

Story number one:

Many years ago, Al Capone virtually owned Chicago. Capone wasn't famous for anything heroic. He was notorious for enmeshing the windy city in everything from bootlegged booze and prostitution to murder.

Capone had a lawyer nicknamed *'Easy Eddie.'* He was Capone's lawyer for a good reason. Eddie was very good! In fact, Eddie's skill at legal manoeuvring kept Big Al out of jail for a long time.

To show his appreciation, Capone paid him very well. Not only was the money big, but Eddie got special dividends, as well. For instance, he and his family occupied a fenced-in mansion with live-in help and all of the conveniences of the day. The estate was so large that it filled an entire Chicago City block.

Eddie lived the high life of the Chicago mob and gave little consideration to the atrocity that went on around him. Eddie did have one soft spot, however. He had a son that he loved dearly. Eddie saw to it that his young son had clothes, cars and a good education. Nothing was withheld. Price was no object.

And, despite his involvement with organised crime, Eddie even tried to teach him right from wrong. Eddie wanted his son to be a better man than he was. Yet, with all his wealth and influence, there were two things he couldn't give his son; he couldn't pass on a good name or a good example.

One day, Easy Eddie reached a difficult decision. Easy Eddie wanted to rectify wrongs he had done. He decided he would go to the authorities and tell the truth about Al 'Scarface' Capone, clean up his tarnished name and offer his son some semblance of integrity. To do this, he would have to testify against The Mob and he knew that the cost would be great. So, he testified.

Within the year, Easy Eddie's life ended in a blaze of gunfire on a lonely Chicago Street. But in his eyes, he had given his son the greatest gift he had to offer, at the greatest price he could ever pay. Police removed from his pockets a rosary, a crucifix, a religious medallion and a poem clipped from a magazine. The poem read:

'The clock of life is wound but once and no man has the power to tell just when the hands will stop, at late or early hour. Now is the only time you own. Live, love, toil with a will. Place no faith in time. For the clock may soon be still.'

Story number two:

World War II produced many heroes. One such man was Lieutenant Commander Butch O'Hare. He was a fighter pilot assigned to the aircraft carrier Lexington in the South Pacific.

One day his entire squadron was sent on a mission. After he was airborne, he looked at his fuel gauge and realised that someone had forgotten to top off his fuel tank. He would not have enough fuel to complete his mission and get back to his ship.

His flight leader told him to return to the carrier. Reluctantly, he dropped out of formation and headed back to the fleet. As he was returning to the mother ship, he saw something that turned his blood cold; a squadron of Japanese aircraft was speeding its way toward the American fleet.

The American fighters were gone on a sortie and the fleet was all but defenceless. He couldn't reach his squadron and bring them back in time to save the fleet. Nor could he warn the fleet of the approaching danger. There was only one thing to do. He must somehow divert them from the fleet.

Laying aside all thoughts of personal safety, he dove into the formation of Japanese planes. Wing-mounted 50 calibre's blazed as he charged in, attacking one surprised enemy plane and then another. Butch wove in and out of the now broken formation and fired at as many planes as possible until all his ammunition was finally spent.

Undaunted, he continued the assault. He dove at the planes, trying to clip a wing or tail in hopes of damaging as many enemy planes as possible, rendering them unfit to fly. Finally, the exasperated Japanese squadron took off in another direction.

Deeply relieved, Butch O'Hare and his tattered fighter limped back to the carrier. Upon arrival, he reported in and related the event surrounding his return. The film from the gun-camera mounted on his plane told the tale. It showed the extent of Butch's daring attempt to protect his fleet. He had, in fact, destroyed five enemy aircraft.

This took place on February 20, 1942 and for that action Butch became the Navy's first Ace of WWII and the first Naval Aviator to win the Congressional Medal of Honour.

A year later Butch was killed in aerial combat at the age of 29. His home town would not allow the memory of this WW II hero to fade and today, O'Hare Airport in Chicago is named in tribute to the courage of this great man.

So, the next time you find yourself at O'Hare International, give some thought to visiting Butch's memorial displaying his statue and his Medal of Honour. It's located between Terminals 1 and 2.

So what do these two stories have to do with each other?
Butch O'Hare was *'Easy Eddie's'* son.

Still watching over you

They said a drunken man in an Oldsmobile had run the light that caused the six-car pileup on 109 that night.

When broken bodies lay about and blood was everywhere, the sirens screamed out eulogies, for death was in the air.

A mother, trapped inside her car, was heard above the noise; her plaintive plea near split the air: *'Oh, God, please spare my boys!'*

She fought to loosen her pinned hands; she struggled to get free, but mangled metal held her fast in grim captivity.

Her frightened eyes then focused on where the back seat once had been, but all she saw was broken glass and two children's seats crushed in.

Her twins were nowhere to be seen; she did not hear them cry and then she prayed they'd been thrown free, *'Oh, God, don't let them die!'*

Then firemen came and cut her loose, but when they searched the back, they found no little boys, but the seat belts were intact.

They thought the woman had gone mad and was travelling alone, but when they turned to question her, they discovered she was gone.

Policemen saw her running wild and screaming above the noise in beseeching supplication, *'Please help me find my boys! They're four years old and wear blue shirts; their jeans are blue to match.'*

One cop spoke up, *'They're in my car and they don't have a scratch. They said their daddy put them there and gave them each a cone, then told them both to wait for Mom to come and take them home. I've searched the area high and low, but I can't find their dad. He must have fled the scene, I guess and that is very bad.'*

The mother hugged the twins and said, while wiping at a tear, *'He could not flee the scene, you see, for he's been dead a year.'*

The cop just looked confused and asked, *'Now, how can that be true?'*

The boys said, *'Mommy, Daddy came and left a kiss for you. He told us not to worry and that you would be all right and then he put us in this car with the pretty, flashing light.*

We wanted him to stay with us, because we miss him so, but Mommy, he just hugged us tight and said he had to go. He said someday we'd understand and told us not to fuss and he said to tell you, Mommy, he's watching over us.'

The mother knew without a doubt that what they spoke was true, for she recalled their dad's last words, *'I will watch over you.'*

The firemen's notes could not explain the twisted, mangled car and how the three of them escaped without a single scar. But on the cop's report was scribed, in print so very fine, *'An angel walked the beat tonight on Highway 109.'*

Sisters

A young wife sat on a sofa on a hot humid day, drinking iced tea and visiting with her mother. As they talked about life, about marriage, about the responsibilities of life and the obligations of adulthood, the mother clinked the ice cubes in her glass thoughtfully and turned a clear, sober glance upon her daughter.

'Don't forget your sisters,' she advised, swirling the tea leaves to the bottom of her glass. *'They'll be more important as you get older. No matter how much you love your husband, no matter how much you love the children you may have, you are still going to need sisters. Remember to go places with them now and then; do things with them.'*

'Remember that sisters means all the women ... your girlfriends, your daughters and all your other women relatives too. You'll need other women. Women always do.'

'What a funny piece of advice!' the young woman thought. *'Haven't I just been married? Haven't I just joined the couple-world? I'm now a married woman, for goodness sake! A grownup! Surely my husband and the family we may start will be all I need to make my life worthwhile!'*

But she listened to her mother. She kept contact with her sisters and made more women friends each year. As the years tumbled by, one after another, she gradually came to understand that her mother really knew what she was talking about. As time and nature work their changes and their mysteries upon a woman, sisters are the mainstays of her life.

Here is what I've learned. This says it all:

Time passes. Life happens;. distance separates; children grow up; jobs come and go; love waxes and wanes; men don't do what we expect them to do; hearts break; parents die; colleagues forget favours and careers end.

But ... sisters are there, no matter how much time and how many miles are between you. A girl friend is never farther away than needing her can reach. When you have to walk that lonesome valley and you have to walk it by yourself, the women in your life will be on the valley's rim, cheering you on, praying for you, pulling for you, intervening on your behalf and waiting with open arms at the valley's end.

Three Yellow Roses:

I walked into the grocery store not particularly interested in buying groceries. I wasn't hungry. The pain of losing my husband of thirty-seven years was still too raw. And this grocery store held so many sweet memories. Rudy often came with me and almost every time he'd pretend to go off and look for something special. I knew what he was going to do.

I'd always spot him walking down the aisle with the three yellow roses in his hands. Rudy knew I loved yellow roses. With a heart filled with grief, I only wanted to buy my few items and leave, but even grocery shopping was different since Rudy had passed on. Shopping for one took time, a little more thought than it had for two. Standing by the meat, I searched for the perfect small steak and remembered how Rudy had loved his steak.

Suddenly a woman came beside me. She was blonde, slim and lovely in a soft green pantsuit. I watched as she picked up a pack of T-bone steaks, dropped them in her basket, hesitated and then put them back. She turned to go and once again reached for the pack of steaks. She saw me watching her and she smiled. *'My husband loves T-bones, but honestly, at these prices, I don't know.'* I swallowed the emotion down my throat and met her pale blue eyes.

'My husband passed away eight days ago,' I told her. Glancing at the package in her hands, I fought to control the tremble in my voice. *'Buy him the steaks. And cherish every moment you're together.'*

She shook her head and I saw the emotion in her eyes as she placed the package in her basket and wheeled it away. I turned and pushed my cart across the length of the store to the dairy products. There I stood; trying to decide which size milk I should buy. A litre, I finally decide and moved on to the ice cream section near the front of the store. If nothing else, I could always fix myself an ice cream cone. I placed the ice cream in my cart and looked down the aisle toward the front. I saw first the green suit and then recognised the pretty lady coming towards me. In her arms she carried a package.

On her face was the brightest smile I had ever seen. I would swear a soft halo encircled her blonde hair as she kept walking towards me, her eyes holding mine. As she came closer, I saw what she held and tears began misting in my eyes. *'These are for you,'* she said and placed three beautiful long-stemmed yellow roses in my arms. *'They are paid for.'*

She leaned over and placed a gentle kiss on my cheek, then smiled again. I wanted to tell her what she'd done, what the roses meant, but still unable to speak, I watched as she walked away as tears clouded my vision. I looked down at the beautiful roses nestled in the green tissue wrapping and found it almost unreal. How did she know? Suddenly the answer seemed so clear. I wasn't alone. *'Oh Rudy. You haven't forgotten me, have you?'* I whispered, with tears in my eyes. He was still with me and she was his angel.

Lifestyles:

An American businessman was at a pier in a small coastal Mexican village when a small boat with just one fisherman docked. Inside the small boat were several large yellow-fin tuna. The American complimented the Mexican on the quality of his fish and asked how long it took to catch them.

The Mexican replied, *'Only a little while.'*

The American then asked, *'Why don't you stay out longer and catch more fish?'*

The Mexican said, *'I have enough to support my family's immediate needs.'*

The American then asked, *'How do you spend the rest of your time?'*

The Mexican fisherman said, *'I sleep late, fish a little, play with my children, take siesta with my wife Maria, stroll into the village each evening where I sip wine and play guitar with my amigos. I have a full and busy life senor.'*

The American scoffed, *'I am a Harvard MBA and could help you. You could spend more time fishing and, with the proceeds, buy a bigger boat. With the proceeds from the bigger boat, you could buy several boats. Eventually you would have a fleet of fishing boats. Instead of selling your catch to a middleman, you would sell directly to the processor, eventually opening your own cannery. You would control the product, processing and distribution.*

'You would need to leave this small coastal fishing village and move to Mexico City, then Los Angeles and eventually New York City where you will run your expanding enterprise.'

The Mexican fisherman asked, *'But senor, how long will this all take?'*

To which the American replied, *'Fifteen to twenty years.'*

'But what then, senor?' asked the Mexican.

The American laughed and said, *'That's the best part! When the time is right, you could sell your company stock to the public. You'll become very rich, you will make millions!'*

'Millions, senor?' replied the Mexican. *'Then what?'*

The American said, *'Then you could retire. Move to a small coastal fishing village where you would sleep late, fish a little, play with your kids, take a siesta with your wife, stroll to the village in the evenings where you could sip wine and play your guitar with your amigos.'*

Who Packs Your Parachute?

Charles Plumb was a US Navy jet pilot in Vietnam. After 75 combat missions, his plane was destroyed by a surface-to-air missile. Plumb ejected and parachuted into enemy hands. He was captured and spent six years in a communist Vietnamese prison. He survived the ordeal and then conducted lectures on lessons learned from that experience.

One day, when Plumb and his wife were sitting in a restaurant, a man at another table came up and said, *'You're Plumb! You flew jet fighters in Vietnam from the aircraft carrier Kitty Hawk. You were shot down!'*

'How in the world did you know that?' asked Plumb.

'I packed your parachute,' the man replied. Plumb gasped in surprise and gratitude. The man pumped his hand and said, *'I guess it worked!'*

Plumb assured him, *'It sure did. If your chute hadn't worked, I wouldn't be here today.'*

Plumb couldn't sleep that night, thinking about that man.

Plumb said, *'I kept wondering what he had looked like in a Navy uniform: a white hat; a bib in the back; and bell-bottom trousers. I wonder how many times I might have seen him and not even said 'Good morning, how are you?' or anything because, you see, I was a fighter pilot and he was **just** a sailor.'*

Plumb thought of the many hours the sailor had spent at a long wooden table in the bowels of the ship, carefully weaving the shrouds and folding the silks of each chute, holding in his hands each time the fate of someone he didn't know.

Then Plumb asked his audience, *'Who's packing your parachute?'*

Everyone has someone who provides what s/he needs to make it through the day. He also pointed out that he needed many kinds of parachutes when his plane was shot down over enemy territory - he needed his physical parachute, his mental parachute, his emotional parachute and his spiritual parachute. He called on all these supports before reaching safety.

Sometimes in the daily challenges that life gives us, we miss what is really important. We may fail to say, *'Hello, please or thank you,'* congratulate someone on something wonderful that has happened to them, give a compliment or just do something nice for no reason. As you go through this week, this month, this year, recognise people who pack your parachutes.

I am sending you this as my way of thanking you for your part in packing my parachute. And I hope you will send it on to those who have helped pack yours! Sometimes, we wonder why friends keep forwarding jokes to us without writing a word. Maybe this could explain it: When you are very busy, but still want to keep in touch, guess what you do – you forward jokes. And to let you know that you are still remembered, you are still important, you are still loved, you are still cared for, guess what you get? A forwarded joke.

So my friend, next time when you get a joke, don't think that you've been sent just another forwarded joke, but that you've been thought of today and your friend on the other end of your computer wanted to send you a smile, just helping you pack your parachute. Have a great day and stay in touch ...

You are the exception:

If you woke up this morning with more health than illness, you are more blessed than the millions who won't survive the week.

If you have never experienced the danger of battle, the loneliness of imprisonment, the agony of torture or the pangs of starvation, you are ahead of 20 million people around the world.

If you attend a church meeting without fear of harassment, arrest, torture or death, you are more blessed than almost three billion people in the world.

If you have food in your refrigerator, clothes on your back, a roof over your head and a place to sleep, you are richer than 75% of this world.

If you have money in the bank, in your wallet and spare change in a dish someplace, you are among the top 8% of the world's wealthy.

If you hold up your head with a smile on your face and are truly thankful, you are blessed because the majority can, but most do not.

If you can hold someone's hand, hug them or even touch them on the shoulder, you are blessed with friendship.

If you can read this message, you are more blessed than over two billion people in the world that cannot read anything at all.

You are so blessed in ways you may never even know

God Not Allowed in Schools

How did this get started? Let's see, I think it started when Madeline Murray O'Hare complained she didn't want any prayer in our schools. And we said, okay.

Then, someone said you'd better not read the Bible in school - the Bible that says *'thou shalt not kill, thou shalt not steal and love your neighbours as yourself,'* and we said, okay.

Dr. Benjamin Spock said we shouldn't spank our children when they misbehaved because their little personalities would be warped and we might damage their self-esteem. And we said, an expert should know what he's talking about so we won't spank them any more.

Then someone said teachers and principals had better not discipline our children when they misbehave. And the school administrators said no faculty member in school had better touch a student when they misbehave because we don't want any bad publicity and we surely don't want to be sued. And we accepted their reasoning ...

Then someone said, let's let our daughters have abortions if they want and they won't even have to tell their parents. And we said, that's a grand idea.

Then some wise school board member said, since boys will be boys and they're going to do it anyway, let's give our sons all the condoms they want, so they can have all the fun they desire and we won't have to tell their parents they got them at school. And we said, that's another great idea.

Then some of our top elected officials said it doesn't matter what we do in private as long as we do our jobs. And we said, it doesn't matter what anybody, including the President, does in private as long as we have jobs and the economy is good.

And someone else took that appreciation a step further and published pictures of nude children and then stepped further still by making them available on the Internet. And we said, *'everyone's entitled to free speech.'*

And the entertainment industry said; let's make TV shows and movies that promote profanity, violence and illicit sex. And let's record music that encourages rape, drugs, murder, suicide and satanic themes. And we said, it's just entertainment and it has no adverse effect and nobody takes it seriously anyway, so go right ahead.

Now we're asking ourselves why our children have no conscience, why they don't know right from wrong and why it doesn't bother them to kill strangers, classmates or even themselves.

Undoubtedly, if we thought about it long and hard enough, we could figure it out. I'm sure it has a great deal to do with ... *'We reap what we sow!'*

To Kill an American/Canadian/Australian

You probably missed it in the rush of news last week, but there was actually a report that someone in Pakistan had published in a newspaper an offer of a reward to anyone who killed an American, any American. So an Australian dentist wrote an editorial the following day to let everyone know what an American is. So they would know when they found one. [Good one, mate!!!!]

'An American is English or French or Italian, Irish, German, Spanish, Polish, Russian or Greek. An American may also be Canadian, Mexican, African, Indian, Chinese, Japanese, Korean, Australian, Iranian, Asian or Arab or Pakistani or Afghan.

An American may also be a Comanche, Cherokee, Osage, Blackfoot, Navaho, Apache, Seminole or one of the many other tribes known as Native Americans. An American is Christian or he could be Jewish or Buddhist or Muslim. In fact there are more Muslims in America than in Afghanistan. The only difference is that in America they are free to worship as each chooses.

An American is also free to believe in no religion. For that he will answer only to God, not to the government or to armed thugs claiming to speak for the government and for God.

An American lives in the most prosperous land in the history of the world. The root of that prosperity can be found in the Declaration of Independence, which recognises the God-given right of each person to the pursuit of happiness.

An American is generous. Americans have helped out just about every other nation in the world in their time of need, never asking a thing in return.

When Afghanistan was over-run by the Soviet army twenty years ago, Americans came with arms and supplies to enable the people to win back their country.

As of the morning of September 11, Americans had given more than any other nation to the poor of Afghanistan. Americans welcome the best of everything ... the best products, the best books, the best music, the best food, the best services. But they also welcome the least.

The national symbol of America, The Statue of Liberty, welcomes your tired and your poor, the wretched refuse of your teeming shores, the homeless, tempest tossed. These in fact are the people who built America. Some of them were working in the Twin Towers the morning of September 11, 2001 earning a better life for their families. It's been told that the World Trade Centre victims were from at least 30 different countries, cultures and first languages, including those that aided and abetted the terrorists.

So you can try to kill an American if you must. Hitler did. So did General Tojo and Stalin and Mao Tse-Tung and other blood-thirsty tyrants in the world. But, in doing so you would just be killing yourself. Because Americans are not a particular people from a particular place. They are the embodiment of the human spirit of freedom. Everyone who holds to that spirit, everywhere, is an American.' [This applies to Canada. Australia and all other free countries too.]

The Sandpiper [by Robert Peterson]

She was six years old when I first met her on the beach near where I live. I drive to this beach, a distance of three or four miles, whenever the world begins to close in on me. She was building a sand castle or something and looked up, her eyes wereas blue as the sea.

'Hello,' she said. I answered with a nod, not really in the mood to bother with a small child. *'I'm building,'* she said

'I see that. What is it?' I asked, not really caring.

'Oh, I don't know, I just like the feel of sand.'

That sounds good, I thought and slipped off my shoes. A sandpiper glided by. *'That's a joy,'* the child said.

'It's a what?'

'It's a joy. My mama says sandpipers come to bring us joy.'

The bird went gliding down the beach. Good-bye joy, I muttered to myself, hello pain and turned to walk on. I was depressed; my life seemed completely out of balance.

'What's your name?' She wouldn't give up.

'Robert,' I answered. *'I'm Robert Peterson.'*

'Mine's Wendy ... I'm six.'

'Hi, Wendy.'

She giggled. *'You're funny,'* she said.

In spite of my gloom, I laughed too and walked on. Her musical giggle followed me. *'Come again, Mr. P,'* she called. *'We'll have another happy day.'*

The next few days consisted of a group of unruly Boy Scouts, PTA meetings and an ailing mother. The sun was shining one morning as I took my hands out of the dishwater. I need a sandpiper, I said to myself, gathering up my coat. The ever-changing balm of the seashore awaited me. The breeze was chilly but I strode along, trying to recapture the serenity I needed. *'Hello, Mr. P,'* she said. *'Do you want to play?'*

'What did you have in mind?' I asked, with a twinge of annoyance.

'I don't know.'

'How about charades?' I asked sarcastically.

The tinkling laughter burst forth again. *'I don't know what that is.'*

'Then let's just walk.' Looking at her and noticed the delicate fairness of her face.

'Where do you live?' I asked.

'Over there.' She pointed towards a row of summer cottages.

Strange, I thought, in winter. *'Where do you go to school?'*

'I don't go to school. Mommy says we're on vacation.' She chattered little girl talk as we strolled up the beach, but my mind was on other things. When I left for home, Wendy said it had been a happy day.

Feeling surprisingly better, I smiled at her and agreed.

Three weeks later, I rushed to my beach in a state of near panic. I was in no mood to even greet Wendy. I thought I saw her mother on the porch and felt like demanding she keep her child at home.

'Look, if you don't mind,' I said crossly when Wendy caught up with me, *'I'd rather be alone today.'*

She seemed unusually pale and out of breath. *'Why?'* she asked.

I turned to her and shouted, *'Because my mother died!'* and thought, My God, why was I saying this to a little child?

'Oh,' she said quietly, *'then this is a bad day.'*

'Yes,' I said, *'and yesterday and the day before and - oh, go away!'*

'Did it hurt?' she inquired.

'Did what hurt?' I was exasperated with her, with myself.

'When she died?'

'Of course it hurt!' I snapped, misunderstanding, wrapped up in myself. I strode off. A month or so after that, when I next went to the beach, she wasn't there. Feeling guilty, ashamed and admitting to myself I missed her, I went up to the cottage after my walk and knocked at the door. A drawn looking young woman with honey-coloured hair opened the door.

'Hello,' I said, *'I'm Robert Peterson. I missed your little girl today and wondered where she was.'*

'Oh yes, Mr. Peterson, please come in. Wendy spoke of you so much. I'm afraid I allowed her to bother you. If she was a nuisance, please accept my apologies.'

'Not at all - she's a delightful child.' I said, suddenly realising that I meant what I had just said.

'Wendy died last week, Mr. Peterson. She had leukaemia. Maybe she didn't tell you.'

Struck dumb, I groped for a chair. I had to catch my breath.

'She loved this beach, so when she asked to come, we couldn't say no. She seemed so much better here and had a lot of what she called happy days. But the last few weeks, she declined rapidly ...' Her voice faltered, *'She left something for you, if only I can find it. Could you wait a moment while I look?'*

I nodded stupidly, my mind racing for something to say to this lovely young woman. She handed me a smeared envelope with *'MR. P'* printed in bold childish letters. Inside was a drawing in bright crayon hues - a yellow beach, a blue sea and a brown bird. Underneath was carefully printed: A Sandpiper to bring you joy!

Tears welled up in my eyes and a heart that had almost forgotten to love opened wide. I took Wendy's mother in my arms. *'I'm so sorry, I'm so sorry, I'm so sorry,'* I uttered over and over and we wept together.

The precious little picture is framed now and hangs in my study. Six words - one for each year of her life - that speak to me of harmony, courage and undemanding love. A gift from a child with sea blue eyes and hair the colour of sand - who taught me the gift of love.

I realise now that people come into your life for a reason, a season or a lifetime. When you know which one it is, you will know what to do for that person. When someone is in your life for a reason, it is usually to meet a need you have expressed. They have come to assist you through a difficulty, to provide you with guidance and support, to aid you physically, emotionally or spiritually. They may seem like a godsend and they are.

They are there for the reason you need them to be. Then, without any wrongdoing on your part or at an inconvenient time, this person will say or do something to bring the relationship to an end. Sometimes they die. Sometimes they walk away. Sometimes they act up and force you to take a stand. What we must realise is that our need has been met, our desire fulfilled, their work is done.

Some people come into your life for a season, because your turn has come to share, grow or learn. They bring you an experience of peace or make you laugh. They may teach you something you have never done. They usually give you an unbelievable amount of joy. Believe it, it is real. But only for a season.

Lifetime relationships teach you lifetime lessons, things you must build upon in order to have a solid emotional foundation. Your job is to accept the lesson, love the person and put what you have learned to use in all other relationships and areas of your life. It is said that love is blind but friendship is clairvoyant.

Are you happy?

On a certain occasion, during an elegant welcoming reception for the new Director of Marketing of an important London company, some of the wives of the other directors, who wanted to get acquainted with the new spouse, asked her with some hesitation.

'Does your spouse make you happy, truly happy?'

The husband, who at the moment was not at her side, but was sufficiently near to hear the question, paid attention to the conversation, sitting up slightly, feeling secure, even filling his chest lightly in pride, knowing that his spouse would answer affirmatively, since she had always been there for him during their marriage.

Nevertheless, to both his and the others' surprise, she replied simply, *'No, no he doesn't make me happy ...'*

The room became uncomfortably silent, as if everyone were listening to the spouse's response. The husband was petrified. He couldn't believe what his wife was saying, especially at such an important occasion for him.

To the amazement of her husband and of everyone, she simply placed enigmatically on her head an elegant black silk scarf and continued: *'No, he doesn't make me happy ... I am happy! The fact that I am happy or not, doesn't depend on him, but on me. I am the only person upon which my happiness depends. I make the choice to be happy in each situation and in each moment of my life.*

If my happiness were to depend on other people, on other things or circumstances on the face of this earth, I would be in serious trouble! Everything that exists in this life changes continually: humans, wealth, my body, the climate, pleasures, etc. I could enumerate an infinite list ... Over my life I have learned a couple of things: I decide to be happy and the rest is a matter of experiences or circumstances; like helping and understanding, accepting, listening, consoling; and with my spouse, I have lived and practiced this many times ... Happiness will always be found in forgiveness and in loving yourself and others.

It's not the responsibility of my spouse to make me happy ... He also has his experiences or circumstances. I love him and he loves me, often in spite of his circumstances and of mine. He changes, I change, the environment changes, everything changes. Having forgiveness and true love and observing these changes that can be, big or little, but always happen, we must face them with the love that exists in each one of us.

If the two of us love and forgive each other, the changes will only be experiences or circumstances that enrich us and give us strength. Otherwise we would only be 'living together.' For some, divorce is the only solution; [in reality it is the easiest.]

To truly love, is difficult. It is to forgive unconditionally, to live, to take the experiences or circumstances as they are, facing them together and being happy with conviction.

There are those who say: 'I cannot be happy because I am sick, because I have no money, because it's too cool, because they insulted me; because someone stopped loving me; because someone didn't appreciate me!

But what you don't know is that you can be happy even though you are sick, whether it is too hot, whether you have money or not; whether someone has insulted you or someone didn't love you or hasn't valued you.

Being happy is an attitude about life and each one of us must decide! Being happy, depends on you!'

I've never been so proud of my wife as at that moment!

Daffodil Principle

Several times my daughter had telephoned to say, *'Mother, you must come to see the daffodils before they are over.'*

I wanted to go, but it was a two-hour drive from Laguna to Lake Arrowhead. *'I will come next Tuesday'* I promised a little reluctantly on her third call.

Next Tuesday dawned cold and rainy. Still, I had promised and reluctantly I drove there. When I finally walked into Carolyn's house I was welcomed by the joyful sounds of happy children. I delightedly hugged and greeted my grandchildren.

'Forget the daffodils, Carolyn! The road is invisible in these clouds and fog and there is nothing in the world except you and these children that I want to see badly enough to drive another inch!'

My daughter smiled calmly and said, *'We drive in this all the time, Mother.'*

'Well, you won't get me back on the road until it clears and then I'm heading for home!' I assured her.

'But first we're going to see the daffodils. It's just a few blocks,' Carolyn said. *'I'll drive. I'm used to this.'*

'Carolyn,' I said sternly, *'Please turn around.'*

207

'It's all right, Mother, I promise. You will never forgive yourself if you miss this experience.'

After about twenty minutes, we turned onto a small gravel road and I saw a small church. On the far side of the church, I saw a hand lettered sign with an arrow that read, *'Daffodil Garden.'* We got out of the car, each took a child's hand and I followed Carolyn down the path. Then, as we turned a corner, I looked up and gasped. Before me lay the most glorious sight.

It looked as though someone had taken a great vat of gold and poured it over the mountain and its surrounding slopes. The flowers were planted in majestic, swirling patterns, great ribbons and swaths of deep orange, creamy white, lemon yellow, salmon pink and saffron and butter yellow. Each different coloured variety was planted in large groups so that it swirled and flowed like its own river with its own unique hue. There were five acres of flowers.

'Who did this?' I asked Carolyn. *'Just one woman,'* Carolyn answered. *'She lives on the property. That's her home.'* Carolyn pointed to a well-kept A-frame house, small and modestly sitting in the midst of all that glory. We walked up to the house.

On the patio, we saw a poster. *'Answers to the Questions I Know You Are Asking'*, was the headline. The first answer was a simple one. *'50,000 bulbs,'* it read. The second answer was, *'One at a time, by one woman. Two hands, two feet and one brain.'* The third answer was, *'Began in 1958.'*

For me, that moment was a life-changing experience. I thought of this woman whom I had never met, who, more than fifty years before, had begun, one bulb at a time, to bring her vision of beauty and joy to an obscure mountaintop. Planting one bulb at a time, year after year, this unknown woman had forever changed the world in which she lived. One day at a time, she had created something of extraordinary magnificence, beauty and inspiration. The principle her daffodil garden taught is one of the greatest principles of celebration.

That is, learning to move toward our goals and desires one step at a time - often just one baby-step at time - and learning to love the doing, learning to use the accumulation of time. When we multiply tiny pieces of time with small increments of daily effort, we too will find we can accomplish magnificent things. We can change the world.

'It makes me sad in a way,' I admitted to Carolyn. *'What might I have accomplished if I had thought of a wonderful goal thirty-five or*

forty years ago and had worked away at it 'one bulb at a time' through all those years? Just think what I might have been able to achieve!'

My daughter summed up the message of the day in her usual direct way. *'Start tomorrow,'* she said.

She was right. It's so pointless to think of the lost hours of yesterdays. The way to make learning a lesson of celebration instead of a cause for regret is to only ask, *'How can I put this to use today?'* Use the Daffodil Principle. Stop waiting until ...

* your car or home is paid off
* you get a new car or home
* your kids leave the house
* you go back to school
* you finish school
* you clean the house
* you organise the garage
* you clean off your desk
* you lose 10 lbs.
* you gain 10 lbs.
* you get married
* you get a divorce
* you have kids
* the kids go to school
* you retire
* summer / spring / winter / fall
* you die ...

There is no better time than right now to be happy. Happiness is a journey, not a destination. So work like you don't need money. Love like you've never been hurt and dance like no one's watching. Don't be afraid that your life will end, be afraid that it will never begin.

What comes around - goes around

One day a man saw an old lady, stranded on the side of the road, but even in the dim light of day, he could see she needed help. So he pulled up in front of her Mercedes and got out. His Pontiac was still sputtering when he approached her.

Even with the smile on his face, she was worried. No one had stopped to help for the longest time.

He could see that she was frightened, standing out there in the cold. He knew how she felt. It was those chills which only fear can put in you.

He said, *'I'm here to help you, ma'am. Why don't you wait in the car where it's warm? By the way, my name is Bryan Anderson.'*

Well, all she had was a flat tire, but for an old lady, that was bad enough. Bryan crawled under the car looking for a place to put the jack, skinning his knuckles a time or two. Soon he was able to change the tire. But he had to get dirty and his hands hurt.

As he was tightening up the lug nuts, she rolled down the window and began to talk to him. She told him that she was from St. Louis and was only just passing through. She couldn't thank him enough for coming to her aid.

Bryan just smiled as he closed her trunk. The lady asked how much she owed him. Any amount would have been all right with her. She already imagined all the awful things that could have happened had he not stopped. Bryan never thought twice about being paid.

This was not a job to him. This was helping someone in need and God knows there were plenty, who had given him a hand in the past. He had lived his whole life that way and it never occurred to him to act any other way.

He told her that if she really wanted to pay him back, the next time she saw someone who needed help, she could give that person the assistance they needed and Bryan added, *'And think of me.'*

He waited until she started her car and drove off. It had been a cold and depressing day, but he felt good as he headed for home, disappearing into the twilight.

A few miles down the road the lady saw a small l cafe. She went in to grab a bite to eat and take the chill off before she made the last leg of her trip home. It was a dingy looking restaurant. Outside were two old gas pumps. The whole scene was unfamiliar to her. The waitress came over and brought a clean towel to wipe her wet hair. She had a sweet smile, one that even being on her feet for the whole day couldn't erase.

The lady noticed the waitress was nearly eight months pregnant, but she never let the strain and aches change her attitude. The old lady wondered how someone who had so little could be so giving to a stranger. Then she remembered Bryan.

After the lady finished her meal, she paid with a hundred dollar bill. The waitress quickly went to get change for her hundred dollar bill, but the old lady had slipped right out the door. She was gone by

210

the time the waitress came back. The waitress wondered where the lady could be. Then she noticed something written on the napkin.

There were tears in her eyes when she read what the lady wrote: *'You don't owe me anything. I have been there too. Somebody once helped me out, the way I'm helping you. If you really want to pay me back, here is what you do: Do not let this chain of love end with you.'*

Under the napkin were four more $100 bills. Well, there were tables to clear, sugar bowls to fill and people to serve, but the waitress made it through another day. That night when she got home from work and climbed into bed, she was thinking about the money and what the lady had written. How could the lady have known how much she and her husband needed it? With the baby due next month, it was going to be hard ...

She knew how worried her husband was and as he lay sleeping next to her, she gave him a soft kiss and whispered soft and low, *'Everything's going to be all right. I love you, Bryan Anderson.'*

There is an old saying *'What comes around goes around.'*

Teddy Stoddard

As she stood in front of her fifth grade class on the very first day of school, she told the children an untruth. Like most teachers, she looked at her students and said that she loved them all the same. However, that was impossible, because there in the front row, slumped in his seat, was a little boy named Teddy Stoddard.

Mrs. Thompson had watched Teddy the year before and noticed that he did not play well with the other children, that his clothes were messy and that he constantly needed a bath. In addition, Teddy could be unpleasant. It got to the point where Mrs. Thompson would actually take delight in marking his papers with a broad red pen, making bold X's and then putting a big 'F' at the top of his papers.

At the school where Mrs. Thompson taught, she was required to review each child's past records and she put Teddy's off until last. However, when she reviewed his file, she was in for a surprise.

Teddy's first grade teacher wrote, *'Teddy is a bright child with a ready laugh. He does his work neatly and has good manners ... he is a joy to be around.'*

His second grade teacher wrote, *'Teddy is an excellent student, well liked by his classmates, but he is troubled because his mother has a terminal illness and life at home must be a struggle.'*

His third grade teacher wrote, *'His mother's death has been hard on him. He tries to do his best, but his father doesn't show much interest and his home life will soon affect him if some steps aren't taken.'*

Teddy's fourth grade teacher wrote, *'Teddy is withdrawn and doesn't show much interest in school. He doesn't have many friends and he sometimes sleeps in class.'*

By now, Mrs. Thompson realised the problem and she was ashamed of herself. She felt even worse when her students brought her Christmas presents, wrapped in beautiful ribbons and bright paper, except for Teddy's. His present was clumsily wrapped in the heavy, brown paper that he got from a grocery bag. Mrs. Thompson took pains to open it in the middle of the other presents. Some of the children started to laugh when she found a rhinestone bracelet with some of the stones missing and a bottle that was one-quarter full of perfume. But she stifled the children's laughter when she exclaimed how pretty the bracelet was, putting it on and dabbing some of the perfume on her wrist. Teddy Stoddard stayed after school that day just long enough to say, *'Mrs. Thompson, today you smelled just like my Mom used to.'*

After the children left, she cried for at least an hour. On that very day, she quit teaching reading, writing and arithmetic. Instead, she began to teach children. Mrs. Thompson paid particular attention to Teddy. As she worked with him, his mind seemed to come alive. The more she encouraged him, the faster he responded. By the end of the year, Teddy had become one of the smartest children in the class and, despite her lie that she would love all the children the same, Teddy became one of her 'teacher's pets.'

A year later, she found a note under her door, from Teddy, telling her that she was the best teacher he ever had in his whole life.

Six years went by before she got another note from Teddy. He then wrote that he had finished high school, third in his class and she was still the best teacher he ever had in life.

Four years after that, she got another letter, saying that while things had been tough at times, he'd stayed in school, had stuck with it and would soon graduate from college with the highest of honours. He assured Mrs. Thompson that she was still the best and favourite teacher he had ever had in his whole life.

Then four more years passed and yet another letter came. This time he explained that after he got his bachelor's degree, he decided

212

to go a little further. The letter explained that she was still the best and favourite teacher he ever had. But now his name was a little longer ... The letter was signed, Theodore F. Stoddard, MD.

The story does not end there. You see, there was yet another letter that spring. Teddy said he had met this girl and was going to be married. He explained that his father had died a couple of years ago and he was wondering if Mrs. Thompson might agree to sit at the wedding in the place that was usually reserved for the mother of the groom. Of course, Mrs. Thompson did. And guess what? She wore that bracelet, the one with several rhinestones missing. Moreover, she made sure she was wearing the perfume that Teddy remembered his mother wearing on their last Christmas together.

They hugged each other and Dr. Stoddard whispered in Mrs. Thompson's ear, *'Thank you Mrs. Thompson for believing in me. Thank you so much for making me feel important and showing me that I could make a difference.'*

Mrs. Thompson, with tears in her eyes, whispered back. She said, *'Teddy, you have it all wrong. You were the one who taught me that I could make a difference. I didn't know how to teach until I met you.'*

[For you that don't know, Teddy Stoddard is the Doctor at Iowa Methodist in Des Moines that has the Stoddard Cancer Wing.]

Burnt biscuit story

When I was a kid, my mom liked to make breakfast food for dinner every now and then. And I remember one night in particular when she had made breakfast after a long, hard day at work.

On that evening so long ago, my mom placed a plate of eggs, sausage and extremely burned biscuits in front of my dad. I remember waiting to see if anyone noticed! Yet all my dad did was reach for his biscuit, smile at my mom and ask me how my day was at school. I don't remember what I told him that night, but I do remember watching him smear butter and jelly on that biscuit and eat every bite!

When I got up from the table that evening, I remember hearing my mom apologise to my dad for burning the biscuits. And I'll never forget what he said: *'Honey, I love burned biscuits.'*

Later that night, I went to kiss Daddy good night and I asked him if he really liked his biscuits burned. He wrapped me in his arms and said, *'Your Momma put in a hard day at work today and she's real tired. And besides - a little burnt biscuit never hurt anyone.'*

Life is full of imperfect things ... and imperfect people. I'm not the best at hardly anything and I forget birthdays and anniversaries just like everyone else. But what I've learned over the years is that learning to accept each others' faults - and choosing to celebrate each others' differences - is one of the most important keys to creating a healthy, growing and lasting relationship

We could extend this to any relationship. In fact, understanding is the base of any relationship, be it a husband-wife or parent-child or brother-sister or friendship!

'Don't put the key to your happiness in someone else's pocket - keep it in your own. So please pass me a biscuit and yes, the burnt one will do just fine!'

Kyle

One day, when I was a freshman in high school, I saw a kid from my class was walking home from school. His name was Kyle. It looked like he was carrying all of his books. I thought to myself, *'Why would anyone bring home all his books on a Friday? He must really be a nerd.'*

I had quite a weekend planned [parties and a football game with my friends tomorrow afternoon] so I shrugged my shoulders and went on. As I was walking, I saw a bunch of kids running toward him. They ran at him, knocking all his books out of his arms and tripping him so he landed in the dirt.

His glasses went flying and I saw them land in the grass about ten feet from him. He looked up and I saw this terrible sadness in his eyes. My heart went out to him. So, I jogged over to him as he crawled around looking for his glasses and I saw a tear in his eye. As I handed him his glasses, I said, *'Those guys are jerks. They really should get lives.'*

He looked at me and said, *'Hey thanks!'* There was a big smile on his face. It was one of those smiles that showed real gratitude. I helped him pick up his books and asked him where he lived. As it turned out, he lived near me, so I asked him why I had never seen him before. He said he had gone to private school before now. I would have never hung out with a private school kid before.

We talked all the way home and I carried some of his books. He turned out to be a pretty cool kid. I asked him if he wanted to play a little football with my friends. He said yes.

We hung out all weekend and the more I got to know Kyle, the more I liked him and my friends thought the same of him.

Monday morning came and there was Kyle with the huge stack of books again.

I stopped him and said, *'Boy, you are gonna really build some serious muscles with this pile of books every day!'* He just laughed and handed me half the books.

Over the next four years, Kyle and I became best friends. When we were seniors we began to think about college. Kyle decided on Georgetown and I was going to Duke. I knew that we would always be friends, that the miles would never be a problem.

He was going to be a doctor and I was going for business on a football scholarship.

Kyle was valedictorian of our class. I teased him all the time about being a nerd. He had to prepare a speech for graduation. I was so glad it wasn't me having to get up there and speak.

Graduation day, I saw Kyle. He looked great. He was one of those guys that really found himself during high school. He filled out and actually looked good in glasses. He had more dates than I had and all the girls loved him. Boy, sometimes I was jealous! Today was one of those days.

I could see that he was nervous about his speech. So, I smacked him on the back and said, *'Hey, big guy, you'll be great!'* He looked at me with one of those looks [the really grateful one] and smiled. *'Thanks,'* he said.

As he started his speech, he cleared his throat and began *'Graduation is a time to thank those who helped you make it through those tough years. Your parents, your teachers, your siblings, maybe a coach ... but mostly your friends ... I am here to tell all of you that being a friend to someone is the best gift you can give them. I am going to tell you a story.'*

I just looked at my friend with disbelief as he told the story of the first day we met. He had planned to kill himself over the weekend. He talked of how he had cleaned out his locker so his Mom wouldn't have to do it later and was carrying his stuff home.

He looked hard at me and gave me a little smile. *'Thankfully, I was saved. My friend saved me from doing the unspeakable.'*

I heard the gasp go through the crowd as this handsome, popular boy told us all about his weakest moment. I saw his Mom and dad looking at me and smiling that same grateful smile. Not until that moment did I realise its depth.

Never underestimate the power of your actions. With one small gesture you can change a person's life.

Five lessons about the way we treat people

First Important Lesson - Cleaning Lady.
During my second month of college, our professor gave us a pop quiz. I was a conscientious student and had breezed through the questions until I read the last one: *'What is the first name of the woman who cleans the school?'* Surely this was some kind of joke. I had seen the cleaning woman several times. She was tall, dark-haired and in her 50s, but how would I know her name?

I handed in my paper, leaving the last question blank. Just before class ended, one student asked if the last question would count toward our quiz grade.

'Absolutely,' said the professor. *'In your careers, you will meet many people. All are significant. They deserve your attention and care, even if all you do is smile and say 'hello.''*

I've never forgotten that lesson. I also learned her name was Dorothy.

Second Important Lesson - Pickup in the Rain.
One night, at 11:30 pm, an older African American woman was standing on the side of an Alabama highway trying to endure a lashing rain storm. Her car had broken down and she desperately needed a ride. Soaking wet, she decided to flag down the next car. A young white man stopped to help her, generally unheard of in those conflict-filled 1960's. The man took her to safety, helped her get assistance and put her into a taxicab.

She seemed to be in a big hurry, but wrote down his address and thanked him. Seven days went by and a knock came on the man's door. To his surprise, a giant console colour TV was delivered to his home. A special note was attached. It read:

'Thank you so much for assisting me on the highway the other night. The rain drenched not only my clothes, but also my spirits. Then you came along. Because of you, I was able to make it to my dying husband's bedside just before he passed away ... God bless you for helping me and unselfishly serving others.'
Sincerely,
Mrs. Nat King Cole.

Third Important Lesson - Always remember those who serve.
In the days when an ice cream sundae cost much less, a 10-year-old boy entered a hotel coffee shop and sat at a table. A waitress put a glass of water in front of him.

216

'How much is an ice cream sundae?' he asked.

'Fifty cents,' replied the waitress.

The little boy pulled is hand out of his pocket and studied the coins in it.

'Well, how much is a plain dish of ice cream?' he inquired.

By now more people were waiting for a table and the waitress was growing impatient. *'Thirty-five cents,'* she brusquely replied.

The little boy again counted his coins.

'I'll have the plain ice cream,' he said.

The waitress brought the ice cream, put the bill on the table and walked away. The boy finished the ice cream, paid the cashier and left. When the waitress came back, she began to cry as she wiped down the table. There, placed neatly beside the empty dish, were two nickels and five pennies.

You see, he couldn't have the sundae, because he had to have enough left to leave her a tip.

Fourth Important Lesson. - The obstacle in Our Path.

In ancient times, a King had a boulder placed on a roadway. Then he hid himself and watched to see if anyone would remove the huge rock. Some of the king's wealthiest merchants and courtiers came by and simply walked around it. Many loudly blamed the King for not keeping the roads clear, but none did anything about getting the stone out of the way.

Then a peasant came along carrying a load of vegetables. Upon approaching the boulder, the peasant laid down his burden and tried to move the stone to the side of the road. After much pushing and straining, he finally succeeded. After the peasant picked up his load of vegetables, he noticed a purse lying in the road where the boulder had been. The purse contained many gold coins and a note from the King indicating that the gold was for the person who removed the boulder from the roadway. The peasant learned what many of us never understand! Every obstacle presents an opportunity to improve our condition.

Fifth Important Lesson - Giving When it Counts ...

Many years ago, when I worked as a volunteer at a hospital, I got to know a little girl named Liz who was suffering from a rare and serious disease. Her only chance of recovery appeared to be a blood transfusion from her five-year old brother, who had miraculously survived the same disease and had developed the antibodies needed to combat the illness.

The doctor explained the situation to her little brother and asked the little boy if he would be willing to give his blood to his sister. I saw him hesitate for only a moment before taking a deep breath and saying in a quivering voice, *'Yes I'll do it if it will save her.'* As the transfusion progressed, he lay in bed next to his sister and smiled, as we all did, seeing the colour returning to her cheek. Then his face grew pale and his smile faded.

He looked up at the doctor and asked with a trembling voice, *'Will I start to die right away?'*

Being young, the little boy had misunderstood the doctor; he thought he was going to have to give his sister all of his blood in order to save her.

Dear God

There was a man who worked for the Post Office whose job was to process all the mail that had illegible addresses. One day, a letter came addressed, written in a shaky handwriting, to God with no actual address. He thought he should open it to see what it was about. The letter read:

Dear God,

I am an 83 year old widow, living on a very small pension. Yesterday someone stole my purse. It had $100 in it, which was all the money I had until my next pension payment.

Next Sunday is Christmas and I had invited two of my friends over for dinner. Without that money, I have nothing to buy food with, have no family to turn to and you are my only hope. Can you please help me?
Sincerely, Edna

The postal worker was touched. He showed the letter to all the other workers. Each one dug into his or her wallet and came up with a few dollars. By the time he made the rounds, he had collected $96, which they put into an envelope and sent to the woman.

The rest of the day, all the workers felt a warm glow thinking of Edna and the dinner she would be able to share with her friends.

Christmas came and went. A few days later, another letter came from the same old lady to God. All the workers gathered around while the letter was opened. It read:

Dear God,

How can I ever thank you enough for what you did for me? Because of your gift of love, I was able to fix a glorious dinner for my friends. We had a very nice day and I told my friends of your wonderful gift. By the way, there was $4 missing. I think it might have been those bastards at the post office.

Sincerely,

Edna

Just stay

A nurse took the tired, anxious serviceman to the bedside.

'Your son is here,' she said to the old man.

She had to repeat the words several times before the patient's eyes opened.

Heavily sedated because of the pain of his heart attack, he dimly saw the young uniformed Marine standing outside the oxygen tent. He reached out his hand. The Marine wrapped his toughened fingers around the old man's limp ones, squeezing a message of love and encouragement.

The nurse brought a chair so that the Marine could sit beside the bed. All through the night the young Marine sat there in the poorly lighted ward, holding the old man's hand and offering him words of love and strength. Occasionally, the nurse suggested that the Marine move away and rest awhile.

He refused. Whenever the nurse came into the ward, the Marine was oblivious of her and of the night noises of the hospital - the clanking of the oxygen tank, the laughter of the night staff members exchanging greetings, the cries and moans of the other patients.

Now and then she heard him say a few gentle words. The dying man said nothing, only held tightly to his son all through the night.

Along towards dawn, the old man died. The Marine released the now lifeless hand he had been holding and went to tell the nurse. While she did what she had to do, he waited.

Finally, she returned. She started to offer words of sympathy, but the Marine interrupted her.

'Who was that man?' he asked.

The nurse was startled, *'He was your father,'* she answered.

'No, he wasn't,' the Marine replied. *'I never saw him before in my life.'*

'Then why didn't you say something when I took you to him?'

'I knew right away there had been a mistake, but I also knew he needed his son and his son just wasn't here. When I realised that he was too sick to tell whether or not I was his son, knowing how much he needed me, I stayed. I came here tonight to find a Mr. William Grey. His son was killed in Iraq today and I was sent to inform him. What was this gentleman's name?'

The Nurse with Tears in her eyes answered, *'Mr. William Grey.*

The next time someone needs you ... just be there.

Mr. Belser

A young man learned what is most important in life from the man next door. It had been some time since Jack had seen the old man. College, girls, career and life itself got in the way. In fact, Jack moved clear across the country in pursuit of his dreams.

There, in the rush of his busy life, Jack had little time to think about the past and often no time to spend with his wife and son. He was working on his future and nothing could stop him.

Over the phone, his mother told him, *'Mr. Belser died last night. The funeral is Wednesday.'*

Memories flashed through his mind like an old newsreel as he sat quietly remembering his childhood days.

'Jack, did you hear me?'

'Oh, sorry, Mom. Yes, I heard you. It's been so long since I thought of him. I'm sorry, but I honestly thought he died years ago,' Jack said.

'Well, he didn't forget you. Every time I saw him he'd ask how you were doing. He'd reminisce about the many days you spent over 'his side of the fence' as he put it,' Mom told him.

'I loved that old house he lived in,' Jack said.

'You know, Jack, after your father died, Mr. Belser stepped in to make sure you had a man's influence in your life,' she said

'He's the one who taught me carpentry,' he said. *'I wouldn't be in this business if it weren't for him. He spent a lot of time teaching me things he thought were important... Mom, I'll be there for the funeral,'* Jack said.

As busy as he was, he kept his word. Jack caught the next flight to his home town. Mr. Belser's funeral was small and uneventful. He had no children of his own and most of his relatives had passed away.

The night before he had to return home, Jack and his Mom stopped by to see the old house next door one more time. Standing in the doorway, Jack paused for a moment. It was like crossing over into another dimension, a leap through space and time. The house was exactly as he remembered. Every step held memories. Every picture, every piece of furniture ... Jack stopped suddenly.

'What's wrong, Jack?' his Mom asked.

'The box is gone,' he said.

'What box?' Mom asked.

'There was a small gold box that he kept locked on top of his desk. I must have asked him a thousand times what was inside. All he'd ever tell me was 'the thing I value most," Jack said.

It was gone. Everything about the house was exactly how Jack remembered it, except for the box. He figured someone from the Belser family had taken it.

'Now I'll never know what was so valuable to him,' Jack said. *'I'd better get some sleep. I have an early flight home, Mom.'*

It had been about two weeks since Mr. Belser died. Returning home from work one day Jack discovered a note in his mailbox. *'Signature required on a package. No one at home. Please stop by the main post office within the next three days,'* the note read.

Early the next day Jack retrieved the package. The small box was old and looked like it had been mailed a hundred years ago. The handwriting was difficult to read, but the return address caught his attention. 'Mr. Harold Belser' it read. Jack took the box out to his car and ripped open the package. There inside was the gold box and an envelope. Jack's hands shook as he read the note inside.

'Upon my death, please forward this box and its contents to Jack Bennett. It's the thing I valued most in my life.' A small key was taped to the letter. His heart racing, as tears filling his eyes, Jack carefully unlocked the box. There inside he found a beautiful gold pocket watch.

Running his fingers slowly over the finely etched casing, he unlatched the cover. Inside he found these words engraved: *'Jack, Thanks for your time! Harold Belser.'*

'The thing he valued most was ... my time'

Jack held the watch for a few minutes, then called his office and cleared his appointments for the next two days. *'Why?'* Janet, his assistant asked.

'I need some time to spend with my son,' he said.

'Oh, by the way Janet, thanks for your time!'

Life is not measured by the number of breaths we take but by the moments that take our breath away. Think about this. You may not realise it, but it's 100% true.

1. At least 2 people in this world love you so much they would die for you.
2. At least 15 people in this world love you in some way.
3. A smile from you can bring happiness to anyone, even if they don't like you.
4. Every night, someone thinks about you before they go to sleep.
5. You mean the world to someone.
6. If not for you, someone may not be living.
7. You are special and unique.
8. When you think you have no chance of getting what you want, you probably won't get it, but if you trust and wait, sooner or later, you will get it or something better.
9. When you make the biggest mistake ever, something good can still come from it.
10. When you think the world has turned its back on you, take a look: you most likely turned your back on the world.
11. Someone that you don't even know exists loves you.
12. Always remember the compliments you received. Forget about the rude remarks.
13. Always tell someone how you feel about them; you will feel much better when they know and you'll both be happy.
14. If you have a great friend, take the time to let them know that they are great.

A Truckers Story

I try not to be biased, but I had my doubts about hiring Stevie. His placement counsellor assured me that he would be a good, reliable busboy. But I had never had a mentally handicapped employee and wasn't sure I wanted one. I wasn't sure how my customers would react to Stevie.

He was short, a little dumpy with the smooth facial features and thick-tongued speech of Down's Syndrome. I wasn't worried about most of my trucker customers because truckers don't generally care who buses tables as long as the meatloaf platter is good and the pies are homemade.

The four-wheeler drivers were the ones who concerned me; the mouthy college kids travelling to school; the yuppie snobs who secretly polish their silverware with their napkins for fear of catching some dreaded 'truck stop germ' the pairs of white-shirted business men on expense accounts who think every truck stop waitress wants to be flirted with. I knew those people would be uncomfortable around Stevie so I closely watched him for the first few weeks.

I shouldn't have worried. After the first week, Stevie had my staff wrapped around his stubby little finger and within a month my truck regulars had adopted him as their official truck stop mascot.

After that, I really didn't care what the rest of the customers thought of him. He was like a 21-year-old in blue jeans and Nikes, eager to laugh and eager to please, but fierce in his attention to his duties. Every salt and pepper shaker was exactly in its place, not a bread crumb or coffee spill was visible when Stevie got done with the table. Our only problem was persuading him to wait to clean a table until after the customers were finished. He would hover in the background, shifting his weight from one foot to the other, scanning the dining room until a table was empty. Then he would scurry to the empty table and carefully bus dishes and glasses onto his cart and meticulously wipe the table up with a practiced flourish of his rag.

If he thought a customer was watching, his brow would pucker with added concentration. He took pride in doing his job exactly right and you had to love how hard he tried to please each and every person he met.

Over time, we learned that he lived with his mother, a widow who was disabled after repeated surgeries for cancer. They lived on their Social Security benefits in public housing two miles from the truck stop. Their social worker, who stopped to check on him every so often, admitted they had fallen between the cracks. Money was tight and what I paid him was probably the difference between them being able to live together and Stevie being sent to a group home. That's why the restaurant was a gloomy place that morning last August, the first morning in three years that Stevie had missed work.

He was at the Mayo Clinic in Rochester getting a new valve or something put in his heart. His social worker said that people with Down's Syndrome often have heart problems at an early age so this wasn't unexpected and there was a good chance he would come through the surgery in good shape and be back at work in a few months.

A ripple of excitement ran through the staff later that morning when word came that he was out of surgery, in recovery and doing fine. Frannie, the head waitress, let out a war hoop and did a little dance in the aisle when she heard the good news.

Belle Ringer, one of our regular trucker customers, stared at the sight of this 50-year-old grandmother of four doing a victory shimmy beside his table. Frannie blushed, smoothed her apron and shot Belle Ringer a withering look.

He grinned. *'OK, Frannie, what was that all about?'* he asked.

'We just got word that Stevie is out of surgery and going to be okay.'

'I was wondering where he was. I had a new joke to tell him. What was the surgery about?'

Frannie quickly told Belle Ringer and the other two drivers sitting at his booth about Stevie's surgery and then sighed: *'Yeah, I'm glad he is going to be OK,'* she said. *'But I don't know how he and his Mom are going to handle all the bills. From what I hear, they're barely getting by as it is.'*

Belle Ringer nodded thoughtfully and Frannie hurried off to wait on the rest of her tables. Since I hadn't had time to round up a busboy to replace Stevie and really didn't want to replace him, the girls were bussing their own tables that day until we decided what to do.

After the morning rush, Frannie walked into my office. She had a couple of paper napkins in her hand and a funny look on her face.

'What's up?' I asked.

'I didn't get that table where Belle Ringer and his friends were sitting cleared off after they left and Pony Pete and Tony Tipper were sitting there when I got back to clean it off,' she said. *'This was folded and tucked under a coffee cup.'*

She handed the napkin to me and three $20 bills fell onto my desk when I opened it. On the outside, in big, bold letters, was printed *'Something for Stevie.'*

'Pony Pete asked me what that was all about,' she said, *'so I told him about Stevie and his Mom and everything and Pete looked at Tony and Tony looked at Pete and they ended up giving me this.'* She handed me another paper napkin that had, *'Something For Stevie'* scrawled on its outside. Two $50 bills were tucked within its folds.

Frannie looked at me with wet, shiny eyes, shook her head and said simply: *'truckers.'*

That was three months ago. Today is Thanksgiving, the first day Stevie is supposed to be back to work. His placement worker said he's been counting the days until the doctor said he could work and it didn't matter at all that it was a holiday. He called ten times in the past week, making sure we knew he was coming, fearful that we had forgotten him or that his job was in jeopardy. I arranged to have his mother bring him to work. I then met them in the parking lot and invited them both to celebrate his day back.

Stevie was thinner and paler, but couldn't stop grinning as he pushed through the doors and headed for the back room where his apron and bussing cart were waiting.

'*Hold up there, Stevie, not so fast,*' I said I took him and his mother by their arms. '*Work can wait for a minute. To celebrate you coming back, breakfast for you and your mother is on me!*' I led them toward a large corner booth at the rear of the room.

I could feel and hear the rest of the staff following behind as we marched through the dining room. Glancing over my shoulder, I saw booth after booth of grinning truckers empty and join the procession. We stopped in front of the big table. Its surface was covered with coffee cups, saucers and dinner plates, all sitting slightly crooked on dozens of folded paper napkins.

'*First thing you have to do, Stevie, is clean up this mess,*' I said. I tried to sound stern. Stevie looked at me and then at his mother, then pulled out one of the napkins. It had '*Something for Stevie*' printed on the outside. As he picked it up, two $10 bills fell onto the table.

Stevie stared at the money, then at all the napkins peeking from beneath the tableware, each with his name printed or scrawled on it. I turned to his mother. '*There's more than $10,000 in cash and checks on that table, all from truckers and trucking companies that heard about your problems. Happy Thanksgiving.*'

Well, it got real noisy about that time, with everybody hollering and shouting and there were a few tears, as well. But you know what's funny? While everybody else was busy shaking hands and hugging each other, Stevie, with a big, big smile on his face, was busy clearing all the cups and dishes from the table.

Best worker I ever hired. Plant a seed and watch it grow.

Crabby old man

When an old man died in the geriatric ward of a small hospital near Tampa, Florida, it was believed that he had nothing left of any value.

225

Later, when the nurses were going through his meagre possessions, they found this poem. Its quality and content so impressed the staff that copies were made and distributed to every nurse in the hospital.

One nurse took her copy to Missouri.

The old man's sole bequest to posterity has since appeared in the Christmas edition of the News Magazine of the St. Louis Association for Mental Health.

A slide presentation has also been made based on his simple, but eloquent poem.

And this little old man, with nothing left to give to the world is now the author of this 'anonymous' poem winging across the Internet:

What do you see nurses? What do you see?
What are you thinking ... when you're looking at me?
A crabby old man ... not very wise,
Uncertain of habit ... with faraway eyes?
Who dribbles his food ... and makes no reply.
When you say in a loud voice ... *'I do wish you'd try!'*
Who seems not to notice ... the things that you do.
And forever is losing ... A sock or a shoe?
Who, resisting or not ... lets you do as you will,
With bathing and feeding ... the long day to fill?
Is that what you're thinking? Is that what you u see?
Then open your eyes, nurse ... you're not looking at me.
I'll tell you who I am ... As I sit here so still,
As I do what you're bidding ... as I eat at your will.
I'm a small child of ten ... with a father and mother,
Brothers and sisters ... who love one another.
A young boy of sixteen ... with wings on his feet,
Dreaming that soon now ... a lover he'll meet.
A groom soon at twenty ... my heart gives a leap.
Remembering, the vows ... that I promised to keep.
At twenty-five, now ... I have young of my own.
Who need me to guide ... and a secure happy home.
A man of thirty ... my young now grown fast,
Bound to each other ... with ties that should last.
At forty, my young sons ... have grown and are gone,
But my woman's beside me ... to see I don't mourn.
At fifty, once more ... babies play 'round my knee,

Again, we know children ... my loved one and me.
Dark days are upon me ... my wife is now dead.
I look at the future ... I shudder with dread.
For my young are all rearing ... young of their own.
And I think of the years ... and the love that I've known.
I'm now an old man ... and nature is cruel.
'Tis jest to make old age ... look like a fool.
The body, it crumbles ... grace and vigour, depart.
There is now a stone ... where I once had a heart.
But inside this old carcase ... a young guy still dwells,
And now and again ... my battered heart swells
I remember the joys ... I remember the pain.
And I'm loving and living ... life over again.
I think of the years all too few ... gone too fast.
And accept the stark fact ... that nothing can last.
So open your eyes, people ... open and see,
Not a crabby old man. Look closer ... see ... ME!!

Remember this poem when you next meet an older person who you might brush aside without looking at the young soul within ... we will all, one day, be there, too!

You have two choices

Jerry is the manager of a restaurant. He is always in a good mood. When someone would ask him how he was doing, he would always reply: 'If I were any better, I would be twins!'

Many of the waiters at his restaurant quit their jobs when he changed jobs, so they could follow him around from restaurant to restaurant. Why? Because Jerry was a natural motivator.

If an employee was having a bad day, Jerry was always there, telling him how to look on the positive side of the situation. Seeing this style really made me curious, so one day I went up to Jerry and asked him 'I don't get it! No one can be a positive person all of the time. How do you do it?'

Jerry replied, 'Each morning I wake up and say to myself, I have two choices today. I can choose to be in a good mood or I can choose to be in a bad mood. I always choose to be in a good mood. Each time something bad happens, I can choose to be victim or I can choose to learn from it. I always choose to learn from it. Every time someone comes to me complaining, I can choose to accept their complaining or I can point out the positive side of life. I always choose the positive side of life.'

'But it's not always that easy,' I protested.

'Yes it is,' Jerry said. *'Life is all about choices. When you cut away all the junk every situation is a choice. You choose how you react to situations. You choose how people will affect your mood. You choose to be in a good mood or bad mood. It's your choice how you live your life.'*

Several years later, I heard that Jerry accidentally did something you are never supposed to do in the restaurant business. He left the back door of his restaurant open and then in the morning, he was robbed by three armed men. While Jerry was trying to open the safe box, his hand, shaking from nervousness, slipped off the combination. The robbers panicked and shot him.

Luckily, Jerry was found quickly and rushed to the hospital. After 18 hours of surgery and weeks of intensive care, Jerry was released from the hospital with fragments of the bullets still in his body.

I saw Jerry about six months after the accident. When I asked him how he was, he replied, *'If I were any better, I'd be twins. Want to see my scars?'*

I declined to see his wounds, but did ask him what had gone through his mind as the robbery took place. *'The first thing that went through my mind was that I should have locked the back door,'* Jerry replied. *'Then, after they shot me, as I lay on the floor, I remembered that I had two choices: I could choose to live or could choose to die. I chose to live.'*

'Weren't you scared?' I asked. Jerry continued, *'The paramedics were great. They kept telling me I was going to be fine, but when they wheeled me into the Emergency Room and I saw the expression on the faces of the doctors and nurses, I got really scared. In their eyes, I read 'He's a dead man. I knew I needed to take action.'*

'What did you do?' I asked.

'Well, there was a big nurse shouting questions at me,' said Jerry. *'She asked if I was allergic to anything.'*

'Yes, to bullets,' I replied.

Over their laughter, I told them: *'I am choosing to live. Please operate on me as if I am alive, not dead.'*

Jerry lived thanks to the skill of his doctors, but also because of his amazing attitude. I learned from him that every day you have the choice to either enjoy your life or to hate it. The only thing that is truly yours - that no one can control or take from you is your attitude, so if you can take care of that, everything else in life becomes much easier.

Nails in the fence

There once was a little boy who had a bad temper. His Father gave him a bag of nails and told him that every time he lost his temper, he must hammer a nail into the back of the fence. The first day the boy had driven 37 nails into the fence. Over the next few weeks, as he learned to control his anger, the number of nails he hammered daily, gradually dwindled down. He discovered it was easier to hold his temper than to drive nails into the fence. Finally the day came when the boy didn't lose his temper at all.

He told his father about it and the father suggested that the boy now pull out one nail for each day that he was able to hold his temper. The days passed and the young boy was finally able to tell his father that all the nails were gone.

The father took his son by the hand and led him to the fence. He said, *'You have done well, my son, but look at the holes in the fence. The fence will never be the same. When you say things in anger, they leave a scar just like this one. You can put a knife in a man and draw it out, but it won't matter how many times you say I'm sorry, the wound will still be there. A verbal wound is as bad as a physical one.*

Remember that friends are very rare jewels, indeed. They make you smile and encourage you to succeed. They lend an ear, they share words of praise and they always want to open their hearts to us.'

The Cab Ride

I arrived at the address and honked the horn. After waiting a few minutes I walked to the door and knocked. *'Just a minute,'* answered a frail, elderly voice. I could hear something being dragged across the floor.

After a long pause, the door opened. A small woman in her 90's stood before me. She was wearing a print dress and a pillbox hat with a veil pinned on it, like somebody out of a 1940's movie.

By her side was a small nylon suitcase. The apartment looked as if no one had lived in it for years. All the furniture was covered with sheets. There were no clocks on the walls, no knickknacks or utensils on the counters. In the corner was a cardboard box filled with photos and glassware.

229

'Would you carry my bag out to the car?' she said. I took the suitcase to the cab, then returned to assist the woman. She took my arm and we walked slowly toward the curb.

She kept thanking me for my kindness. *'It's nothing',* I told her. *'I just try to treat my passengers the way I would want my mother treated.'*

'Oh, you're such a good boy,' she said. When we got in the cab, she gave me an address and then asked, *'Could you drive through downtown?'*

'It's not the shortest way,' I answered quickly.

'Oh, I don't mind,' she said. *'I'm in no hurry. I'm on my way to a hospice.'*

I looked in the rear-view mirror. Her eyes were glistening. *'I don't have any family left,'* she continued in a soft voice. *'The doctor says I don't have very long.'* I quietly reached over and shut off the meter.

'What route would you like me to take?' I asked.

For the next two hours, we drove through the city. She showed me the building where she had once worked as an elevator operator.

We drove through the neighbourhood where she and her husband had lived when they were newlyweds. She had me pull up in front of a furniture warehouse that had once been a ballroom where she had gone dancing as a girl.

Sometimes she'd ask me to slow in front of a particular building or corner and would sit staring into the darkness, saying nothing.

As the first hint of sun was creasing the horizon, she suddenly said, *'I'm tired. Let's go now.'*

We drove in silence to the address she had given me. It was a low building, like a small convalescent home, with a driveway that passed under a portico. Two orderlies came out to the cab as soon as we pulled up. They were solicitous and intent, watching her every move. They must have been expecting her. I opened the trunk and took the small suitcase to the door. The woman was already seated in a wheelchair.

'How much do I owe you?' she asked, reaching into her purse.

'Nothing,' I said

'You have to make a living,' she answered.

'There are other passengers,' I responded.

Almost without thinking, I bent and gave her a hug. She held onto me tightly.

'You gave an old woman a little moment of joy,' she said.

'Thank you.' I squeezed her hand and then walked into the dim morning light. Behind me, a door shut. It was the sound of the closing of a life.

I didn't pick up any more passengers that shift. I drove aimlessly lost in thought. For the rest of that day, I could hardly talk. What if that woman had gotten an angry driver or one who was impatient to end his shift? What if I had refused to take the run or had honked once, then driven away?

On a quick review, I don't think that I have done anything more important in my life.

We're conditioned to think that our lives revolve around great moments. But great moments often catch us unaware - beautifully wrapped in what others may consider a small one.

People may not remember exactly what you did or what you said but they will always remember how you made them feel.

Treasures

I grew up with practical parents. A mother, God love her, who washed aluminum foil after she cooked in it, then reused it. She was the original recycle queen, before they had a name for it ... A father who was happier getting old shoes fixed than buying new ones. Their marriage was good, their dreams focused. Their best friends lived barely a wave away.

I can see them now, Dad in trousers, tee shirt and a hat and Mom in a house dress, lawn mower in one hand and dish-towel in the other. It was the time for fixing things. A curtain rod, the kitchen radio, screen door, the oven door, the hem in a dress. Things we keep.

It was a way of life and sometimes it made me crazy. All that refixing, eating, renewing, I wanted just once to be wasteful. Waste meant affluence. Throwing things away meant you knew there'd always be more.

But then my father died and on that clear winter's night, in the warmth of the hospital room, I was struck with the pain of learning that sometimes there isn't any more.

Sometimes, what we care about most gets all used up and goes away ... never to return. So, while we have it, it's best we love it and care for it, fix it when it's broken ... and heal it when it's sick.

This is true ... for marriage, old cars, children with bad report cards, dogs with bad hips, aging parents and grandparents. We keep them because they are worth it, because we are worth it.

Some things we keep. Like a best friend that moved away or a classmate we grew up with. There are just some things that make life important, like people we know who are special ... and so, we keep them close! Good friends are like stars ... You don't always see them, but you know they are always there. Keep them close!

[By the way, the word aluminum is spelled correctly. It was invented in the USA and was called aluminum – then the Brits added the extra (i) and made it aluminium.]

The Boy and the Puppy

A farmer had some puppies he needed to sell. He painted a sign advertising the 4 pups and set about nailing it to a post on the edge of his yard. As he was driving the last nail into the post, he felt a tug on his overalls. He looked down into the eyes of little boy.

'Mister,' he said, *'I want to buy one of your puppies.'*

'Well,' said the farmer, as he rubbed the sweat off the back of his neck, *'These puppies come from fine parents and cost a good deal of money.'*

The boy dropped his head for a moment.

Then reaching deep into his pocket, he pulled out a handful of change and held it up to the farmer.

'I've got thirty-nine cents. Is that enough to take a look?'

'Sure,' said the farmer. And with that he let out a whistle.

'Here, Dolly!' he called.

Out from the doghouse and down the ramp ran Dolly followed by four little balls of fur.

The little boy pressed his face against the chain link fence. His eyes danced with delight.

As the dogs made their way to the fence, the little boy noticed something else stirring inside the doghouse. Slowly another little ball appeared, this one noticeably smaller. Down the ramp it slid. Then in a somewhat awkward manner, the little pup began hobbling toward the others, doing its best to catch up.

'I want that one,' the little boy said, pointing to the runt. The farmer knelt down at the boy's side and said, *'Son, you don't want that puppy. He will never be able to run and play with you like these other dogs would.'*

With that the little boy stepped back from the fence, reached down and began rolling up one leg of his trousers. In doing so he revealed a steel brace running down both sides of his leg attaching itself to a specially made shoe.

Looking back up at the farmer, he said, *'You see sir, I don't run too well myself and he will need someone who understands.'*

With tears in his eyes, the farmer reached down and picked up the little pup. Holding it carefully he handed it to the little boy.

'How much?' asked the little boy. *'No charge,'* answered the farmer, *'There's no charge for love.'*

The world is full of people who need someone who understands

The Pickle Jar

The pickle jar as far back as I can remember sat on the floor beside the dresser in my parents' bedroom. When he got ready for bed, Dad would empty his pockets and toss his coins into the jar.

As a small boy, I was always fascinated at the sounds the coins made as they were dropped into the jar. They landed with a merry jingle when the jar was almost empty. Then the tones gradually muted to a dull thud as the jar was filled.

I used to squat on the floor in front of the jar to admire the copper and silver circles that glinted like a pirate's treasure when the sun poured through the bedroom window. When the jar was filled, Dad would sit at the kitchen table and roll the coins before taking them to the bank.

Taking the coins to the bank was always a big production. Stacked neatly in a small cardboard box, the coins were placed between Dad and me on the seat of his old truck.

Each and every time, as we drove to the bank, Dad would look at me hopefully. *'Those coins are going to keep you out of the textile mill, son. You're going to do better than me. This old mill town's not going to hold you back.'*

Also, each and every time, as he slid the box of rolled coins across the counter at the bank toward the cashier, he would grin proudly. *'These are for my son's college fund. He'll never work at the mill all his life like me.'*

We would always celebrate each deposit by stopping for an ice cream cone. I always got chocolate. Dad always got vanilla. When the clerk at the ice cream parlour handed Dad his change, he would show me the few coins nestled in his palm. *'When we get home, we'll start filling the jar again.'* He always let me drop the first coins into the empty jar. As they rattled around with a brief, happy jingle, we grinned at each other.

'You'll get to college on pennies, nickels, dimes and quarters,' he said. *'But you'll get there; I'll see to that.'*

No matter how rough things got at home, Dad continued to doggedly drop his coins into the jar. Even the summer when Dad got laid off from the mill and Mama had to serve dried beans several times a week, not a single dime was taken from the jar.

To the contrary, as Dad looked across the table at me, pouring catsup over my beans to make them more palatable, he became more determined than ever to make a way out for me *'When you finish college, Son,'* he told me, his eyes glistening, *'You'll never have to eat beans again - unless you want to.'*

The years passed and I finished college and took a job in another town. Once, while visiting my parents, I used the phone in their bedroom and noticed that the pickle jar was gone. It had served its purpose and had been removed. A lump rose in my throat as I stared at the spot beside the dresser where the jar had always stood. My dad was a man of few words: he never lectured me on the values of determination, perseverance and faith. The pickle jar had taught me all these virtues far more eloquently than the most flowery of words could have done.

When I married, I told my wife Susan about the significant part the lowly pickle jar had played in my life as a boy. In my mind, it defined, more than anything else, how much my dad had loved me.

The first Christmas after our daughter Jessica was born, we spent the holiday with my parents. After dinner, Mom and Dad sat next to each other on the sofa, taking turns cuddling their first grandchild. Jessica began to whimper softly and Susan took her from Dad's arms. *'She probably needs to be changed,'* she said, carrying the baby into my parents' bedroom to diaper her. When Susan came back into the living room, there was a strange mist in her eyes.

She handed Jessica back to Dad before taking my hand and leading me into the room. *'Look,'* she said softly, her eyes directing me to a spot on the floor beside the dresser. To my amazement, there, as if it had never been removed, stood the old pickle jar, the bottom already covered with coins. I walked over to the pickle jar, dug down into my pocket and pulled out a fistful of coins. With a gamut of emotions choking me, I dropped the coins into the jar. I looked up and saw that Dad, carrying Jessica, had slipped quietly into the room. Our eyes locked and I knew he was feeling the same emotions I felt. Neither one of us could speak.

This truly touched my heart. Sometimes we are so busy adding up our troubles that we forget to count our blessings. Never underestimate the power of your actions. With one small gesture you can change a person's life, for better or for worse.

Flawed friends

Here's a good old Chinese piece of wisdom.

An elderly Chinese woman had two large pots that hung on the ends of a pole that she carried across her neck. One of the pots had a crack in it, while the other was perfect and always delivered a full portion of water.

At the end of the long walk from the stream to the house, the cracked pot arrived only half full. For two years this went on daily with the woman bringing home only one and a half pots of water.

Of course the perfect pot was proud of its accomplishment, but the poor cracked pot was ashamed of its own imperfection.

After two years, it spoke to the woman by the stream. *'I'm ashamed of myself because this crack in my side causes water to leak out all the way back to the house.'*

The old woman smiled, *'Did you notice that there were lovely flowers on your side of the path, but not on the other pot's side? That's because I have always known about your flaw, so I planted flower seeds on your side of the path and every day while I walk back, you water them. For two years I have been able to pick those beautiful flowers to decorate the table. Without you being just the way you are, there would not be this beauty to grace the house.*

Each of us has our own unique flaws ... but it's the cracks and flaws we each have that make our lives together so interesting and rewarding. You've just got to take each person for what they are and look for the good in them.

An Obituary printed in the London Times.

Interesting and sadly rather true:

Today we mourn the passing of a beloved old friend, Common Sense, who has been with us for many years. No one knows for sure how old he was, since his birth records were long ago lost in bureaucratic red tape. He will be remembered as having cultivated such valuable lessons as:

- Knowing when to come in out of the rain;
- Why the early bird gets the worm;
- Life isn't always fair;
- Maybe it was my fault;

Common Sense lived by simple, sound financial policies:
- Don't spend more than you can earn and

235

- Reliable strategies such as adults - not children, are in charge.

His health began to deteriorate rapidly when well-intentioned but overbearing regulations were set in place. Reports of a six-year-old boy charged with sexual harassment for kissing a classmate; teens suspended from school for using mouthwash after lunch; and a teacher fired for reprimanding an unruly student, only worsened his condition.

Common Sense lost ground when parents attacked teachers for doing the job that they themselves had failed to do in disciplining their unruly children. It declined even further when schools were required to get parental consent to administer sun lotion or an aspirin to a student; but could not inform parents when a student became pregnant and wanted to have an abortion.

Common Sense lost the will to live as the churches became businesses; and criminals received better treatment than their victims.

Common Sense took a beating when you couldn't defend yourself from a burglar in your own home and the burglar could sue you for assault.

Common Sense finally gave up the will to live, after a woman failed to realise that a steaming cup of coffee was hot. She spilled a little in her lap and was promptly awarded a huge settlement.

Common Sense was preceded in death, by his parents, Truth and Trust, by his wife, Discretion, by his daughter, Responsibility and by his son, Reason.

He is survived by his 4 stepbrothers;

I Know My Rights;

I Want It Now;

Someone Else Is To Blame; and

I'm A Victim

Not many attended his funeral because so few realised he was gone.

It's what you scatter

I was at the corner grocery store buying some early potatoes and noticed a small boy, delicate of bone and feature, ragged but clean, hungrily appraising a basket of freshly picked green peas.

I paid for my potatoes but was also drawn to the display of fresh green peas. I am a pushover for creamed peas and new potatoes. Pondering the peas, I couldn't help overhearing the conversation between Mr. Miller [the store owner] and the ragged boy next to me.

'Hello Barry, how are you today?'

'H'lo, Mr. Miller. Fine, thank ya. Jus' admirin' them peas. They sure look good.'

'They are good, Barry. How's your Ma?'

'Fine. Gittin' stronger alla' time.'

'Good. Anything I can help you with?'

'No, Sir. Jus' admirin' them peas.'

'Would you like to take some home?' asked Mr. Miller.

'No, Sir. Got nuthin' to pay for 'em with.'

'Well, what have you to trade me for some of those peas?'

'All I got's my prize marble here.'

'Is that right? Let me see it,' said Miller.

'Here 'tis. She's a dandy.'

'I can see that. Hmm mmm, only thing is this one is blue and I sort of go for red. Do you have a red one like this at home?' the store owner asked.

'Not zackley but almost.'

'Tell you what. Take this sack of peas home with you and next trip this way let me look at that red marble'. Mr. Miller told the boy.

'Sure will. Thanks Mr. Miller.'

Mrs. Miller, who had been standing nearby, came over to help me. With a smile she said, *'There are two other boys like him in our community, all three are in very poor circumstances. Jim just loves to bargain with them for peas, apples, tomatoes or whatever. When they come back with their red marbles and they always do, he decides he doesn't like red after all and he sends them home with a bag of produce for a green marble or an orange one, when they come on their next trip to the store.'*

I left the store smiling to myself, impressed with this man. A short time later I moved to Colorado, but I never forgot the story of this man, the boys and their bartering for marbles.

Several years went by, each more rapid than the previous one. Just recently I had occasion to visit some old friends in that Idaho community and while I was there learned that Mr. Miller had died. They were having his visitation that evening and knowing my friends wanted to go, I agreed to accompany them. Upon arrival at the mortuary we fell into line to meet the relatives of the deceased and to offer whatever words of comfort we could.

Ahead of us in line were three young men. One was in an army uniform and the other two wore nice haircuts, dark suits and white shirts ... all very professional looking. They approached Mrs. Miller, standing composed and smiling by her husband's casket.

Each of the young men hugged her, kissed her on the cheek, spoke briefly with her and moved on to the casket. Her misty light blue eyes followed them as, one by one; each young man stopped briefly and placed his own warm hand over the cold pale hand in the casket. Each left the mortuary awkwardly, wiping his eyes.

Our turn came to meet Mrs. Miller. I told her who I was and reminded her of the story from those many years ago and what she had told me about her husband's bartering for marbles. With her eyes glistening, she took my hand and led me to the casket. *'Those three young men who just left were the boys I told you about. They just told me how they appreciated the things Jim 'traded' them. Now, at last, when Jim could not change his mind about colour or size ... they came to pay their debt.'*

'We've never had a great deal of the wealth of this world,' she confided, *'but right now, Jim would consider himself the richest man in Idaho ...'*

With loving gentleness she lifted the lifeless fingers of her deceased husband. Resting underneath were three exquisitely shined red marbles.

The Moral: We will not be remembered by our words, but by our kind deeds. Life is not measured by the breaths we take, but by the moments that take our breath. Today I wish you a day of ordinary miracles:

- ❖ A fresh pot of tea you didn't make yourself.
- ❖ An unexpected phone call from an old friend.
- ❖ Green stoplights on your way to work.
- ❖ The fastest line at the grocery store.
- ❖ A good sing-along song on the radio.
- ❖ Your keys found right where you left them.

It's not what you gather, but what you scatter that tells what kind of life you have lived!

Cost of a Miracle

A little girl went to her bedroom and pulled a glass jelly jar from its hiding place in the closet. She poured the change out on the floor and counted it carefully. Three times, even ... The total had to be exactly perfect ... No chance here for mistakes. Carefully placing the coins back in the jar and twisting on the cap, she slipped out the back door and made her way six blocks to Rexall's Drug Store with the big red Indian Chief sign above the door.

She waited patiently for the pharmacist to give her some attention, but he was too busy at this moment. Tess twisted her feet to make a scuffing noise. Nothing. She cleared her throat with the most disgusting sound she could muster. No good. Finally she took a quarter from her jar and banged it on the glass counter... That did it!

'*And what do you want?*' the pharmacist asked in an annoyed tone of voice. I'm talking to my brother from Chicago whom I haven't seen in ages,' he said without waiting for a reply to his question.

'*Well, I want to talk to you about my brother,*' Tess answered back in the same annoyed tone. '*He's really, really sick ... and I want to buy a miracle.*'

'*I beg your pardon?*' said the pharmacist.

'*His name is Andrew and he has something bad growing inside his head and my Daddy says only a miracle can save him now. So how much does a miracle cost?*'

'*We don't sell miracles here, little girl. I'm sorry but I can't help you,*' the pharmacist said, softening a little.

'*Listen, I have the money to pay for it. If it isn't enough, I will get the rest. Just tell me how much it costs.*'

The pharmacist's brother was a well dressed man. He stooped down and asked the little girl, '*What kind of a miracle does your brother need?*'

'*I don't know,*' Tess replied with her eyes welling up. '*I just know he's really sick and Mommy says he needs an operation. But my Daddy can't pay for it, so I want to use my money ...*'

'*How much do you have?*' asked the man from Chicago.

'*One dollar and eleven cents,*' Tess answered barely audible. '*And it's all the money I have, but I can get some more if I need to.*'

'*Well, what a coincidence,*' smiled the man. '*A dollar and eleven cents is the exact price of a miracle for little brothers.*'

He took her money in one hand and with the other hand he grasped her mitten and said '*Take me to where you live. I want to see your brother and meet your parents. Let's see if I have the miracle you need.*'

That well-dressed man was Dr. Carlton Armstrong, a surgeon, specialising in neuron-surgery. The operation was completed free of charge and it wasn't long until Andrew was home again and doing well.

Mom and Dad were happily talking about the chain of events that had led them to this place.

'That surgery,' her Mom whispered, *'was a real miracle. I wonder how much it would have cost?'*

Tess smiled. She knew exactly how much a miracle cost ... one dollar and eleven cents, plus the faith of a little child. In our lives, we never know how many miracles we will need. A miracle is not the suspension of natural law, but the operation of a higher law.

The Whale

If you read the front page story of the SF Chronicle, you would have read about a female humpback whale that had become entangled in a spider web of crab traps and lines. She was weighted down by hundreds of pounds of traps that caused her to struggle to stay afloat. She also had hundreds of yards of line rope wrapped around her body, her tail, her torso and a line tugging in her mouth.

A fisherman spotted her just east of the Golden Gate Bridge and radioed an environmental group for help. Within a few hours, the rescue team arrived and determined that she was so bad off, the only way to save her was to dive in and untangle her - *a very dangerous proposition.* One slap of her tail could kill a rescuer. They worked for hours with curved knives and eventually freed her.

When she was free, the divers say she swam in what seemed like joyous circles. She then came back to each and every diver, one at a time and nudged them, pushed gently around - she thanked them. Some said it was the most incredibly beautiful experience of their lives. The man who cut the rope out of her mouth says her eye was following him the whole time and he will never be the same.

A true story by Catherine Moore

'Watch out! You nearly broad-sided that car!' My father yelled at me. *'Can't you do anything right?'*

Those words hurt worse than blows. I turned my head towards the elderly man in the seat beside me, daring me to challenge him. A lump rose in my throat as I averted my eyes. I wasn't prepared for another battle.

'I saw the car, Dad. Please don't yell at me when I'm driving' My voice was measured and steady, sounding far calmer than I really felt.

Dad glared at me, then turned away and settled back. At home I left Dad in front of the television and went outside to collect my thoughts ... Dark, heavy clouds hung in the air with a promise of rain. The rumble of distant thunder seemed to echo my inner turmoil. What could I do about him?

Dad had been a lumberjack. He had enjoyed being outdoors and had reveled in pitting his strength against the forces of nature. He had entered grueling lumberjack competitions. The shelves in his house were filled with trophies that attested to his prowess.

The years marched on relentlessly. The first time he couldn't lift a heavy log, he joked about it; but later that same day I saw him outside alone, straining to lift it. He became irritable whenever anyone teased him about his advancing age or when he couldn't do something he had done as a younger man.

Four days after his sixty-seventh birthday, he had a heart attack. An ambulance sped him to the hospital. He was lucky; he survived. But something inside Dad died. His zest for life was gone. Suggestions and offers of help were turned aside with sarcasm and insults. The number of visitors thinned and then finally stopped altogether. Dad was left alone.

My husband, Dick and I asked Dad to come live with us on our small farm. We hoped the fresh air and rustic atmosphere would help him adjust. Within a week after he moved in, I regretted the invitation. It seemed nothing was satisfactory. He criticised everything I did. I became frustrated and moody. Soon I was taking my pent-up anger out on Dick. We began to bicker and argue.

Something had to be done and it was up to me to do it. The next day I methodically called each of the mental health clinics listed in the Yellow Pages. I explained my problem to each of the sympathetic voices that answered in vain. Just when I was giving up hope, one of the voices suddenly exclaimed, *'I just read something that might help you! Let me go get the article.'*

The article described a remarkable study done at a nursing home. All of the patients were under treatment for chronic depression. Yet their attitudes had proved dramatically when they were given responsibility for a dog.

I drove to the animal shelter that afternoon. I studied each one but rejected one after the other for various reasons. As I neared the last pen, a dog in the shadows of the far corner struggled to his feet, walked to the front of the run and sat down. It was a pointer, one of the dog world's aristocrats. But this was a caricature of the breed. Years had etched his face and muzzle with shades of gray. His hip bones jutted out in lopsided triangles. But it was his eyes that caught and held my attention. Calm and clear, they beheld me unwaveringly.

I pointed to the dog. *'Can you tell me about him?'*

The officer replied, *'He's a funny one. Appeared out of nowhere and sat in front of the gate. We brought him in, figuring someone would be right down to claim him. That was two weeks ago and we've heard nothing. His time is up tomorrow.'*

As the words sank in I turned to the man in horror. *'You mean you're going to kill him?'*

'Ma'am,' he said gently, *'that's our policy. We don't have room for every unclaimed dog.'*

I looked at the pointer again. The calm brown eyes awaited my decision. *'I'll take him,'* I said.

I was helping my prize out of the car when Dad shuffled onto the front porch ... *'Ta-da! Look what I got for you, Dad!'* I said excitedly.

Dad looked and then wrinkled his face in disgust. *'If I had wanted a dog I would have gotten one. And I would have picked out a better specimen than that bag of bones. Keep it! I don't want it'* Dad waved his arm scornfully and turned back toward the house.

Anger rose inside me. It squeezed together my throat muscles and pounded into my temples. *'You'd better get used to him, Dad. He's staying!'*

Dad ignored me. *'Did you hear me, Dad'* I screamed. At those words Dad whirled angrily, his hands clenched at his sides, his eyes narrowed and blazing with hate. We stood glaring at each other like duelists, when suddenly the pointer pulled free from my grasp. He wobbled toward my dad and sat down in front of him. Then slowly, carefully, he raised his paw.

Dad's lower jaw trembled as he stared at the uplifted paw. Confusion replaced the anger in his eyes. The pointer waited patiently. Then Dad was on his knees hugging the animal.

It was the beginning of a warm and intimate friendship. Dad named the pointer Cheyenne. Together he and Cheyenne explored the community. They spent long hours walking down dusty lanes. They spent reflective moments on the banks of streams, angling for tasty trout. Dad and Cheyenne were inseparable throughout the next three years. Dad's bitterness faded and he and Cheyenne made many friends.

Then late one night I was startled to feel Cheyenne's cold nose burrowing through our bed covers. He had never before come into

our bedroom at night. I woke Dick, put on my robe and ran into my father's room. Dad lay in his bed, his face serene. But his spirit had left quietly sometime during the night. Two days later my shock and grief deepened when I discovered Cheyenne lying dead beside Dad's bed. I wrapped his still form in the rag rug he had slept on. As Dick and I buried him near a favourite fishing hole, I silently thanked the dog for the help he had given me in restoring Dad's peace of mind.

I was thankful that I had reached out and helped my father, knowing that if I had not, I would never have forgiven myself.

Shay

At a fundraising dinner for a school that serves children with learning disabilities, the father of one of the students delivered a speech that would never be forgotten by all who attended. After extolling the school and its dedicated staff, he offered a question:

'When not interfered with by outside influences, everything nature does, is done with perfection. Yet my son, Shay, cannot learn things as other children do. He cannot understand things as other children do. Where is the natural order of things in my son?'

The audience was stilled by the query.

The father continued. *'I believe that when a child like Shay, who was mentally and physically disabled comes into the world, an opportunity to realise true human nature presents itself and it comes in the way other people treat that child.'*

Then he told the following story:

Shay and I had walked past a park where some boys Shay knew were playing baseball. Shay asked, *'Do you think they'll let me play?'* I knew that most of the boys would not want someone like Shay on their team, but as a father. I also understood that if my son were allowed to play, it would give him a much-needed sense of belonging and some confidence to be accepted by others in spite of his handicaps.

I approached one of the boys on the field and asked [not expecting much] if Shay could play. The boy looked around for guidance and said, *'We're losing by six runs and the game is in the eighth inning. I guess he can be on our team and we'll try to put him in to bat in the ninth inning.'*

Shay struggled over to the team's bench and, with a broad smile, put on a team shirt. I watched with a small tear in my eye and warmth in my heart. The boys saw my joy at my son being accepted.

In the bottom of the eighth inning, Shay's team scored a few runs but was still behind by three.

In the top of the ninth inning, Shay put on a glove and played in the right field. Even though no hits came his way, he was obviously ecstatic just to be in the game and on the field, grinning from ear to ear as I waved to him from the stands.

In the bottom of the ninth inning, Shay's team scored again.

Now, with two outs and the bases loaded, the potential winning run was on base and Shay was scheduled to be next at bat.

At this juncture, do they let Shay bat and give away their chance to win the game?

Surprisingly, Shay was given the bat. Everyone knew that a hit was all but impossible because Shay didn't even know how to hold the bat properly, much less connect with the ball.

However, as Shay stepped up to the plate, the pitcher, recognising that the other team was putting winning aside for this moment in Shay's life, moved in a few steps to lob the ball in softly so Shay could at least make contact.

The first pitch came and Shay swung clumsily and missed.

The pitcher again took a few steps forward to toss the ball softly towards Shay.

As the pitch came in, Shay swung at the ball and hit a slow ground ball right back to the pitcher.

The game would now be over.

The pitcher picked up the soft grounder and could have easily thrown the ball to the first baseman.

Shay would have been out and that would have been the end of the game.

Instead, the pitcher threw the ball right over the first baseman's head, out of reach of all team mates.

Everyone from the stands and both teams started yelling, *'Shay, run to first! Run to first!'*

Never in his life had Shay ever run that far, but he made it to first base.

He scampered down the baseline, wide-eyed and startled.

Everyone yelled, *'Run to second, run to second!'*

Catching his breath, Shay awkwardly ran towards second, gleaming and struggling to make it to the base.

By the time Shay rounded towards second base, the right fielder had the ball, the smallest guy on their team, who now had his first chance to be the hero for his team.

He could have thrown the ball to the second-baseman for the tag, but he understood the pitcher's intentions so he, too, intentionally threw the ball high and far over the third-baseman's head.

Shay ran toward third base deliriously as the runners ahead of him circled the bases toward home.

All were screaming, *'Shay, Shay, Shay, all the Way to go Shay'*

Shay reached third base because the opposing shortstop ran to help him by turning him in the direction of third base and shouted, *'Run to third! Shay, run to third!'*

As Shay rounded third, the boys from both teams and the spectators, were on their feet screaming, *'Shay, run home! Run home!'*

Shay ran to home, stepped on the plate and was cheered as the hero who hit the grand slam and won the game for his team.

'That day,' said the father softly with tears now rolling down his face, *'the boys from both teams helped bring a piece of true love and humanity into this world. I saw many of the parents quietly congratulating their sons for their heroic deed and I smiled at them as I walked my gleaming son to our car.'*

Shay didn't make it to another summer. He died that winter, having never forgotten being the hero and making me so happy and coming home and seeing his Mother tearfully embrace her little hero of the day!

And now a little foot note to this story:

We all send thousands of jokes through the e-mail without a second thought, but when it comes to sending messages about life choices, people hesitate.

The crude, vulgar and often obscene pass freely through cyberspace, but public discussion about decency is too often suppressed in our schools and workplaces.

If you're thinking about forwarding this message, chances are that you're probably sorting out the people in your address book who aren't the 'appropriate' ones to receive this type of message Well, the person who sent you this believes that we all can make a difference.

We all have thousands of opportunities every single day to help realise the 'natural order of things.'

So many seemingly trivial interactions between two people present us with a choice:

Do we pass along a little spark of love and humanity or do we pass up those opportunities and leave the world a little bit colder in the process?

A wise man once said every society is judged by how it treats it's least fortunate amongst them.

CONCLUSION

We sometimes take life too seriously and at other times we become selfish and think only of ourselves. Life is not easy, but with a good mixture of laughter, tears and caring for others – we can say at the end of our lives, that we have made an impact and lived a good life.

Let's all aim to stop hurting others intentionally; regularly give help, joy and laughter to others and keep the balance right.